A LILY FOR LILLIAN

Lillian forced her trembling fingers to close around the wooden handle, and she lifted the brand. Averting her eyes from the angry orange tip, she brought it to her stepmother, prepared to hand it over. Yet the older woman shook her head, smiling. "It is yours, so you will have the honor of setting the mark."

Lillian swallowed, then looked at the bound man, who was watching them warily, his blue gaze even more intense than before.

"Very well."

Camille pointed. "Go along."

Lillian took a deep breath and met the man's eyes. *I am sorry,* she said with her own. *I am so sorry.* Then, as she went forward, her gaze dropped to his heaving chest, to the smooth place above the left nipple. Steadying herself, gripping the handle with both hands, she pressed the branding iron against his skin and tried not to notice the way his body jerked or the smell of scorched flesh.

THE LILY BRAND

SANDRA SCHWAB

LEISURE BOOKS NEW YORK CITY

To Amazie, as promised.

A LEISURE BOOK®

July 2005

Published by

Dorchester Publishing Co., Inc.
200 Madison Avenue
New York, NY 10016

ISBN 0-8439-5552-X

Visit us on the web at www.dorchesterpub.com.

ACKNOWLEDGMENTS

For the most part, writing is a solitary business, yet this book wouldn't have come about without the help of many lovely people:

First and foremost my thanks go to the wonderful ladies of the Literary Forum: Thank you for teaching me how to fly! I wouldn't have been able to do it without you!

Extra-special thanks to our own Lady LaLa, for being an inspiration for us all, but also for letting herself be bullied into proofreading the last few chapters.

A million thanks to my editor, Chris, for taking a chance on this bumbling new author. Many thanks to Teresa, for her enthusiasm and the cover quote; to Gaelen, for her friendship and advice; to Ulla, who knows why; to the members of La porte de pierre, who helped me with the French swear words; to Martin, for Debrett's; and to Dee, for giving me confidence when I needed it. Meeting you was like meeting my very own fairy godmother!

Furthermore, I'm deeply grateful to everybody who patted my hand during last-minute panic attacks: Jen, Trish, Ulla, the other Sandy and the members of the Beau Monde.

Last but not least, I would like to thank my parents for always enabling me to pursue my dreams.

THE LILY
BRAND

Part I

The varying year with blade and sheaf
Clothes and reclothes the happy plains,
Here rests the sap within the leaf,
Here stays the blood along the veins.
Faint shadows, vapours lightly curl'd,
Faint murmurs from the meadows come,
Like hints and echoes of the world
To spirits folded in the womb.

—Tennyson, The Day Dream

Chapter 1

France, Autumn 1815

The rattling of the doors was what alerted him first. In this stinking, dim-lit hell where he was imprisoned, the sound meant food at best and the step of the hangman at worst. But then, most of the men had been here for so long that they welcomed even that.

The shuffling of bodies around him meant his fellow inmates were getting up—both food and hangman were better met standing, if only to rob the prison guards of the glee of hauling one to one's feet. Warily, Troy stood, ignoring his left leg. The pain there had been a constant comrade ever since his last battle, when shot had peppered his thigh, taking him down, rendering him helpless when he had been taken prisoner. Bringing him *here*.

Absentmindedly, he scratched his matted beard, which was dark with dirt. A flea shell cracked under the pressure of two of his grimy fingers, their nails broken, and was flicked away, discarded without conscious thought. Too long. It had been too long since he had been brought here.

3

He had lost track of the days and weeks and months; they had blurred together and eventually formed eternity. Eternal damnation.

There had been a rumor that the war was over, that Bonaparte had been overcome. Wasn't it the custom to release the prisoners of war in case of a defeat? If he had been an officer, they probably would have ransomed him even before that. He *had* been an officer, he seemed to remember, but he hadn't been wearing his normal uniform in that last battle. And so he had been treated like a common soldier, had been dragged into an available prison nearby, thrown into the company of thieves and cutthroats, and had been forgotten along with them.

A small prison at the end of the world, at the edge of the sea—or was it? He could not trust his memories on that score, could not be sure whether the roaring in his ears during the drive on the back of that coarse wagon had been the sound of the waves or just his own blood.

As the rattling grew louder, his neighbor dug his elbow into Troy's ribs, causing the chains which tied them to the wall to rattle in counterpoint. "Ey, *rouquin*," the man mumbled in coarse French, "what do you think it'll be today?"

Troy shrugged.

The other prisoner licked his gray lips. "A flogging? Has been some time since we had one of those. Gratien will be impatient by now. Lusting after our blood." A strange light entered his eyes. Troy had seen the likes of it too often to be shocked. If it was to be a flogging they would all be crowded into the small courtyard to watch the spectacle.

The prisoners liked floggings. It meant an interruption of the gray time in their cells.

Gratien came into view, shuffling down the aisle between the cells. It might have been a peculiar joke of the

Fates that a man whose name meant "pleasing" had grown into a short, red-faced specimen with faded yellow hair, his breath wheezing in his lungs. Yet when Gratien descended into the bowels of his prison, nobody dared laugh. All the men feared his violent temper.

This time, however, he did not come alone.

When the men spotted who was walking behind him, tall and graceful as Death itself, a murmur rippled through them as if a stone had been thrown into a dark, depthless lake.

"*La Veuve Noire.*"

"Silence!" The handle of Gratien's whip banged against the bars before he turned to bow low. "Here are more, *madame.*" He had stopped in front of Troy's cell.

All around him, the men stepped back from the bars in a fruitless attempt to melt into the walls. The Black Widow, with her eyes like cold jewels, was a woman to be feared. Every once in a while she came to the prison to collect . . . a prize. These men were taken away, never to be heard of again. But there were rumors, strange rumors, strange enough for the prisoners not to seek to become a prize.

The black silk of the woman's dress rustled as she turned to look into the cell. "I see." She spoke with the polished accent of an aristocrat, yet her voice was cold enough to freeze the blood in the veins of a man. Against the black of her clothes, her face seemed ghostly white, the eyes painted in such a way that they appeared to be slanted like a cat's. A slight smile curved her ruby-red lips, and she snapped her gloved fingers. "Light!"

Two prison guards hurried forward, each holding a torch that threw a flickering light on the inhabitants of the cell. The Black Widow studied each man as if she were at market and they were the cattle she wished to purchase.

Troy straightened his back and stared at her, refusing to

lower his eyes as everybody else did. Once he had been a man to wield power. Even after all this time, there was enough pride left in him. He would *not* grovel in front of such a woman.

"Ah," she said in pleased tones. "Open the cell."

Gratien hurried to obey her command and waved the torchbearers to follow her inside.

The men shrank away, yet Troy did not notice. Unblinkingly, he continued to stare at the woman until his eyes began to water.

She halted in front of him, and the torchlight glittered on the golden net that held back the mass of her charcoal hair. "Oh, yes." Her smile intensified. "Come here, *chérie*."

At first, Troy thought she meant him, but when the Black Widow looked back over her shoulder, he noticed another woman standing in the aisle outside, shoulders slightly hunched upward. Her dress of muted gray made her appear like the sad shadow of her companion. Reluctantly, she stepped into the cell, her eyes darting to the filthy men in chains, to the bare stone floor, to the few dirty rushes.

"Don't be so shy, *chérie*." *La Veuve Noire* extended her hand, fingers beckoning.

Troy blinked.

The other woman, he now saw, was hardly more than a girl. A girl who tightly pressed her lips together. He watched as she laid her hand in the hand of the widow and was drawn forward.

"What do you think of that?"

Looking down, the girl shuffled her foot in the rushes, refusing to acknowledge the question, refusing to meet Troy's gaze.

"Great, great . . ." Gratien hurried to the widow's side, closing his fingers around Troy's forearm. "A good one, that.

Young. *Madame* wished for young, *non?* Good shape, very good shape . . ."

Madame deigned to smile some more. "Everywhere?" she asked with arched eyebrows.

"*Pardon?* Oh . . . well . . ." Huffing and puffing, Gratien abruptly released Troy's arm. "I'm sure . . . if *madame* would like to feel . . ."

"Indeed." The widow let go of the girl's hand in order to strip the glove from her own. Long, white fingers came into view, crowned by long nails, their color matching her red lips.

Troy wanted to jerk out of reach, yet his back was already against the wall, and now Gratien was pressing the end of his whip into the soft spot under his chin, forcing Troy's head upwards and back so that he would not move. Troy swallowed convulsively, feeling the hard wood pressing against his windpipe, before the woman's fingers closed over the worn material of his breeches and around his manhood. He shuddered with revulsion as, chuckling, she roughly measured the width and length of him.

"Not bad," she murmured, "not bad. *Chérie?*" She reached back with her free hand and again brought the girl to her side. "Your glove."

From the corner of his eyes, Troy saw Gratien lick his lips. He was dimly aware of the soft clinking of his fellow inmates' chains as they watched this spectacle in uncomfortable silence.

Then the pressure of the widow's long fingers eased, only to be replaced by another, softer grip. All Troy could see was the girl's bent head, with the torchlight flickering over dark brown curls.

"Well," *la Veuve Noire* said. "What do you think, Lillian?"

The girl raised her head and, for the first time, looked at Troy. Her eyes, he saw, were very wide, and it appeared as if the pupil had swallowed up the iris. She was, he realized, not just embarrassed by this situation, but very much afraid.

"Stroke him some," the woman commanded. "After all, we want to know whether it is in good working order."

Over the reek of the prison cell that he had long ago ceased to notice, Troy suddenly became aware of another smell, fresh and sweet, of flowers, perhaps, whose names he had forgotten. He felt the girl's hand quiver, and her teeth came down to bite her lower lip, hard. Yet she did as she was told.

As the perfume wafted around him and the girl's fingers worked on him, stroking, stroking, arousing, he closed his eyes and remembered how long it had been since he had last lain with a woman. Soon sweat beaded his forehead, while fire ran through his body, pooling in his loins. His hips jerked forward. It was obscene. Troy gritted his teeth.

"Very nice," the widow commented. "I think it will do."

Abruptly, the fingers were removed and the pressure against his windpipe disappeared. Troy staggered, the blood roaring in his ears. With something akin to surprise he realized that he was quivering like a cornered animal.

La Veuve Noire spoke one last time. "We will take that one, then. Clean it and shave it—we would not want any vermin to come along. Then put it in the second carriage as usual. We will wait outside."

On the coarse road, washed out by recent rain, the carriage was rocking like a ship on high seas. Nevertheless, Lillian sat ramrod-straight, counterbalancing the motion of the vehicle with movements of her hips. Her stepmother lounged in the opposite corner, a thin smile on her blood-red lips. *Like the cat who got the canary.* But then, Camille *had* got a canary of some sort—even if it was not for herself.

The key on Lillian's golden necklace seemed to burn through cloth and skin, a visible promise of the things to come. She resisted the urge to tug her coat tighter around herself. Emotion, she had learned from an early age, was a weakness that one could not afford to show at Château du Marais. Instead she looked outside, to where the mist rose from the ground to blur all shapes and to render the landscape a gray, ghostly place of hopelessness. *Like that prison.*

Involuntarily, her hands tightened into fists on her lap.

The prison, the manor house, and the mines—they all were part of the land her stepmother owned, and they all formed a unity that fed on people's despair, a well for Camille's pleasure. On these outskirts of civilization Camille had spun a tight, powerful web, with herself holding all the threads. And those who got entangled were doomed, one way or another.

From beneath her lashes, Lillian shot a look at her stepmother.

Camille's smile deepened. "You were quite shy today, *chérie*. Did Gratien's little institution overwhelm you?"

"It was my first time, *maman*." Lillian chose her words with care. It would endanger her plans to anger Camille even in the smallest way. Better to pretend submission, compliance. "But let me thank you for my present. It is . . . lovely."

Her stepmother nodded amiably. "It is quite a nice specimen. And so much . . . spirit." She licked her lips as if in anticipation. "It will be a pleasure to break it in. A challenge." She raised a brow at Lillian. "Naturally, you will have to do that yourself."

"*Oui, maman*." Outside, the world seemed even bleaker than before.

When they arrived at Château du Marais, dinner had already been prepared for them, giving the servants time to prepare the man. Lillian did not taste any of the food she forced down her throat; she could have eaten sand and it would not have made any difference.

The candlelight gleamed off Antoine's bronzed chest, sparkled on the gold bands around his arms. He stood behind Camille's chair, serving his mistress in silence, his face expressionless, the mark on his forehead smooth. Lillian tried very hard not to stare at the golden breeches that hugged his hips, blending in quite nicely with the cherry-wood and golden furnishings of the dining room. Trust Camille to mind the details.

Finally, the door opened to admit Maurice, his short black curls spanning his head like a cap. He, too, was wearing golden breeches, yet his torso was covered in a white silk shirt and his forehead was flawless. The mark, Lillian knew, could be found on his right biceps.

He stopped at the table and bowed low. "Everything has been prepared, *madame*."

"*Trés bien*." Camille clapped her hands together, delight shining on her face, and she turned toward her stepdaughter. "Shall we go upstairs, then, *chérie*, and admire the results?"

"*Oui, maman*." Lillian put her napkin on the table, praying for strength to get through the next half hour. Never had it been more difficult to force a smile onto her lips than at that moment. Composure had been easier to gather even when her father's coffin was lowered into the grave, leaving her alone with Camille.

But Lillian stood, straight and graceful, her face as blank as those of the servants.

Her stepmother led them through the wide hall and up the marble staircase, stone horses rearing up at the end of the rail. It was not far, then, to Lillian's room, as she had moved rooms on her nineteenth birthday.

The door opened to reveal another selection of cherry-wood furnishings in combination with white, diaphanous drapes on the windows and the four-poster bed. Even the bed linen shone like untouched snow.

Blood showed so well on white.

Across the room loomed one of Camille's constructions. It had been unused and empty all these past weeks since Lillian's birthday, but it now held the spread-eagled form of a man, chains stretching his legs and arms so that movement was impossible. Also made impossible was speech, as a gag filled his mouth, the leather strings wrapping around his shaven head, rendering him more helpless than at the prison.

"Ahhh," Camille breathed, "magnificent."

Lillian forced herself to step forward, to approach the man who had been reduced to something less than an animal.

Gone were his beard and hair, revealing a strong-boned face that for the most part had been invisible before. He had been shaved back at the prison, and the guards had been careless enough to cover his skull with the thin red lines of small cuts. Under Maurice's supervision, Lillian knew, he had been cleaned again until the last stench of prison disappeared. Now, the light of the candles lent a soft, healthy glow to his skin, which gleamed with the oil that had been rubbed onto his body. Like Antoine, he was naked except for a pair of golden breeches.

But the eyes, Lillian saw, the eyes were the same—an intense cornflower-blue that seemed to burn to her very soul.

Camille turned to look at Maurice, who lingered on the threshold, and nodded. "Very nice, very nice indeed." At that he bowed and left. He would be given his treat later on.

11

Camille went over to the small table that held a collection of her . . . instruments. "As I have already told you, *chérie*, you will have to break it in yourself." She chose two short whips and strolled back to the man, slowly walking around him. "For tonight, I advise you to leave it like that. Tomorrow we might consider the cage. *If* . . ." She raised her perfectly trimmed brows. "If it behaves. If not. . . ." She lightly touched one of the whips to his back, causing the muscles to ripple under the smooth skin. "Come here, *chérie*."

Dutifully, Lillian walked around the construction, her face a calm mask while inside she wanted to scream and weep.

"If not, you might start with this. *This*"—with an expert move of her right wrist Camille brought the leather string of the first whip cracking down on the man's back—"will leave red weals, sometimes drawing blood and sometimes not; whereas *this*"—she used the other whip, a vicious-looking thing with numerous straps that had small pieces of metal knotted at the ends—"will take away skin and draw blood for sure."

At each lash, Lillian closed her eyes so as not to see the flesh quiver or the body flinch. Yet the results of each lash glared at her when she looked again, an angry red welt and a set of bloody rips in the man's skin.

"You must learn how to use them well," Camille continued while she put the whips back with the rest of her other instruments. "For after a month we will have to decide whether it is fit."

Whether his spirit could be broken and the man controlled, Lillian knew. Whether he could be reduced to a mere toy for Camille's pleasure . . . or not.

Smiling, Camille stepped in front of the man. "Then we will have to decide what has to go: its tongue . . ." She laid a finger against the gag, laughing as the man tried to flinch away. In swift retribution she slapped his face, hard, leaving an imprint of her hand on his cheek. "Its tongue," Camille went on and reached between his legs, "or its balls." Because Camille had no wish to mar her body with an unwanted pregnancy.

By now, the man was breathing noisily through his nose, his body taut like a bowstring.

Lillian nodded, praying for a swift end of this. "*Oui, maman.*"

"Yes." Her stepmother let go of their captive and patted Lillian's cheek instead. "You are an intelligent girl, *n'est-ce pas?* You will handle this well. And for now, it is all yours." She lowered her voice to a conspiratorial whisper. "And there is one last surprise waiting for you. Look in the fire, *chérie.*"

With a sinking feeling in the pit of her stomach, Lillian went over to the fireplace, where, in a bowl of red hot coals, was stuck another of Camille's instruments.

"Bring it here," her stepmother commanded.

Lillian forced her trembling fingers to close around the wooden handle, and she lifted the brand. Averting her eyes from the angry orange tip, she brought it to Camille, prepared to hand it over. Yet the older woman shook her head, smiling. "It is yours, so you will have the honor of setting the mark."

Lillian swallowed, then looked at the bound man, who was watching them warily, his blue gaze even more intense than before.

"Where would you like to place it?" Camille studied the expanse of glistening flesh before her. "I am very partial to the forehead, as you know. Or the arm?" One red fingernail scratched across the man's helplessly extended arm. "What shall it be?"

Lillian gripped the handle tighter. "The . . . the . . ." Where could such a thing most easily be concealed? "The . . . chest."

"Very well." Camille pointed. "Go along."

Lillian took a deep breath and met the man's eyes. *I am sorry*, she said with her own. *I am so sorry.* Then, as she went forward, her gaze dropped to his heaving chest, to the smooth place above the left nipple. Steadying herself, gripping the handle with both hands, she pressed the branding iron against his skin and tried not to notice the way his body jerked or the smell of scorched flesh that tickled her nose.

Finally, she stepped back. With detached surprise she registered the different design: a lily, instead of Camille's rose.

Her stepmother clapped. "A lily for Lillian. Very fine, *chérie, n'est-ce pas?* Now that you have marked it, you should also decide on a name for it. How about Olivier? Think about it."

Lillian hardly noticed the kiss that was blown onto her cheek or the sound of the door as it opened and closed, leaving her alone with the man. She kept staring at the small spot of flesh, now raw and burnt, kept staring and staring until her legs gave way and she sat down on the floor rather abruptly. She had enough sense left to hold the iron upright so that it would not set the floor on fire.

Drawing her knees to her chest, she used them as a cushion for her forehead. Her ears buzzed and the room was swimming, so she closed her eyes to draw long, even breaths. Cursed be the day when she had attracted Camille's attention. And cursed be the day when she had first set foot onto the threshold of Camille's mansion all those years ago.

Lillian had no idea how long she sat on the floor, yet when she finally raised her head, the room was still the same—of course. Filled with the stench of burnt flesh, which not even the scented candles had been able to eclipse.

She shuddered, once.

As horrid as it was, the smell, however, helped her to settle her nerves and to focus her thoughts on the most urgent issues at hand. Looking up, she found the man staring at her, his eyes even darker than before. Staring at her like he had stared at her stepmother back in the prison.

God, why hadn't he possessed enough sense to lower his eyes, to show proper submission? Didn't he know that Camille owned not just the land but the people as well, body and soul? That all resistance was futile and would be met with savage retribution? Lillian suppressed the memory of the song of the dogs at night, out to hunt those who tried to escape Camille's web. Futile . . . futile. . . .

But, *everything needs balance*, even if, as always, the choice had been taken away from her. She had set the mark; he was hers, and she had to act accordingly.

Her responsibility.

Determinedly, she stood, putting the iron away before she pulled a bell cord beside her bed. She did not have to wait long for her maid to amble through the door, a sly grin on the servant's face when she spotted the shackled man.

"So, you got one all for yourself." Chuckling, Marie approached the rack-like construction, reaching out to touch oil-smooth flesh. "My, and such a fine one. . . ."

Lillian narrowed her eyes. "I called you," she said in her iciest voice, "because I need hot water to wash. Also, I have a desire for some wine, fresh fruit and rosemary bread." He would not have been given any fruit or vegetables in the prison.

A sullen look replaced the maid's slyness, rendering her features ugly as those of a toad.

Lillian straightened her shoulders. Casually she reached

out to take hold of one of the discarded whips, letting the leather strap run through her fingers. "I gave you an order, Marie. Now make haste—or shall I use this on you?" She raised her brows.

Even though it had been but a bad imitation of her stepmother, the trick worked and the servant hurried out of the room. Lillian turned to glance at the man once more. His chest was still heaving, his breath whistling through his nose. Lillian fiddled with the whip, glad that her hands had something to do while she was waiting for Marie's return.

However, it was Gabriel who knocked at the door and entered. Golden-haired Gabriel, gangly as a colt, with a certain chubbiness still clinging to his cheeks. He bowed. "Cook sent me to bring you the food, mistress."

Lillian stared at him. She could not be sure whether he was already bearing the mark. He was younger even than herself. Had he already been cut? She forced her lips into a smile. "Thank you. Put it on the table over there." She noticed how he avoided looking at the construction as he went across the room to set the tray down.

Marie came soon after to deliver the pitcher of warm water. While her face remained cast in a sulk, she did not linger this time, and soon Lillian was all alone with the man once more.

She could not help the sigh of relief that escaped her. Swiftly, she went over to the door to slide the bolt in place. No unwelcome surprises from that quarter. Leaning against the door, she surveyed the room and took stock of the situation.

She could not do anything about the chains that kept him shackled to the construction, of course, as Camille would expect to see him in exactly the same place in the morning. But she *could* do something about the man's injuries and his pain.

Everything needs balance: One to do the healing in a place where another does all the wounding. But this time, she herself had done the wounding.

Lillian tried to ignore the bitter twist of her stomach. *She* had set the mark. It was *her* responsibility.

So she dragged a footrest behind the construction in order to reach the strings of the gag. Lightly she rested her hands on the man's shoulders, ignoring the stickiness of the oil under her fingers. At her touch he flinched slightly as if he feared more pain. Yet all she did was lean forward in order to bring her mouth close to his ear. "Listen," she whispered. "I am going to free you of the gag. But you *must not* speak, do you understand? These walls have ears and one never knows who is listening." And whoever it was would report back to Camille, for no one slipped her control easily. By now, most people knew better than to even attempt it.

Not me, came the unbidden thought. Lillian shivered as the enormity of the plan struck her once more. This man was a burden she neither needed nor wanted. He might endanger everything.

For a moment she felt anger that he had been stupid enough to get chosen, to show defiance. She felt a tight, hot ball of anger in the pit of her stomach—and something else. Something which pricked in her eyes, an emotion she dared not name. Compassion, after all, was a luxury and not for her.

She let her gaze shift to the window, where the night, cold and dark, pressed against the glass. She felt the coldness reaching out for her and waited until it touched her heart, erased all feeling inside.

Her fingers steady, she started to work on the knots of the gag. Carefully, she reached around him to take it out of his mouth. "Remember," she reminded him on a murmur. *"Not one sound!"* Again, he nodded.

Satisfied, she stepped down and went over to the chest where she kept her herbs and medicines. Nanette had taught her that. *Everything needs balance*, she heard the old woman's voice whispering in her head. Nanette had been her nanny from the time Lillian's mother was still alive, and later, she had been the only link to a bygone golden life. She had taught Lillian to stay away from the main part of the mansion, never to be heard or seen so as not to attract any attention. So her father had forgotten Lillian and had died. When later on, Camille had finally taken notice of her stepdaughter, Nanette had been sent away and Lillian herself had been forced to move rooms—among other things.

Lillian swallowed. Then she shoved all memories of her nineteenth birthday aside and concentrated on selecting the proper herbs. Oil of St. John's wort for the burn, marigold salve for the cuts.

She straightened and went back to the man, who never once let her out of his sight. She started with his burn, carefully applying the oil to the skin. As she touched the raw flesh, his breath hissed through his teeth, but true to his promise, he did not make any other sound.

The body under her hands was lean, too lean for such a tall man. The ribs, Lillian noticed, seemed to be poking through the skin; the muscles on his arms and belly were not rounded and defined like Antoine's or Maurice's or any other of Camille's men.

When she was finished, Lillian went around the construction to step onto the footrest once more. The cuts on the man's head had already been cleaned, she saw, so all she had to do was to spread salve on them. After that, she pulled the stool in front of him and fed him the fruit and the bread and let him drink part of the wine. Over the rim of the glass, his eyes were very blue.

Lillian tried not to notice.

She only spoke once, when she put the sleeping potion in the rest of the wine and gave it to him. "To make you rest," she explained.

He gazed at her and finally nodded his assent.

Lillian watched the muscles of his throat work as he swallowed. Perhaps she should have given him poison instead. That way, he would never become a danger to her plans. But Camille would not be happy to lose one of her toys overnight. And that was even more certain to put the plan on the line.

Lillian blinked.

Besides, would she be capable of simply ending the life of a human being? Somebody who was just as entrapped in Camille's web as she herself was?

His eyes met hers.

Perhaps. If it meant sparing him the fate that awaited him at the end of the four weeks: either a life as Camille's toy, or the mines.

Chapter 2

Lillian thought about taking a sleeping potion herself. But as she had to rise before dawn to get the man ready, she chose a sleepless night instead, listening to his even breathing. Sometimes he would grow restless, his muscles fighting against the strain of the chains.

When the horizon blushed with the first touch of the sun, she roused him so that she could put the gag back in place. She saw his skin ripple with gooseflesh from the cold. Or perhaps it wasn't from the cold at all; Lillian looked out of the window and forced herself not to care.

When Camille finally walked into the room, black silks rustling, Lillian was cool and poised. Clad in muted gray, she felt as if the mists outside had risen to gather around her body, to freeze her heart and soul.

"*Bonjour, chérie.*" Cold red lips touched her cheek.

"*Bonjour, maman.*"

Behind Camille stood Maurice, her stepmother's golden shadow for today. Arms folded across his naked chest, he wore his face in an expressionless mask. The red marks on his skin were badges of honor. Like all of Camille's favorites, he seemed to crave his mistress's touch.

Camille's gaze shifted to the man in chains, and her lips lifted in the travesty that was her smile. "It looks even better in broad daylight, *n'est-ce pas?*" Slowly, she walked around the construction, appraising the well-made form and shape of the prisoner. Her fingernail trailed his long backbone, making his muscles ripple in revulsion and herself laugh. "Stubborn, is it? Maurice . . ." She turned. "See to it that it learns the error of its ways."

Lillian's eyes darted to the bound man's face. Did he know the meaning of this? Could he guess?

Her stepmother finished her tour in front of the construction. She patted the man's cheek while his eyes shot blue fire at her. "Teach it," she said softly, her fingers mimicking a caress, "that stubbornness is a flaw which we do not tolerate."

In a whirl of black, she turned to Lillian. "We should have breakfast now, *chérie*. Maurice will see after your present." Thoughtfully she touched her fingers to her chin. "Should we put it back here, do you think, or should we consider the cage?"

Lillian stood straight and unblinking. "This morning, I have a desire for a walk in the garden, I think. Could that be arranged?"

"Of course. Maurice will prepare everything. Now come, *chérie*, before the chocolate grows cold in our cups."

Well aware that her stepmother's loyal golden shadow regarded her every move, Lillian followed Camille from the room without once looking back at the spread-eagled man. She did not know why she had spared him the cage. It was just a postponement of the things to come.

* * *

21

All the weeks since her birthday had not yet managed to accustom Lillian to the meals in the dining room. Golden decorations blazed with the light of the early morning, filling the room with a thousand small suns. Hercule was standing next to the sideboard where the chocolate was kept warm, so still he could have been a statue carved out of darkest ebony. Young Gérard of the rosy face cowered beside his mistress to feed her bits of fruit and sweet roll. If the mood took her, she bit his fingers.

Lillian's eyes remained cool over the rim of her cup. The chocolate tasted like acid. On her plate, the sweet rolls crumbled to sand.

A snap of Camille's fingers sent Gérard spreading himself on the table so she could eat the fruits off his body and scorch his skin with droplets of hot chocolate. Hercule brought the pot to fill her cup when it was empty, while Gérard moved sinuously before her, his eyes never once leaving the face of his mistress.

Lillian watched, detached. Hercule did not need to refill her cup.

A dark cherry gleamed between Camille's lips, before she sucked it into her mouth and chewed, smiling. The next was crushed between her fingers, staining her skin. She spread the sticky juice on her throat. Slowly, she leaned her head back, and, lithe as a cat, Gérard rose—the sign to Lillian that she could leave. She saw his tongue sweeping white skin just before the door closed behind her.

Downstairs, Maurice had her coat and the man ready for her. The traces of his punishment were not visible at first glance. Or perhaps the breeches and the shirt covered them; Lillian did not know. The gag still filled his mouth. Better than the bridle Camille so liked.

Wordless, she took the chain that fastened on the ring around his throat, a dog on a leash. Shackles held his hands on his back, where another chain ran up to fasten on the ring at his neck. Thus, he would not get far, should he decide to run away. Camille preferred to make sure nobody slipped her control.

Wordless, Lillian took the riding crop to use when he failed to show appropriate subordination.

Maurice bowed, and she stepped over the threshold outside. The man in shackles followed without resistance. By now he knew better.

Lillian's stepmother did not have much use for gardens. She preferred the games inside the mansion; it was cooler in summer and warmer in winter. Sometimes, though, she would have a man's naked body covered in ice, chilled for her pleasure. Also, she did not like flowers except for roses. She liked it when the men brushed her body with roses while the thorns were buried deep in the flesh of their hands. Thus, with the exception of the rose garden, the grounds had not been tended in years. The bushes had grown over the statues of stone and over the small benches scattered around the garden. The paths hid behind curtains of greenery, which had rendered them almost invisible.

Yet Lillian did not hesitate to pick her way through the overgrown garden. She walked carefully, of course, mindful of the thorny branches which lay waiting to trap the folds of her coat and dress. The man had been given boots, she saw, so they would not have to clean him up later.

At this time of the year, the leaves had already started to fall and reveal the branches gray and bare. In many ways, the garden was as ghostly as the mansion itself. But, oh, how many times she had wished that the plants would reach out and envelop the house, bury it under a green blanket!

La belle au bois dormant.

Lillian's lips turned up in a humorless smile. There would be no prince coming to release *her* from the evil spell.

In her dreams, the plants would grow and cover the walls of the mansion, would press against the glass of the windows, would seek out the tiniest cracks in the walls. And, once inside, they would grow and grow and twine themselves around Camille. Around and around her until there would be no trace left—

Lillian gave herself a mental shake and looked over her shoulder at the man trudging behind her. His chest rose and fell with laborious breaths. What could she say to ease his troubles? For him, there would be no deliverance. And so, she remained silent.

To the left, a lichen-covered Pan peeked out of the bushes, lounging on a bit of rock, flute raised to his lips as if he were about to compete with the absent birds. Just visible under the dark green tendrils was one of the broad, powerful shoulders, a hint of muscles bouncing in his arm. His very presence seemed to mock the man in shackles, for the faun had achieved what the prisoner had not: escape of Camille's web.

Lillian stepped down moss-covered stairs. Overhead, the tops of the trees touched intimately, while under their feet dead leaves rustled—or perhaps it was the whispering of ghosts, quietly conversing among themselves.

With one hand Lillian drew her coat tighter around her body. The crop, though, was in her way and she wished she could put it down somewhere. But Maurice or Antoine or another of Camille's men would notice, and thus Camille would eventually hear.

Such a tight, suffocating web of control. To break it, one had to destroy the spider in the middle. Drip poison into her drink. Watch her writhe in agony on the marbled floor. Or feed the fire in the kitchen, let it rage out of control until the blaze wrapped the house in its bright red bloom.

The chain and the handle of the crop bit into Lillian's hands.

Futile, futile dreams, these. For how could she ever dare lay hands on her stepmother, the woman her father had loved? Besides, she had been taught to heal, not to hurt. This she had done—with one exception.

Again, she threw a look over her shoulder, watched the man limping behind her. His left leg, it seemed, was giving him pain. Lillian wondered whether punishment had been applied to this part of his body or whether the limp was for other reasons.

The path now curved and wound, twisting like young Gérard on the table in front of Camille, his torso covered with fruit stains and chocolate scorches. A split opened in the greenery to reveal the statue of the half-naked lovers whom creepers had sealed together forevermore. Their hands were bare of whips or branding irons, their ankles free of chains and shackles. Sometimes Lillian wondered whether a love like that belonged to bygone ages, just like the statue itself.

Finally, Lillian and the prisoner reached the banks of a still lake, and Lillian followed the track around the slimy green water, where the grass had already been trampled down on earlier visits. What had been created to resemble nature by now had been devoured by nature. The trees stood tall and at places trunk by trunk, branches intertwining. The bushes and hedges had broken from their intended form and were now growing in wild abandon. In summer, when the air was hot enough to flimmer before one's eyes, the meadows around the lake would be ablaze with grasses and flowers, the deep hum of wild bees the only sound in the new wilderness.

At the other end of the lake, near the hidden garden wall, an imposing formation of rocks rose out of the water to form the mouth of a cave. At its entrance stood two proud horses of stone, nostrils flaring, and two men, on their knees, were offering up bowls of water. The group, Nanette had said, might once have been part of a fountain because the men had fishtails where their legs should be and one of them was holding a large, winding shell on his lap. The water would have flowed from the shell, perhaps, swirling around the horses' feet before dropping over several dark stone steps into the lake. The only way to reach the mouth of the cave was to take the path of the stepping stones that lay scrambled in the water as if thrown there by accident. During heavy rainfalls, the slimy green liquid would rise to cover them completely. Lillian hoped to be spared the rain over the next few days.

She gestured to the man to step to a nearby tree. She wound his chain around the trunk and secured it with the snap link at its loose end. After she took off his gag, she sat down on a fallen log. While she considered which poison was best to use on him, she awaited the call of the thrush.

That evening, dinner served as another lesson.

Nataraj, who had once lived in India, where the air tasted of spices, was the one chosen to stand behind the mistress's chair in his golden-brown glory. As the evening ritual demanded, his only garments were the golden breeches and the golden bands winding around his biceps. His hair as dark as night, his eyes coffee-brown, and his fingers swift and clever, he was another of Camille's favorites. That explained why he was chosen to be the teacher in this.

Lillian sat straight and stiff, ever aware of the prisoner looming at her back. He was similarly adorned as Nataraj, though his hands were still shackled behind him. Camille did not yet consider him suitable to touch. Thus, he was here to watch and to learn.

The first course consisted of mushroom soup, thick and creamy. Spoon after spoon Lillian raised to her mouth. It could have been sour goat milk—it was all the same to her.

The hand-feeding began with the small pastries, filled with fish and herbs, that Gérard brought out next. Nataraj slid to his knees beside his mistress's chair and made his fingers into plates for her pleasure. After each pastry, he would ensure that no crumbs remained to mar Camille's perfection. Nibbling and licking, he removed all lingering traces from her chin and lips.

Lillian sat straight and chewed, even though, with the presence of the man behind her, his breath almost searing the little hairs on her neck, she felt as if she were choking. Through that course and the next, all through the Russian caviar and the Laplander reindeer tongues, Lillian's back remained erect.

After each course, Nataraj would wash his hands so as not to spoil Camille's enjoyment of the different foods. She ate the curry rice from his palm and licked the caviar from his fingertips. Sometimes, when her teeth sank into his flesh, he would blink, but his smile never wavered. While she stroked his chest, he offered her the olives from Spain between his lips.

Lillian ate, her face expressionless, her fingers unfeeling.

On a large silver plate, Gérard brought in the last course, fruit and ginger-flavored cream. At the sight, Lillian's stomach sank. Coldness washed over her—not the numbing cold she so often sought, but the sudden icy flow of despair. For between the juicy pieces of peach and pineapple and the bowls with cream lay one of Camille's short whips. A whip with metal-adorned straps to draw blood at the first lash, which her stepmother only used to punish. So far, there had been no reason to punish Nataraj.

Camille moved her chair backwards, and, smiling over the rim of her wine-filled glass, she beckoned.

Lillian had to swallow hard, but then, turning her head a little, she said to the prisoner: "Go." What else could she say? What else could she do, helplessly caught in Camille's web, just like him, and surrounded by men loyal to her stepmother.

The man walked slowly over, his limp more pronounced than it had been in the garden.

It was enough to make Camille pout. "Has Gratien sold us damaged goods?"

Carefully, Lillian folded her hands in her lap. "As long as the service is good in other quarters. . . ."

She met her stepmother's stare calmly, and after a moment Camille's trilling laughter filled the room. "How right you are, *chérie*." She toasted Lillian with her glass. "And now we shall begin to see how good it is." This time, her smile was directed at the man, who had stopped at her end of the table.

Nataraj got to his feet and, following the silent command of his mistress, took the whip and stepped aside.

Leisurely, Camille's gaze stroked over the man before her, lingered lovingly on the scorched flesh in the form of a lily, before, with a jerk of her chin, she ordered him to his knees. When he would not obey, out of stubbornness or perhaps because he had not understood, another, sideways jerk of her head made Nataraj shove him down. The first blow of the whip tore at skin still bearing the weals from the night before.

Camille reached out and took a piece of peach, obviously enjoying the feel and taste of the fruit. Only when she had licked the last drops of sticky juice from her lips did she lean forward. "Your hands are in bonds, but you may serve in other ways."

Nataraj handed her a bowl of cream. Camille swirled her finger in the concoction, then licked it with relish. Next she dipped two fingers in the cream and proceeded to spread it on the pale expanse of her plunging neckline. While a smile of anticipation started to lift her lips, her hand snaked around the prisoner's neck to draw him near. He would lick it from her.

He resisted, and the whip sounded a second time.

It took ten lashes to make him give up his resistance. By that time, the blood Lillian saw was streaming down his back. Regardless, Camille spread her hand over the man's skin, dug her nails into his ravaged flesh. The smile bloomed on her face as she threw her head back, and Nataraj provided a steady supply of cream.

Soon, the white sweetness stained the top of her dress, traveling lower with each generous spread. It took another touch with the whip to make the man lower his head to her lap. Across the table, Lillian closed her eyes.

Chapter 3

The call came in the middle of the following week, on a cold afternoon when the sky was gray and the clouds hovered low with the promise of more rain. Three times the thrush called out in the long-awaited signal. Yet when Lillian rose from the damp tree trunk, her face was expressionless.

Chained to the other tree, the prisoner stood like a well-raised dog. For his obedience during the last two days or so, he had been spared the gag today.

Lillian turned and shook her head. They would not yet go back to the mansion.

Swiftly, she stepped onto the first stone in the water. The clacking of her shoes on the stones sounded unnaturally loud in the silence of the garden. However, she crossed the path to the mouth of the cave without hesitation. Only when she had climbed up to the statues of the men and their horses did she halt and, taking a deep breath, look back to the man on the banks of the lake. He stood so still that he could have been stone himself.

With a swirl of her coat, Lillian turned to enter the cave. A grotto, Nanette had said it was called. Perhaps the first lord of the mansion had used it for his secret dalliances. If so, his paramour had come from outside the manor.

In the cave, close to the niche with the statues of the horses and the men but well hidden from unsuspecting view, Lillian felt for the flintbox and the candle. When her light flared up, it revealed the fantastic decorations, mythic beasts in stone springing from the walls and the ceiling. Then the light touched upon the metal door at the back, which might have once been concealed by a tapestry.

Lillian's heart rose to her throat as her fingers skimmed the cool metal. But then, as its coolness seeped into her, she straightened her shoulders and slid the door's bolt free.

On the other side, behind the curtain of creepers that had been thinned out weeks ago, stood a bedraggled boy with bare feet. At her sudden appearance he blinked. His eyes surveyed her from head to toe before he nodded briskly, his face suddenly that of a man. "Everything's ready," he said in the broad *patois* of the area. He smelled of the sea; perhaps he was a fisher's son. A smuggler's son.

"When?"

He raised his brows. "Now." And he spat, carelessly. As if spitting was a sign of manliness. "Get your things, *madame.*"

"Now?" She had thought she would have time to prepare.

"The tide'll rise in a few hours." He looked as if he considered spitting again. "We were told that you'd be ready." All of a sudden, his expression became wary. Perhaps he suspected a trap. This was a risky enough enterprise as it was, defying the mistress of the manor. In the past, nobody had dared help. How Nanette had managed to find somebody willing this time, Lillian did not know. To slip the net of control. . . .

Her hands itched to snake around her body, to protect herself from the cold within. She had thought she would have a few hours. She would have packed a bundle with her herbs. She would have poisoned the man.

Her head jerked around as she remembered him, chained to the tree. How long would it take him to die out there? Three days? A week? More?

"*Madame?*" The boy sounded impatient now. Of course they needed to be on their way. The sea was not patient either; it would not wait for them.

"You." Lillian turned around, her decision made even before she realized it. "I will be back. In a few minutes at most. Wait for me."

Displeasure rumbled in the boy's chest. "You better hurry."

Lillian straightened her shoulders and gave him a haughty stare. "You will be paid well for this. Do not forget it." With that, she swung around and stepped back into the grotto. Carefully, she closed the door behind her so the boy would not use the opportunity to nose around the cave. For if he found the purse with all the jewelry she had collected over the last few weeks, he might disappear like a morning mist.

Lillian felt her heart beating hard and fast against her ribs. How strange that the men and their horses still stood frozen at the entrance of the cave, covered with moss and lichen, when she herself seemed to have finally broken free. Across the lake, the man still stood as well.

Her foot slid and she slithered down onto the first step, her legs shaky, her breath a wheezing sound in her ears. Lillian clenched her fingers into fists until her nails bit into the tender skin of her palms. The pain helped her to concentrate, to make the tremors pass. She called upon the coolness of the water, upon the cold air that surrounded her, and let it soak into her skin and her whole being.

Steadily, she took the remaining steps down to lake level

and walked over the stones back to the bank. Her fingers, when they touched the chain to release the prisoner's snap lock, were calm—as calm as her voice. "Come with me."

The chains made it difficult for him to traverse the stepping stones, yet she did not dare loosen them at the moment. A caged animal turned free might well turn against anyone who was near.

The steps up to the cave presented even more of a challenge, but Lillian dragged him on without showing any mercy. There was no time for mercy now. No time at all for mercy at Château du Marais. She gathered the chill that emanated from the stones into herself, a core of ice to hold her upright through the next few hours.

Following the flickering light of the candle, the man's gaze dashed over the grotto's carved animals. Lillian stood on tiptoe and felt behind the wings of the gryphon. The purse she withdrew was heavy with jewelry, her own and some of Camille's. She would need all of it tonight to pay the smugglers for their services. Lillian made it disappear inside her coat. "When we are outside"—she threw a look at him over her shoulder—"be quiet." And she opened the door.

The boy's eyes widened slightly when he caught sight of the man. "That was not the bargain," he spluttered. "'Twas only you—"

"I know." Ever careful, Lillian clicked the door shut. "He will not come the whole way. Do you wish to discuss this? I thought we had not much time."

The boy ran his hands through his hair and muttered some vile curses, then finally led them to the place where he had left his cart. Of course it did not compare with Camille's elegant carriage. It was a farmer's cart, a smuggler's cart, and the two ponies looked strong and sturdy. They remained quiet when the boy approached. Smugglers' animals. A whinny at a wrong time could mean certain death for their owners.

Lillian cast a searching look at the sky. Dusk would settle fast today, and soon night would welcome them into her arms. By the time anybody noticed their disappearance, they would be long gone.

She climbed onto the ramp of the cart, which she had to share with the prisoner. The chains made him clumsy, and a fine film of sweat covered his forehead and throat. She drew her knees against her chest so she would not touch him. She did not look back when the boy took the reins and the cart started to bumble down the muddy path. Soon afterwards it began to drizzle, the wetness clinging to Lillian's coat in a million little droplets, moistening her face and hands. A gray curtain closed off the world.

Beside her, tiny shivers raced through the man's injured body and made his chains click in a grotesque parody of a tune. But Lillian raised her face to the sky and gloried in the rain that dampened her hair. Her brown curls sprang to a wild life of their own, slipping out of her hairpins, escaping her carefully arranged ivory combs.

The wetness that soaked the earth would render their tracks invisible within a very short time. And the drizzle itself would cloak them for the rest of their journey. In weather like this, nobody looked twice at a farmer's cart.

The boy swore and muttered, but the ponies seemed heedless of the rain. They trotted on, and the sodden ground swallowed the sounds of their hooves.

Once, Lillian looked back, yet by then the mansion had disappeared as if it had never been. Nevertheless, she could still feel the dark menace that emanated from it, a bleakness that seemed to have seeped into the land itself. This was cursed soil, where every rose would blacken and all grass would wither.

Lillian closed her eyes, swaying with the motion of the cart. She would not let herself think of Camille's anger upon learning of her escape. By the time they would notice her absence, the oncoming night and the weather would have made it impossible for anyone to follow her straight away. And by tomorrow morning, she would be gone.

If not. . . .

It did not bear thinking about.

Lillian opened her eyes and found the man staring at her, his own eyes very blue. Quickly, she turned her head away. She did not want him here. Why hadn't she left him in the garden, chained to the tree? But then . . . but then, she had pressed the brand into his skin. . . .

Her responsibility.

She watched the indistinct shapes and shades of the gray landscape slide by, all color washed out. Perhaps they had lost their track, had entered the Otherworld long ago. Perhaps they were now forced to travel on and on, forever caught in the small cart.

Lillian shook herself.

Shadows loomed ahead, dark and menacing. As she looked, a forest grew out of the shadows. Untouched trees reached high, and below, bushes formed a seemingly impregnable wall. A forest, perfect for hiding, far away from the prison and the mines alike. It was as good a place as anywhere.

"Stop," Lillian said to the boy. When he just grunted for an answer, she gripped a handful of his jerkin. "Stop. I want to let him go."

The boy reined the ponies in and turned in his seat. "Go on with it." He spat. "And hurry." The wetness had slicked his hair to his head, formed nonexistent grooves in his face so that he looked older, a man instead of a boy.

"Go," Lillian told the prisoner, whose chains rattled

against the wooden cart. She climbed off the vehicle after him, watching as he nearly stumbled and fell. Perhaps his bad leg was hurting. She should have left him in the garden.

Lillian slipped the necklace with the key over her head, and she opened the ring around his neck. The metal was cool and slippery with wetness. Impossible to tell whether it was from the rain or from his sweat.

Behind her, she heard a distinct clicking sound.

When she turned around, the boy was holding a pistol, ready to shoot. At the glance she threw him, he just shrugged. "No need to take risks, is there? Better to get rid of that one soon."

So she ordered the man to turn around for her to open the shackles that bound his wrists. The flesh beneath, she saw, was scraped raw. It did not matter anymore.

Quickly, she scrambled back up the cart, suddenly glad for the boy's pistol. She reminded herself: a caged animal, turned free, might well turn against anyone who was near.

She watched the man spread his hands, free at last, and turn around, his eyes a smoldering blue. Then the cart rumbled on, gathering speed, and his eyes disappeared behind the curtain of the rain. He would not be able to follow them, Lillian knew, not with his limp. He would not make it out of the forest, perhaps. He would surely not make it beyond the forest. Not fast enough. Not without money.

Her responsibility.

All that was in the purse, she had to use to pay the smugglers. It was all she had.

Her responsibility.

Lillian touched her muslin-covered throat, where under the layer of cloth another necklace dangled, pure gold. Without thinking, she reached inside and unfastened it.

For a brief, precious moment she held the locket clutched in her hand; then she threw it, hoping he would see it in the waning light. "Here!"

He hopped and bent—he had caught it, she saw.

The rain was running down her face, while she looked back on the solitary figure in the middle of the muddy road. She looked and looked until the rain swallowed him completely.

Shivering, Lillian drew her coat tighter around her body. "How far is it?" she asked the boy.

"Not far."

By the time they reached the small group of cottages huddled against the hill, night had fallen and Lillian had lost all sense of time. The boy urged the ponies on to one of the houses, whose inviting yellow lights were a merry counterpart to the flickering light of the lantern he'd lit when the darkness came upon them. Over the sounds of the rain, Lillian could now hear the song of the sea. The wind smelled of salt and fish and rotten seaweed. The taste of it filled her mouth, strange and foreign.

The cart came to a squelching halt in front of one of the cottages. The light of the lantern danced over a faded red door; somewhere a dog started barking. At that, the door opened, throwing more light into the darkness outside. It cast the man on the threshold in shadow, a hulk of blackness and gleaming edges. "There you are," he said, his voice gruff, his French even rougher than the boy's. "What took you so long?"

The boy sprang from the box seat. "Roads were bad."

Another, much smaller figure appeared in the door and hovered behind the man, like a bird looking for a way out of its cage. Lillian recognized the bent shape of Nanette, and, with a sigh of relief, she jumped to the ground. Her light boots disappeared in the mud up to well over her ankle. But she did not notice.

"*Oh, mon petit chou-chou!*" The birdlike figure pushed past the man, who surprisingly stepped aside without a word. Straightening, the form became a petite old woman, her white hair floating around her head like a cloud of white wool. Hands outstretched, she gathered Lillian into her arms. Parchment-like skin touched Lillian's icy-cold cheeks, and bony hands ran over her sodden coat, shaping shoulders and arms and waist as if to reassure themselves that everything was still there.

For a moment, Lillian allowed herself to close her eyes and to lay her head on the fragile shoulder, inhaling the familiar scent of crushed lavender blossoms that rose from the old woman's clothes. For a while, she allowed her own shoulders to sag before she finally straightened. Yet when she went to step back, the old woman's hands came up to frame her face. The thumbs brushed over her cheekbones, warming her skin.

"How have you been?"

Lillian tried a smile. "I'm fine. Truly."

The man, who until now had held a respectful silence, interrupted them. "The time's almost here."

"Yes, of course." Nanette turned to smile at him. "We will be ready quite soon. Come in, *chou-chou*, you are all wet and dripping. You need some warm clothes before we go."

In the house it smelled of fish and smoke. A fire lit the room, revealed a smoke-darkened ceiling, a table with a bench and some chairs. At a spinning wheel sat a woman, an apron over her coarse dress. Beside her on the floor sat a grubby child in a short frock, chubby legs and feet bare. Eyes as round as marbles, it gnawed thoughtfully on its fist. Another child, a girl of ten, maybe, led Lillian up a ladder to a low room under the roof. At the far end stood a candle waiting for them, chasing the shadows away and revealing enough of the surroundings that Lillian saw they were in the sleeping quarters of the family. Here Lillian shed her silk and cotton and donned rough wool instead: underskirts, a plain dress, thick socks, and, finally a heavy dark coat with a cape which would ward off the wind and the spray of the sea.

When they returned downstairs, Nanette put on a huge oilskin coat, looking like a child playing at dress-up. A new shaft of fear darted through Lillian as she became aware once again how very vulnerable they were: Should the smugglers decide to forgo their bargain, to take their gold and jewels and dump them on high seas, she and Nanette would be helpless to stop them.

Lillian bit her lip.

Better the sea than Camille's wrath.

Better the sea than living under Camille's roof for another day, another night.

Catching sight of Lillian's worried face, Nanette stepped up and tutted under her breath. With deft fingers the old woman made to close the top button of Lillian's borrowed oilskin coat, as if Lillian were still a little girl. When Nanette's knuckles brushed over the naked skin at the base of Lillian's throat, she halted. Frowning, she looked up. "Your locket, *chou-chou*, your mother's locket—where is it?"

Lillian felt the cold of the night squeeze through the chinks in the wall, through the slits under the closed shutters, through the small cracks in the door. It filled the room until coldness whirled all around her and soaked her body in ice. She smiled the tight little smile she had come to perform so well, and said: "I had to hide it and leave it in my room." She remembered the light glinting on its golden surface as it had sailed through the rain. "She will never find it."

The man coughed. "We need to go." He led them down to the beach, where the wet sand crunched under all of their boots. The song of the sea increased in a threatening crescendo until it had become a roar, filling Lillian's ears. The cold water was calling out to her.

She remembered the feeling of the locket in her hand, warm on one side where it had rested against her skin, cold on the other. The miniatures of her mother and father inside had been holding the memory of her parents alive when it would have slipped away and faded into nothingness.

Lillian forced her back to remain straight, even though the wind was chilling her cheeks and trying to wedge under the borrowed coat. Any sign of weakness might be deadly—it was a lesson she had learned well in the years under her stepmother's roof.

Ahead, flickering lights danced on the seashore—more lanterns just like theirs. Figures separated from the shadows, took on human forms: the crew of the ship that would bring them over the channel.

The men who might cut their throats.

Half hidden by the rain, the waves rocked a black shell of a boat too small to seem trustworthy. Surely too small to be able to cross the sea.

Wordlessly, the big man picked up Nanette and carried her through the water to the boat, while another man approached Lillian. Her world lurched as he heaved her up into his arms and followed the others. The smell of stale sweat and rancid fish filled her nose and burnt the back of her throat, and yet it was more appealing than the odor of crushed rose petals or of Camille's scented body oil.

In order to be out of the men's way, the two women huddled between some barrels, dark bulky shapes in the night, their oilskin coats all that protected them from the wind and the rain. A lonely mast rose up as if to touch the cloudy sky, with the bulk of the sail waiting to be hoisted.

The men worked in silence, and soon, cloth rustled and wood creaked; the sail billowed with wind in the ghostly gray and pulled the vessel out to the sea. Salty spray joined the steady rain, while the wind rocked the ship from side to side and the waves rolled under them. Their course seemed awkward, changing now and then, but perhaps it was just the sea, bucking like a horse that wants to throw its rider. In the wet darkness of the small vessel, Lillian forgot all about her earlier fears. She no longer worried about a slit throat, but about a cold grave in the endless black water.

Better than another night under Camille's roof.

After a while, Lillian lost all feeling of time, and the memories of Château du Marais faded into insignificance. It seemed to her as if her journey stretched to cover past and present, reaching for an eternity of miserable, rolling night. Perhaps they had long slipped through the web of time and now were doomed to sail onward forever after.

Lillian let the icy dampness numb her body and mind, and moved with the motions of the ship as she had moved with the motions of Camille's carriage. The wetness soaked even her oilskin coat, and the rain and the spray dampened her coarse woolen clothes, chilling the skin beneath.

After what seemed like ages or perhaps no time at all, one of the men struck a tinder and lit a lantern. The flame threw a flickering light over the people in the boat, creating nightmarish beings from black hollows and moving shadows and the unfamiliar shapes of fishermen's coats.

Nanette patted Lillian's arm. "Soon," she whispered, while in the distance an answering light flared, almost invisible in the endless rain.

Sandra Schwab

Once more, wood creaked as the sails filled with wind and carried them forward. The darkness looming ahead slowly took on form and revealed the bulky shape of a coastline. The single light ahead rose high the nearer they came and then was joined by a chain of moving lights, twinkling in and out of existence in the steady downpour.

Again the little vessel changed its course, sailing parallel to the coast, before the men let the wind fill the sails to the full for the last time. With a crunch they came to a halt, and the sails were hurriedly brought in. "We're there," said the big man unnecessarily. The light of his lantern flickered over his face, gleamed on his wet skin. Lillian no longer smelled the fish.

He jumped into the water and reached for Nanette to carry her the last steps to the shore. Another man, large and wet as well, held out his arms for Lillian. She could not tell whether it was the same who had carried her before. But then, it did not matter. She reached the land high in his arms, the land she had left over a decade before, the land of her father and mother who would never see it again.

She heard the water gurgling around the man's feet, the rhythmic song of the sea, of the waves lapping at the land. The wet sand sparkled in the dim light of the lanterns, which now joined them on the beach. Shadows shifted and became men or horses and sometimes a cart to be filled with barrels from the boat.

When Lillian's feet touched the ground, the land shifted as if she were still on the boat, rocked by the waves. She wondered what Nanette had done with her purse, whether she had already given it to the smugglers or whether it would be divided between the men who had brought them over the sea and the men who would receive them. She saw

42

the big man talking to one of the latter; tall and slim, as if his daily labor was neither hard nor of his hands.

Lillian felt exhaustion creeping upwards from her feet, trickling through veins and muscles, leaving numbness behind. She felt the cold wind biting her salt-crusted cheeks, cracking her lips until the coppery taste of blood filled her mouth. She remembered the sight of blood on smooth skin, muscles rippling underneath but unable to escape the sting of the whip.

"Are you all right, *chou-chou?*" Lillian almost did not notice the touch of Nanette's hand on her arm, her flesh unfeeling. She let the coldness of the rain and the night seep into her body until all lingering feelings were dead, all memories forgotten.

"Yes," she said. "Where will they take us?"

"Through the heath up north." In the big oilskins, the old woman looked frail and lost, and Lillian's heart gave a strange lurch. "They are friends of Jean's. They have promised to help."

"But are they trustworthy? Is *he* trustworthy?" Lillian swayed a little in the soft wind as she thought about being at these men's mercy.

"I saved his wife from the fever," Nanette answered softly. "We will come to no harm."

Everything needs balance. One to do the healing in a place where another does all the wounding. And sometimes the healing could be used as coin, could be used to win people's trust.

An alien word, this *trust.*

Lillian drew her oilskin coat tighter around herself as if to wrap her body in its cool wetness, numbing her limbs.

Then the two men came forward, and the one whom Nanette had called Jean said: "You'll go with Mr. Collins here and warm yourselves up for a bit. Later, they'll bring you away." He reached out, and his large fingers closed around one of Nanette's withered hands. "I thank you for what you did for us. May the Lord keep you safe."

Lillian thought she saw Nanette smile, but with the steady rain and the dim light of the lanterns she could not be sure. The old woman bowed her head. "Good-bye, Jean. And God bless you."

The man, Mr. Collins, led them up the beach while the sand crunched under their feet, and before long they saw the twinkling lights of a village just awakening to a new morn. They followed him past small cottages that hovered near the ground like great, black beasts; past the disgruntled bark of a dog, the early cry of a newborn babe, until they walked in the shadow of the village church, whose bell tower rose crookedly above them. The man beckoned them to another small house that nestled close to the crumbling wall of the churchyard. Beside the well-trodden front steps stood a pot with flowers whose scent, despite the night and the rain, wafted up to tickle Lillian's nose and summon the memory of summers long bygone, when small girls and fat puppies had played in flower gardens kissed by the sun.

Lillian shook her head to chase away these unbidden thoughts. One last time, she gathered the cold night around herself before entering the warmth and the light of the house, where the smell of newly baked bread lingered in the hallway, underlaid by the fragrance of fresh tea.

At the other end of the corridor, a door opened and emitted a middle-aged woman with cheeks like red apples. She wore a gray, woolly scarf over a high-collared nightgown, and from underneath her white nightcap a few tendrils of faded blond hair tumbled onto her forehead, whirled around her earlobes. "There you are, there you are," she said. The fragrances of bread and tea were stronger now, seemed to surround the woman like a cloud.

"This is my sister," said the tall, slim man. "Miss Hilda Collins." The golden light of the house revealed him to be clothed all in black with the exception of his white collar. With a start, Lillian realized that he must be the priest of the village.

How strange a land this is, she thought, *where priests know smugglers' secrets*. She was glad that she had kept to the shadowy place near the front door, where nobody would see her sudden shiver. Seeking the shadows even further, she glided backwards and observed how Nanette smiled and greeted the other woman.

"How do you do?" As easy as that, Nanette switched to English, no trace left of the years spent in France. It was strange to hear her speak without the usual melodious singsong to her voice, strange and frightening, as if another person had appeared in Nanette's place. So easily she chatted with the other woman, who clicked her tongue over the state of their clothes and finally ushered them to a room to wash and to change.

Afterwards, they were given tea and food. Lillian ate as if in a hazy dream, English chatter filling her ears, hurting them with foreign sounds. She almost wished to be back over the sea. But then images of dark blood on white linen rose and hovered in front of her inner eye; images of blood trickling over smooth skin, a lily burnt into human flesh. Briefly she wondered whether he was already dead. Yet it was too soon, just hours, even though it seemed like a lifetime. He would live a little longer.

Lillian imagined him curled up under a duvet of moldy leaves, running, tumbling through the undergrowth of the forest, the angry sounds of Camille's big dogs never far away, dogs ready to sink their teeth into skin and muscle,

45

to tear apart human flesh until the body resembled an overlarge doll, all smeared with blood. . . .

Lillian balled her hands to fists in her lap. It had been raining when they left France. The rain would have washed away all tracks and all lingering scents. Camille would not be able to indulge in one of her hunts; the dogs would be fed with beef and pork instead of human flesh. It would take another day and, hopefully, another man before they could again be used for their foul purpose.

Lillian willed the memories to recede. For a little while longer, he would live.

She was glad when a man came to take them away, Nanette and herself. The warmth of the house and of its people was unfamiliar and seemed to thaw her invisible armor. She preferred the coldness of the night, welcomed it even. She raised her face and let the chilly wind caress her skin, dribble coldness into her pores, until the familiar numbness settled over her once more. So much safer this, than applelike cheeks or the taste and smell of freshly baked bread covered with golden butter.

They had to ride ponies, tough shaggy beasts, and had to bundle their skirts around their legs so they would sit on the ponies like men did on horses. The man who rode with them did not talk much, just led them out of the village, through the heath, which rolled around them in endless abandon.

Dawn was not far away, and they traveled through a world of dim gray. Their lead's lantern cast a lonely light, which flickered and dimmed as if it were a will-o'-the-wisp, luring the unwary wanderer away from the right path. Here and there, naked trees rose up through the veil of rain and strained their skeleton-like arms toward heaven.

Again, it seemed to Lillian as if they had left the real

world behind only to enter a nebulous in-between, a world of shadows and void of warmth. And once more, all feeling of time ceased to exist.

So it might have been hours or days or even just minutes until the rain stopped. Overhead, the wind was chasing the clouds away until the last stars filled the sky like scattered diamonds, blinking and fading with the steady approach of dawn. The dimness lifted, their guide put out the light in the lantern. In the distance they could hear the sleepy bark of a dog, and slim whiffs of smoke bespoke a village.

And still on they rode.

The first birds rose to greet the new day, while the creatures of the night returned to their dens. A fox barked. The undergrowth rustled with scurrying feet.

Around them, grass and heather gave way to orderly fields and hedges, empty meadows that might have held cows or sheep during the summer. And all of a sudden, a rosy hue settled on the land, tinted the sky and the air itself, so it seemed the world had disappeared behind rose-colored glass.

The man dropped them off at a crossroads and, with a tip of his finger to his hat, rode off. Soon, the muffled squelches of the hooves of the ponies in the mud were no more than a distant memory.

"So, my girl, give me your arm and then we will see the rest of our journey done." Nanette slipped her hand into the crook of Lillian's elbow and led them on. It was difficult walking, with the lane covered in mud that stuck to their boots like balls of lead and turned the hems of their dresses an ugly brown. Yet around them the air was clear and fresh, and the birds broke into jubilant song, while all shades of red and orange and yellow flamed across the eastern sky.

In a gentle curve the road wound around a hill, and behind it, the sight of a stately manor greeted them. In the early light of the new day it seemed to be immersed in gold. An exhausted smile spread across Nanette's face. "Abberley House," she sighed. "Come on, *chou-chou*, we are nearly home."

Bemused, Lillian followed. *Home* was another strange word, foreign to her experience, except as a dim memory that did not bear thinking about, for there was no return to the times of her earliest childhood when her mother had still been alive. Now her parents were only pictures in a golden locket, which, flying through the rain, had sparkled with the waning light of day.

Trees rose up on each side of the road, hiding the house from view, and gravel crunched under their feet. Finally, the trees opened into a semicircle forecourt. With the rising sun, the house seemed to glow from within, as if the stones themselves were consumed by fire. Nanette trudged up the wide steps to the front door, where she lifted the heavy-looking knocker and let it bang against the wooden door. She had to repeat this four times, until the door was opened by a disgruntled servant, hastily dressed, hair still awry.

"What's the racket?" he snapped, when he caught sight of their bedraggled appearance. "There's no place for your likes."

"Kennett, what is it?" another voice inquired from within.

Suddenly the man at the door stood stiff as a board. " 'Tis nothing, your lordship. A few tramps, that's all."

"Tramps?" The voice sounded nearer now, and then the door was opened wider to reveal an elderly man in a dark green dressing gown. He blinked, once, twice, before his gaze fastened on Nanette. Lillian saw his eyes widen in surprise, then they shifted on to her, and she thought they widened even further.

"My lord." Nanette curtsied. "May I present your granddaughter? Lady Lillian Marianne Abberley."

PART II

She sleeps: her breathings are not heard
In palace chambers far apart.
The fragrant tresses are not stirr'd
That lie upon her charmed heart.
She sleeps: on either hand upswells
The gold-fringed pillow lightly prest:
She sleeps, nor dreams, but ever dwells
A perfect form in perfect rest.

—Tennyson, The Day Dream

Chapter 4

London, Spring 1816

Like beacons the three large chandeliers spread their light over the ballroom below, and the bright light of a hundred candles glittered on silver and diamonds, was caught by the shimmering material of swirling dresses and reflected a hundredfold by the many mirrors along the walls. Music mingled with the sounds of laughter and conversation, rising and falling like the waves of an unseen ocean. The perfume of the flower arrangements, lush bouquets of fragrant roses, of Canterbury bells and heliotropes, drifted up to blend with the scent of Imperial water, sandalwood and rose water, overlaid by the aroma of rich soup spiked with negus, which was served in the adjoining room. There, the refreshments were given out: sparkling wine that tickled the nose, sweet elderflower or sour lime lemonade, tiny tarts filled with strawberry marmalade, bitter coffee or soothing tea, old-fashioned ratafia ice cream and fragrant violet parfait. From the cardroom at the other side of the ballroom drifted hazy clouds of smoke, for not only the widows and dowagers enjoyed a game of whist or loo, but also some of the gentlemen who had grown bored with having to impress nubile maidens with fluttering eyelashes.

If Lillian had stepped into fairyland, she could not have felt more out of place. Her back ramrod straight, she went through the steps of a dance whose name she had forgotten, the folds of her white dress whirling around her ankles. Her lips were lifted in a smile, even though her fingers itched under the material of her long gloves. When the figures of the dance demanded, she went and linked arms or hands with her partner, only to depart again and to continue to stand, watching and waiting for her next turn. And when asked, she commented upon the pleasant sound of the orchestra, the lovely weather, or the beautiful decoration, while trying to forget the alien pressure of the waxen bust-improver against her ribs.

Throughout all of winter she had been trained for her entrance into London society. Teachers of all kind had come to her grandfather's country estate, had passed through her life in a seemingly endless procession: one to teach her English etiquette, one for singing, one for dancing, one to reacquaint her with the piano, one with whom to practice polite conversation, one to prepare her for presentation at court. And then an unknown aunt had appeared to chaperone her through the bustle of the London season.

Yes, she had been trained well, and for the sake of her aunt and grandfather she intended to perform well. Thus she smiled and smiled and smiled until her cheeks hurt and her face felt as if, like glass, it might shatter any moment. So far, she had never once misstepped during a dance, her complexion had been deemed perfect and her dresses the height of fashion. And yet. . . .

She, who had perfected silence at a very early age, did not know how to converse with people. Discussions of fashion or beaux or the latest scandal seemed strange to her, and the delicate dance of courtship, in which she saw others engaged, appeared as alien as a foreign language. She did not understand why on the cheeks of her dance partner, a pale young man with stylish blond curls, flaming blotches of excitement bloomed, and why he needed continual reassurance that she liked the music, the dance, and the ball in general. She did not understand why her aunt had ordered the best food to be served when he came to her grandfather's town house for dinner, why it had been necessary for her to wear one of her best dresses, to have her hair done in such an uncomfortable style that her scalp hurt. And then he could not even look at her without blushing a fierce red. Throughout the whole meal she had sat in silence, listening as the conversation around her moved from topic to topic, lightly, as if these people's tongues had wings to carry them through dinner talks.

She did not understand why he would want to come back after that. She did not understand why all these men with whom she scarcely talked came back to ask for a dance or offered to guide her to the refreshment room. As if she could not find the way by herself.

But then, perhaps, she wouldn't be able to find the way by herself. Back at Château du Marais she had known where to walk, where to go to. Now, life had turned into a puzzle whose bits and pieces no longer fit together. And so, she came to yearn for the overgrown garden, for Pan hiding in the greenery and for the stone lovers bound together by creepers forevermore. Secure in the garden, where no one had tread but her, it had not mattered that the world outside had whirled through the months and years without her. Yet here, even as she followed the motions of the dance, she was still not engaged in the greater dance of the world, and here she did not have the solitude of a green haven.

She had . . . nothing.

The dance ended. She was offered an arm so they could walk around the room in a long procession with the other couples. Another thing she did not understand.

However, she understood how to smile even when the matrons at the sides of the room flipped their fans and whispered to each other, none too quietly.

"What does that young Perrin want with *her?*"

". . . the Marquis of Larkmoor's granddaughter . . ."

". . . appeared out of nowhere . . ."

". . . I wouldn't have thought him to be so bird-witted as that . . ."

Perhaps Alexander Markham, Viscount Perrin, did not hear these comments as he walked around the room with Lillian's hand on his arm. Once again, he leaned his head toward her and inquired whether she had liked that dance.

"Yes, my lord." Lillian glanced at him from the corner of her eyes, glanced into his kind, round face, which had not yet lost the chubbiness of adolescence. She wondered how his naïveté could have survived for so long.

Not that it mattered.

A giggle from the sidelines diverted her attention. Her gaze flitted over a woman whose breasts seemed ready to spill over the low neckline of her dress, and was caught by the man at her side, well into his prime. With his ginger hair and whiskers, the Marquis of Hertford looked like a sly fox. Right now, he appeared to regard Lillian as his prey, for he eyed her with a leering grin on his lips, even as he playfully pinched the arm of the woman beside him.

"Ice Maiden," the woman repeated, and this time her giggle was even louder than before. She looked at Lillian, triumph clearly etched on her face just like the wrinkles that bracketed her mouth. The wife of some baron or duke, she might hope to become the marquis's next mistress. And if a younger woman, silent and unapproachable, had been given such a name, *Ice Maiden*, it was well worth a gloat or two.

Lillian understood *that*.

She looked through the woman and the man, her face a careful blank. This, too, she had been taught and taught well—back in France. She knew all about games of power and how to gather the chill that hovered in the corners of the large room and let it numb her skin, soak into her body.

And she knew how not to smirk when from the chandeliers above wax dropped onto the bosom of the woman, scorching white skin just like hot chocolate would. With a shriek, the woman jumped back. Yet the eyes of the man at her side remained fixed on Lillian.

Still Lillian looked through him, refusing to acknowledge the incident, refusing to acknowledge him and how his face twisted, sharpened.

"Lady Medlycott," the Viscount Perrin mumbled, irritated. When Lillian turned her eyes to him, the hectic red blotches appeared on his cheeks, and he made an impatient movement with his free hand. "She is a jade . . . a . . . a vulgar, that woman. Always creating scenes."

"I believe a drop of wax fell on her," Lillian replied quietly.

He stared at her with eyes like round blue marbles, as if he had never heard of such a thing as dripping candles before. Then they both turned and watched as the Marquis of Hertford flicked the offending drop of wax away and let his finger linger on the expanse of heaving white flesh, let it slip under the neckline of the Clarence blue dress.

The Viscount Perrin blushed an even deeper shade of red, very much like the strawberries he had sent Lillian this afternoon before the ball.

Her stepmother would have preferred cherries.

The viscount put a gloved hand over Lillian's fingers on his arm. "I am sorry you had to witness that." His voice sounded both angry and embarrassed, and with a slight tug on her arm, he drew her on. Lillian wondered what he would have thought had he known what she witnessed at Château du Marais.

But then, nobody knew.

Nobody even suspected.

Not even Nanette.

"The daughter of a commoner," Perrin muttered. "Medlycott only married her for the money, and now she . . . she . . ." His voice was lost in a splutter.

"She wants to climb," Lillian said softly. "The Marquis of Hertford is a friend of the Prince Regent, is he not?"

Again, the round blue eyes were turned on her, clearly showing surprise at her insight. Then they darkened ominously. "He is, but . . . he is not a man a respectable woman would want her name linked to. A gamester of the worst sort, a . . . a . . ." Apparently he had difficulties finding a fitting term that would not shock his fair partner's sensibilities. "A scapegrace and . . . and a libertine."

Compared to her stepmother, the Marquis of Hertford sounded like a puppy dog. But, of course, Lillian could not tell Viscount Perrin that. Graciously, she bowed her head. "I see," she murmured.

The young nobleman frowned. "Medlycott should call him out, demand satisfaction. I would, if I were him. This . . . this is an affront to his honor."

Lillian looked straight ahead, focusing on the bright orange feather stuck in the turban of the lady in front of them. "So you would kill a man for this?" It seemed to her as if she could hear the song of the dogs in the distance, yearning to sink their teeth into flesh and bone. She could almost see ruby droplets blooming on white linen, and perhaps a pistol shot would sound like the crack of a whip searing skin.

Lillian blinked.

Beside her, she felt Perrin square his shoulders. "My honor would demand it. As would the honor of every respectable man." Her question seemed to have affronted him. "You might think me inexperienced in battle. True, I have not been to the war as my cousin, but he has no father who would have prevented him from going." All at once, he sounded wistful. "I would have liked to gain glories on the battlefield. How sublime it must have been to fight at Wellington's side at Waterloo. . . ." Here his voice trailed off, and his blue marble eyes turned to the distance, shimmering, as if he would burst into tears any moment, so moved was he by his glorious visions of heroic deeds for king and country.

All Lillian could envision, however, were nightmarish sights of blood and gore, the smell of scorched flesh, the cries of men. She suppressed a shudder. To banish these images, she grabbed at the next best question she could think of. "So your cousin was at Waterloo?"

Perrin frowned, blinked, then shook his head as if to clear his thoughts. "No, he was not. He was wounded in some skirmish or other several months before and taken prisoner." Their round through the room had almost come to an end. This seemed to make him remember his gentlemanly obligations. His fingers pressed reverently down on Lillian's. "Would you like some refreshments, my lady?"

Refreshments meant that she could forego the next dance. "Yes, my lord." She bowed her head. "Thank you."

With purposeful steps the viscount guided her toward the refreshments room, a man with a mission. When they arrived, the smaller room was already filled with other thirsty dancers, smiling, talking, and sipping sparkling wine. Debutantes fingered their necklaces, rows of pearls or sparkling stones, and giggled while they stood beside their dance partners, who in turn puffed out their chests and held their wineglasses with elegant nonchalance.

"Could I tempt you with a cup of soup?" Perrin asked solicitously. His hand still rested over hers in an oddly protective gesture.

Lillian looked at it.

Or perhaps it was just possessive.

Yet who would think such a thing of Alexander Markham, Viscount Perrin, with his innocent blue eyes and blushing cheeks? She lifted her gaze and met his, stared at him as if to penetrate all his secrets. But in the end, it did not matter. What ever did?

His eyes darted away.

"I would like a glass of lemonade," Lillian said softly.

He sent her a delicately painted fan the next day, which Lillian's aunt could not stop admiring. "He must be in love with you, my child!" she exclaimed, obviously pleased with herself that she had managed to secure a good *parti* for her niece during her very first season. Aunt Louisa, a woman with an ample bosom and a preference for rainbow-colored dresses and cheerful turbans, exuded the soft scent of violets as she bowed over the viscount's latest present. "Charming, absolutely charming," she murmured. "Come and see, Lillian, my dear. Such an exquisite miniature. A scene from *A Midsummer Night's Dream*, I believe."

Lillian stood up from the window seat of her grandfather's drawing room, which conveniently overlooked the busy street outside. This way, the ladies of the house could observe what was going on in the neighborhood, who was paying a visit on whom, who had a new bonnet or a new walking dress. Lillian usually just stared out of the window without seeing anything.

"Nanette, have you seen it?" Aunt Louisa asked the older woman, who sat knitting in a corner of the room. "It is truly charming, is it not?"

Lillian magicked a smile on her face as she stepped beside her aunt to admire the fan, which was laid out on the small side table in front of them. The smooth ivory plates of the fan were, indeed, embellished with an Arcadian scene, showing a woman in a shift cuddling close to a donkey-headed man. Lillian touched the fan with the tip of her finger. How curious this was—a man with a donkey head.

"And so very clever," Aunt Louisa went on and clapped her hands in delight. "To send you a fan with a scene from the play we are to attend tonight."

Lillian, now truly enveloped in violet perfume, nodded and smiled and kept her ignorance to herself. There had not been many books in Château du Marais. They were things Camille had no use for.

All at once, clouds seemed to darken the sunny March sky, and Lillian had to fight to keep her smile in place. "Will I take it with me to the theater, then?" she asked quietly.

"Of *course*, my dear, of course." Aunt Louisa turned to Nanette for support. "We want our Lillian to encourage the viscount's suit, do we not? A very eligible young man, that Alexander Markham. And very handsome, too, if I may say so. I know his mother." This hardly came as a surprise to Lillian. Aunt Louisa seemed to know everybody in London. "A very nice woman. Very elegant, very refined.

She was quite a catch in her time. How devastated she was when her nephew was reported to be missing in action two years or so ago. Dreadful story that. But thankfully, the boy returned. He looked horribly haggard for some time, they say, but nothing like poor Ponsonby. Have you heard of Frederick Ponsonby, my dear?"

Lillian nodded. Aunt Louisa had already told her all about Frederick Ponsonby.

"A stab in the lungs is no laughing matter, or so they say. That boy should be happy to be alive. Well, Murgatroyd Sacheverell is probably happy to be alive, too, I say, even though he just looked haggard for a month or two. Now, *that* one is quite a catch, too. The Earl of Ravenhurst. A girl could do worse." She gently patted Lillian's cheek. "But this is nothing *our* girl has to be concerned about. You are quite well off, yourself, my dear, if I may say so. To have caught the attention of Alexander Markham, Viscount Perrin! He will be a marquis one day, you know." Her face took on a dreamy expression. "The Most Honorable the Marchioness of Waldron—wouldn't that be a fine title for our Lillian?"

He came to their box that evening, during the interval. He brought a napkin and oranges, which he proceeded to peel and separate into juicy slices to tempt the ladies. Their fresh scent mingled with the perfume of violets as Aunt Louisa chatted on about dreadful incidents she had seen happening on and off stage. "And the night Drury Lane burnt down. . . ." Like a trapped bird, her fan fluttered against her heaving bosom. "The whole sky across London was lit up by the blaze. And the moon was all red that night, blood red. . . ." She sighed, rather theatrically so.

To Lillian it seemed as if going to the theater had a certain stimulating effect on her aunt, and she nearly smiled when she heard her grandfather's snort behind her. Yet Aunt Louisa carried on, lost in memories of bygone Seasons. "And the elegant Apollo on the roof sank into the sea of flames and was seen nevermore. Very tragic, very tragic that. What a fate for a god! Even for one who was just cast in bronze." She sadly shook her head. "And that just after Covent Garden had burnt down in the year before."

"A dreadful story," the Viscount Perrin said wistfully as if he had seen the blaze reflected on London's sky himself. He offered a slice of orange to Aunt Louisa.

"Ahhh, Covent Garden. . . ." The orange slice disappeared into Aunt Louisa's mouth, and she munched and swallowed thoughtfully. "Master Betty had his debut there, if I remember correctly. Have you heard of Master Betty, my dear?" She turned to look at her niece.

Lillian shook her head.

"An excellent actor," the viscount remarked. "Especially for so young a boy. He was but a boy, Lady Lillian, when he first appeared on a London stage in . . . in. . . ."

Aunt Louisa clicked her tongue. "In 1804. Twelve years ago, in the middle of winter. We would not have been in Town that winter if it had not been for William Betty."

Lillian stared at the young man who sat beside her peeling oranges. He made such an effort to appear all wise and manly, when he could not have been more than a mere boy himself, back in 1804. His slender, graceful fingers made quick work of the oranges. Clever fingers, yet carefully groomed and manicured, they showed no traces of hard labor, and the skin was smooth and white as fresh milk. Lillian imagined his body, the skin pale and unblemished. Smooth, without marks.

No brands.

No scars.

Such an innocent body.

Vividly she remembered another body, another man, tall and lean, but all innocence ripped away, the scorched lily on his chest—

Lillian shook her head to chase the unwanted memory away. *The past is gone.* She folded her hands in her lap to still their trembling. *It is all over.*

Aunt Louisa frowned. "Master Betty. They were all wild for that snooty boy. Even my Lord Wishart." The frown deepened. "*Especially* Wishart. How he would dart backstage to see the boy rubbed down by his father! As if he did not have sons of his own, Wishart. His behavior was rather embarrassing to watch, especially for a wife, if I may say so. But then, he had always been a bit soft in his head, my Wishart. Which is what probably got him killed in the first place." She flipped her fan shut in order to poke it into Perrin's padded waistcoat. "*You* know one end of a gun from the other, do you?"

"Madam!" Clearly affronted, Perrin squared his shoulders and puffed out his chest. "I might not have fought against the Frenchmen, but believe me, I am well renowned for my sportsmanship!"

"What a relief to know," Lillian's grandfather said in a low tone, which seemed meant for Lillian's ears alone. Turning around, she caught his wink. He bent forward and murmured: "Can always bring you home some game, the boy. It's very reassuring to know you won't starve." His clear green eyes twinkled merrily.

Lillian's lips lifted in a shy smile for the man who had been a quiet, benevolent presence in the background during the last few months. He had called in the teachers and Aunt Louisa, had ordered a new wardrobe to be made for his granddaughter, and had remained in his library for most of the time. And yet, he now did not seem to like the thought of parting with Lillian.

Smiling, the Marquis of Larkmoor took his granddaughter's hand and blew a kiss on its back. "Have I already told you, my dear, that you've got your grandmother's eyes?" He patted her hand. "A fine woman, your grandmother. A very fine woman." His voice took on a mellow tone. He squeezed Lillian's fingers, and the warmth of his hand seeped through her gloves to warm the skin below.

As she sat there in the stuffy theater box, looking at her grandfather while her aunt and her suitor discussed guns and the advantages of good fencing skills, a spark, a feeling of belonging ignited in Lillian. The tiny warmth settled in her heart and started to thaw the ice within.

Lillian glanced at Alexander Markham, Viscount Perrin, at his sweet, rosy face, the blond locks that curled around his head like those of the angel she had seen in her mother's prayer book a long time ago. With her forefinger she traced the painted plates of the fan he had given her.

A sweet man, a good man, with innocent skin of milk.

And when, in his conversation with Aunt Louisa, his eyes suddenly darted to Lillian, she gave him, too, a shy smile and watched how warmth suffused his face.

And so, like butterflies, they fluttered on, from soirée to concert, from theater to ball. The Viscount Perrin became a steady companion, forever sending Lillian tokens of his devotion—flowers, sweets and fruit, the latest print from Ackermann's or a slim volume of poetry. By the end of March, Lillian had three of these, and as they sat in the Amphitheater one evening, he pressed her gloved hand, intertwining his fingers with hers while the thunder of the horses' hooves reverberated through the round.

The pleasure gardens were not yet opened, but he joined Lillian and Aunt Louisa on their daily morning drive around Hyde Park, a stately figure on horseback, thighs pressed around the sides of his raven-black horse. Lillian liked looking at him then, when the wind ruffled his blond curls and the sky seemed to be mirrored in his round blue eyes.

By the beginning of April he had kissed Lillian's gloved hand on two occasions, and Aunt Louisa had allowed him to dance the waltz with her niece. Sometimes on the ballroom floor, Lillian would then feel his gloved fingers gently caressing the exposed skin of her shoulders and upper back, a quick, light brush of silk. But she had to force a smile then, for, all at once, his arms around her felt like the bars of a cage. And she would remember another night, another man, and the pressure of the arms around her, imprisoning her. . . .

She would remember the play of candlelight over bronzed skin, over the mark shaped like a rose, over the red droplets blooming on the linen.

Blood shows so well on white.

She would have to reach for the chill gathering in the corners of the room then, would have to cloak herself with cold. Slowly, the spark of warmth inside her, which had kindled that night in the theater, faded and died.

Still, she smiled on, smiled until her cheeks hurt, smiled when his mother and younger sisters were introduced to her, giggling girls not yet old enough to be out, but happy to pursue those pleasures of London that were open to them; smiled when his grandmother came for tea, a stately woman, demanding respect and watching Lillian with sharp eyes like those of an eagle. His family was drawing in, examining the girl their heir might want to bring home—like a cow from the market.

They were subtle about it, for sure; nevertheless images of a prison at the end of the world rose before Lillian's inner eye. The stench of unwashed bodies. The rustling of filthy rushes and the clinking of chains.

The sight of Camille's cold, hard eyes sliding over man after man.

And still, Lillian smiled on, smiled even though she thought that the skin of her face must surely crack; smiled when his breath touched her cheek as he whirled her around and around the room in three-four time.

The past is over . . . over . . .

"You look so lovely tonight," he whispered to her. "So lovely." His fingers clenched around her hand, almost painfully.

Perhaps he would ask her tonight. Aunt Louisa had said that it was to be expected any day now, and Nanette had laid her hand against Lillian's cheek. "*Mon petit chou-chou,*" she had said, "*oh, mon petit chou-chou.*" And her eyes had been swimming in tears, happy tears, that she had seen her charge through all misfortunes to bring her to this, to *this*, to be the Right Honorable the Viscountess Perrin.

A silk-clad finger traced the curve of her neck and shoulder. "So very lovely. I—" His throat worked; fire raced up from underneath his white cravat.

Lillian stared at that bit of starched white linen and willed herself not to flinch under his touch.

The past is over.

"I wish I were a poet." Perrin's breath, warm and moist, touched her ear, his voice hoarse. "So that I might write poems in your praise." The candlelight danced over his blond curls in three-four time, transforming them into spun gold. His voice sank to a breathless whisper. " 'Shall I compare thee to a summer's day . . . ' "

She recalled hot, moist breath touching her skin alongside hands, large hands, arranging her limbs . . . Lillian swayed against the arms currently around her. She seemed to float, weightless, and her ears filled with the roaring of her blood, which shut out the noise of the ballroom.

"Lady Lillian? *Lady Lillian?*"

Lillian blinked.

Round eyes hovered in front of her face like shiny blue marbles. A frown marred the line of his smooth forehead. "Are you all right, Lady Lillian?"

She straightened her back and forced another smile onto her stiff lips. "I am fine, thank you. Just—"

"How very inconsiderate of me." Perrin led her to the side of the dance floor. "To force two of these exhausting waltzes on you. I am sorry, most sorry. Shall I get you some refreshments?" Without waiting for her answer, he led her on, hooking her hand in the crook of his elbow and pressing her arm against his side. Lillian had no choice but to follow, while the other couples swirled on with the music.

"Have I already told you that my cousin is arrived in London?" Perrin made a slight bow to an acquaintance he had spotted among the ball guests, before he turned his attention back to Lillian. "Will you do me the honor of letting me introduce him to you? He promised that he would be here this evening. He runs late, I gather. You must not hold it against him, though." Solicitously he saw to it that she would not stumble over the threshold of the refreshments room.

Lillian's gaze was caught by the black dragons that curled threateningly across the bright red wallpaper and chased each other on the Chinese lanterns on the lacquered side tables. The feet of these were formed like the paws of a lion, with sharp golden claws that might tear through a man's flesh and bone.

The past is over.

From the bowls and cups and pots on the main table, the

smell of coffee and beef soup rose to mingle sickeningly with the scent of the ball guests' various sweetwaters.

"He still tires easily, I believe," Perrin continued, his voice full of importance. "And he has not yet regained his old strength. So you will not hold it against him, will you?"

"Of course not," Lillian murmured, without knowing whom he was talking about. She yearned for the cool, fresh night air, for a place of quiet and solitude.

Perrin guided her to an empty chair of black wood. "Please sit down. I will get you something to drink and you will feel much better, soon." With that, he hurried away.

While she waited for him, Lillian watched the coming and going of the people around her, who sipped wine and talked and laughed, talked and laughed and—

"Here you are." Perrin held out a glass of sparkling red wine to her. "Try this. It will revive you."

The thin, elegant stem of the glass felt cool in Lillian's ginger grip, a fragile thing, so easy to break, to destroy, to shatter into a million pieces. . . .

Lillian took a deep breath and let the coolness of the glass soothe her. She took a tentative sip of the chilled wine, the bubbles tickling her nose. She would have preferred lemonade made of sour limes without any trace of sweetness.

"You might think it strange," Perrin said, "that I would wish to introduce my cousin to you. I love him like a brother, you must know. He is one of my best friends."

Lillian took another sip, welcomed the coolness that washed down her throat. "I see," she said softly. But how could she? She had never had any brothers or sisters or friends. Just Nanette. Nanette had always been there.

Perrin's eyes shone merrily. "We grew up together, my coz and I." And how much effort he took to sound like a fashionable gentleman, a man of the world. "A fine pair of rascals we were! Rambling around the Ravenhurst estate, full of boyish mischief and pranks."

"So you are of the same age?" Lillian forced herself to show some interest in what he told her.

"Oh no, he is five years my senior—but what a fine big brother he would have made! I followed him everywhere. . . ."

Like a puppy, a lap dog, Lillian added silently.

". . . admired him ardently. He was the hero of my boyhood."

Another sip of ruby-red wine. It almost looked like blood, Lillian found. She twirled the liquid in her glass, stared at the tiny red waves.

"I would want my future . . ." The hectic blotches lit up his cheeks once more. ". . . my . . . I would want you to know . . ." He squirmed, his eyes darted away, this way and that. Then suddenly they fastened on something beyond Lillian's shoulder. His face broke into a relieved smile. He straightened his posture. "And here he is. As promised." He waved, an enthusiastic young man, full of eagerness to please. "Troy! Over here!"

Lillian watched the glow spreading over his whole face, and for a moment she felt something like envy. That he had *this*. In the next moment, though, she stood and smiled prettily and turned toward the man who had just entered the refreshments room. Black dragons curled on the walls on each side of him as he strode toward them, tall and broad-shouldered, as graceful as a big cat.

Lillian smiled and smiled as the candlelight kindled fires in a shock of auburn hair, fashionably tousled. Smiled as familiar cornflower-blue eyes turned on her, as recognition flared and kindled hatred, twisting his strong-boned face into an ugly mask.

Beaming, Perrin turned to her. "Lady Lillian, may I present my cousin, Murgatroyd Sacheverell, fifth Earl of Ravenhurst."

Lillian smiled and smiled, even as her glass shattered on the floor, spilling wine everywhere, ruby-red droplets blooming on polished wood just like blood would do. She smiled as the floor rose to meet her, as darkness held out its arms and swallowed her up.

Chapter 5

In the upper floor of White's, Troy stood at one of the high windows and watched the bustle of the morning shopping activities in St. James's Street below. Fashionable gentlemen in pursuit of coats and hats and snuff boxes and cravats, sometimes a military man proudly displaying a bright red uniform. Troy never wore his uniform these days, even though Alex had tried to convince him that the ladies would be mad for it.

Alex . . .

Troy clenched his jaw and thumped his fist against the white window frame. Where was that young fool?

"My lord?" Miraculously, as if out of thin air, the Incomparable George Raggett, the Master of the House, appeared at his side. "Shall I have some refreshments sent up? Scotch? Bourbon?"

When Troy had been first elected to White's, barely twenty, it had still been the efficient Martindale who would solicitously inquire after one's wishes. At the time, the elegance of the club had impressed Troy, young fop that he was. He remembered how he had stroked his hand over the soft leather of the deep, comfortable chairs, how he had stared when Brummell held court in the morning room below. How he had wished to belong to that group, to the pinks of the *ton*.

Grimly, Troy shook his head. "No. No, thank you. Has my cousin arrived already?"

"The Viscount Perrin, my lord? I'm afraid not, my lord."

"*Parsanbleu . . .*" Troy suppressed the rest of the obscenities that he had in mind right now. "It is all right, Raggett, thank you."

"As you wish, my lord."

Alone once again, Troy took a deep breath. At this time of day the club was almost deserted, the last gamesters having left the establishment just a few hours ago. Most gentlemen would return after lunch, to meet friends, to discuss politics, but, more likely, to gamble away their fortunes. Or to *bet*.

Troy threw an incensed look at the bedraggled leather-bound volume that rested on the nearest side table.

Damn the young fool, that greenhead of his cousin!

"*Benêt*," Troy murmured. "*Pauvre nigaud.*" Behind him, the door opened, yet he did not pay it any attention. Instead he punched his fist against the window frame once more. "*Merde!*"

The deep mumbling voice behind him distracted him. "What does that young fellow think he is doing? Youth has no respect for old traditions. The country will go to ruins, *to ruins*, I say." Troy turned and found himself almost face to face with Lord Dudlin, who regarded him from under bushy eyebrows. The older man looked him up and down, then noisily cleared his throat. "Now, my young chap, what do you think you are doing? Trashing the furniture and such alike. Most horrid behavior this!" He wagged his finger under Troy's nose.

"My lord." Troy made a slight bow. The man had been a friend of his father's, so he owed him respect at least.

Dudlin squinted at him, and the ensuing frown crumbled his brows, making him look like an annoyed badger. "What's your name, young fellow? Your name?"

"Murgatroyd Sacheverell, my lord."

"Sacheverell, eh?"

"Fifth Earl of Ravenhurst."

"*Ravenhurst!* I knew a Ravenhurst once. A dashing young fellow he was, that particular Raven." Dudlin poked a finger into Troy's chest. "He stole my mistress. Little Sally. Stole her right away from under my nose. And I couldn't even call him out for it. For who's going to call out a man over a mistress? Not to be done, this." Sadness clouded his face, as he shook his head. "No, not to be done." Suddenly, his expression lightened. "But I took 10,000 guineas from him at the card table the following week." Cackling, he rapped Troy's arm with his walking stick.

Troy gave him a bland smile. He was not in the mood right now to hear about his father's amorous liaisons. Luckily for him, the door to the room opened once more and revealed a rosy-faced Viscount Perrin. "Troy, here you are! Raggett told me you've been waiting for ages." Rather belatedly he seemed to become aware of the presence of Lord Dudlin. He bowed, the perfect dandy from the top of his carefully groomed curls, *au coup de vent*, to the tips of his shining black boots. "Good morning, my lord."

Dudlin peered at him thoughtfully. "And who might you be, young fellow?"

Troy watched as his cousin opened and closed his mouth, his face a study of stupefied amazement. *Like a carp.* Troy frowned. *Un carpeau zinzin.* Grinding his teeth, he said: "Would you excuse us, my lord?"

Dudlin's face darkened like a thundercloud. "This will not do, young fellow." Clearly affronted, he whacked his walking stick against Troy's arm. "To be dismissed in one's own house, not to be done, this! There's no respect in these unlicked cubs these days, no respect!"

Troy halted the walking stick in mid-strike. "You are still at White's, my lord," he pointed out patiently.

"At White's?" Dudlin's eyebrows rose, furry little animals skittering up his forehead. "How curious! How can this be?" He tugged at his walking stick, and Troy obligingly released it. "Are you quite sure about this?"

"Quite sure, my lord."

All at once, Dudlin's expression cleared and a beaming smile appeared on his face. "Well, that explains it, then. That's why I couldn't find my library. Ridiculous this, isn't it, not to be able to find one's own library. Well, well, then I should go home now, before the Doodle-Chick becomes too worried." He leaned toward Troy and whispered confidentially: "That's my wife. I call her the Doodle-Chick. Always makes her quite mad. You won't tell anybody, will you?"

"I won't, my lord," Troy assured him gently. "But you should really go home now."

"Yes, yes, I believe I should. Good day to you, sir. Good day." Swinging his walking stick, Dudlin walked out of the room. "At White's. Still at White's. How very curious. And here I am, looking for my library. . . ." The door closed behind him. His footsteps and muttering voice faded as he walked down the stairs.

"Dear me." Alex straightened his cravat, the bulky Mailcoach knot making him look like an oversized turkey. "The fellow becomes queerer with each passing year. I'd rather be shot myself than walking around in such a fashion as him. And what a quiz he is!"

Troy gritted his teeth. *And what a greenhead you are! A foppish young fool* . . . Why couldn't his cousin show some more consideration for an aging man? Compassion for a fellow human being who had been a great man in his youth? But no, his head was filled with rubbish about fashionable living; he was a jingle-brained cub about town, concerned about fashion and fooleries and—

Troy's gaze fell on the leather-bound book on the side table.

His head whipped up, and his eyes bored into his young cousin. "And where have you been?" he asked, carefully pronouncing each word.

Alex's round face registered surprise. "Why, at Larkmoor's, of course."

"At *Larkmoor's?*" Troy felt as if his head was going to burst any moment.

"Of course." Alex sniffed. "After this dreadful fainting fit last night, I had to inquire after Lady Lillian."

Yes, Troy's head was going to burst for sure. "At this time of day? *Are you out of your mind?*"

Alex sniffed some more. "There's no reason for you to roar like . . . like a wild lion."

"It's not yet one o'clock, you fool!" Troy's voice reverberated in the room. "Do you want to let everybody think you're engaged to her?" He grabbed the book from the side table and shoved it against his cousin's chest. "They're already placing *bets* on you and the chit!"

"Really?" Alex's face lit up like a lantern. "I've never had anybody placing bets on me. What do they say?" He started to thumb through the pages of the old book.

"*Christ!*" Troy ran both of his hands through his hair. "Don't be such a goose, Alex!"

"What?" His cousin threw him a quick look, but was already distracted the next moment. "Ahh, here it is: 'Mr.

76

Brummell bets Captain Capel one hundred guineas that the Viscount P. marries the Marquis of L.'s granddaughter within three months from this day.' Did you know that Brummell is rumored to be broke?"

Troy's hands twitched with the urge to slap his cousin. "I do not care what Brummell is rumored to be about! He might jump into the Thames if he so pleases! But I do care that everybody seems to have linked you with the Marquis of Larkmoor's granddaughter!"

Oh yes, Troy knew all about being linked with the Marquis of Larkmoor's granddaughter. He well remembered the click of the chain that had fastened on the ring around his neck. A dog, he had been. A dog on a leash.

Round blue eyes blinked at him. "Well, but . . ." Alex's gaze darted back to the pages of the book. His brows furrowed. "Why, look at that! The cheek! 'Sir J. Copley bets Lord Alvanley eighty guineas that in case of a marriage with Lady L., the Viscount P. freezes to death during his wedding night.'" His chubby cheeks flushed ominously. "I will call him out for this! I swear I will call him out for this! Both of them! How can they? They should be ashamed, they—"

Troy gripped his shoulders, hard, and shook him like a young puppy dog. "Be quiet, Alex, you fool," he snapped. "How far has it gone between you and that woman? Are you already engaged?"

Alex twisted under the iron grip of Troy's hands. "What's the matter with you, coz?" He gave an artificial laugh. "Has the battle-madness come over you?"

Troy had never come so close to punching his fist into his cousin's face. He gripped Alex's lapels and hauled him up, not caring that the voluminous Mailcoach knot nearly choked the young man in the process. "Do not," he said through clenched teeth, "speak to me of battle-madness ever again. Understood? Now tell me: How far has it come between you and that woman?"

That woman.

Whose cold gray eyes had bored into his as the brand had seared his skin with white hot pain. Burning her *mark* into him as if he were no more than cattle. The mark he was forced to look on each morning and each night; the mark he wished he could cut from his skin so he might forget how he had been robbed of his pride and his self-worth as a man.

"N-n-n . . ." Alex gulped, his eyes wide and very blue with fear. "Not f-far. We're n-n-not yet en-engaged."

"You have not yet asked her?"

Beetroot-red, Alex shook his head as far as his restricted throat would allow. "N-no."

"Good." Disgusted with himself and his cousin, Troy shoved him away. "And you won't do it, either."

Alex coughed and bent over, supporting his hands on his bent knees. Without any hint of regret, Troy listened to his wheezing breaths, the choking sounds he made. Finally, Alex straightened up, eyes streaming, and fumbled with his neckcloth, before he turned his disdainful gaze onto Troy. "You, sir, are out of your mind!"

Troy narrowed his eyes at him. "That's fine by me. I don't care what you think about me as long as you don't marry that hussy."

"I . . . I . . ."

"You have no idea what kind of woman that is, Alex. And I just won't allow you to marry her."

"Go to hell!" Alex spat. "I will not take commands from you, a madman! And I won't stand by hearing you slighting Lady Lillian!" His face still very red, he fumbled with his fine leather gloves until he had worked one free.

Troy anticipated his next move, and before Alex could

slap his face with the glove, Troy gripped his wrist. "Don't do this, Alex."

A muscle jumped in his cousin's cheek. "I demand satisfaction."

Fool, fool.

The years of his military training, the years at war enabled Troy to wipe his face clear of any expression. "Well, that's your poor luck, coz," he drawled, "because I won't fight a duel with you."

Even darker color stained his cousin's cheeks. "Then I will tell everybody that you are a coward."

Troy shrugged. "Then do it." Schooling his face into an expression of contempt, he released Alex's wrist and stepped back. He raised an eyebrow. "Do it."

Trembling, Alex lifted his chin in a show of defiance. "We are through with each other. Do not darken my doorstep again." With a whoosh and a click of his spurs, he swirled around and marched out of the room, head held high.

Do not darken my doorstep again. Troy snorted. God, was his cousin into these gothic novels? "Fool," he murmured. "*Sot.*"

Unconsciously, his hand strayed to his left leg, rubbing the thigh that was now peppered with scars instead of lead. Now that the ersttime wounds had been cleaned, the leg hurt only occasionally and the limp had almost gone.

"God. . . ." Tiredly, Troy passed his hand over his forehead, registering the dampness at his temples.

This had not gone well.

Damn it, but why must his cousin choose that woman of all the young girls who scrambled through London's ballrooms?

The memory of the ghostly pale oval of her face taunted him, of her eyes, those ice-cold eyes, watching, watching,

watching, boring into him as the hated lily was burnt into his flesh—

With a roar, he drove his fist against the wall.

No, he could not let Alex marry her. Never. But trust his cousin to do something foolish, something overhasty. Like running to Larkmoor's tomorrow and asking. It did not bear thinking about.

Troy narrowed his eyes.

He needed to act. Fast. If he could not get through to his cousin, well, perhaps he should try the other party. After all, she had a lot to lose, hadn't she? He would bet his right arm that her grandfather did not know the details of her past. The Marquis of Larkmoor had always been an honorable man.

He would talk to her. Tonight.

Tonight . . .

When the *haut ton* assembled at Almack's for the most boring ball in London.

After making some discreet inquiries—yes, Lady Lillian Abberley had indeed been presented with one of the coveted vouchers—Troy climbed the stairs to the entrance of Almack's Assembly Rooms at ten-thirty later that day. His valet had worked a minor miracle by providing him with a pair of knee breeches at short notice, even if they were a rather ill-fitting pair. Knee breeches, a funny pair of silken socks, a snowy white cravat and a dark dress coat with long, batwinged tails—that was the uniform for the seventh heaven of the fashionable world.

Knee breeches. Troy snorted. He felt like a fop. Yet his valet had insisted on this attire, especially since Troy had neither voucher nor ticket that would grant him entrance to the innermost haven of London society. If his master should fail, the trusty valet had said, it should at least not be due to faulty attire.

Troy gritted his teeth. He would *not* fail. Rather more forcefully than intended, he rapped his walking stick against the door. Another thing that his valet had provided him with: a ridiculous golden-knobbed walking stick and an even more ridiculous-looking hat, which was high enough to make even the people of Babylon jealous.

The door opened and a small, wiry man peered up at him. "Good evening, my lord."

Troy lifted his lips in what he hoped looked like a smile. "Good evening . . . Willis, isn't it?"

"Your ticket, my lord?"

"My ticket." Troy sighed and scratched his head. With great show he bent forward and whispered: "I am afraid, sir, that I do not have a ticket."

Almack's Cerberus regarded him stoically. "Then I cannot let you in, my lord."

"But I am properly clothed," Troy protested. "See? Knee breeches!" He wriggled a stockinged leg. "You cannot turn me away because of that as you did with Wellington."

Willis cocked his head to the side and blinked. He very much gave the appearance of a man faced with a lunatic straight out of Bedlam. "But Wellington, my lord, had a ticket."

Troy gave another tragic sigh and looked up and down the street. For the moment there was no carriage in sight. With a lightning-quick move he had grabbed the other man's collar. "See, Willis, the thing is this: I've been to France, I fought against Napoleon, and believe me, most of the times, it was not a picnic. So now that I want to go up to that ballroom, do you really think you could stop me?"

"My lord!" the unfortunate Willis choked.

"Good. I don't think so either." Smiling gently, he released the doorman, patted his shoulder and stepped around him. Swinging his walking stick in the fashion of a Lord Dudlin, Troy walked up to the great staircase inside. As if struck by an afterthought, he turned around one last time. "Oh, and Willis, if you value your life, you won't breathe a word of this incident to anybody."

Then Troy smiled and nodded and proceeded to hurry up the stairs. For all that Willis had looked as if he had been struck by thunder, Troy did not believe the doorman's silence would last long—even with all the ridiculous threats he had uttered.

Merde! Two men he had threatened with strangling that day. If he needed any further proof that the war and the prison and the events thereafter had made him into a barbarian, this was it.

At the top of the stairs another dilemma faced Troy: He had not been to the cloakroom. But he could not possibly walk into a ballroom with a walking stick and a funny hat. Well, he didn't like the hat anyway. So he whipped it off his head and let it fly into the shadows of the landing. The walking stick followed suit—and good riddance to it, too.

Pasting an amiable smile on his face, Troy sauntered through the open doors into the noise and heat of the ballroom. The orchestra musicians on the small balcony played away on their instruments as if their lives depended on it, while the half-naked Greek statues along the walls watched stoically. And held candelabras. And wore something that looked suspiciously like nightcaps.

Heavens! Troy suppressed a shudder and scanned the assembled personages. Not surprisingly, the gentlemen looked all the same: bored expressions and coats with bat-winged tails. This season's debutantes—

"Lord Ravenhurst! What a nice surprise!" Lady Jersey, clad in Turkey red, sailed toward him.

Trust the society queen to hone in on him even before he had quite crossed the threshold to her kingdom! His hands spasmed into fists before he forced himself into a relaxed attitude.

"Madam." He bowed low. "Good evening." Smiling, he looked her in the eye and added: "Lady Sefton was kind enough to give me a voucher on short notice so that I might see the hallowed halls of Almack's for myself. I guess she pitied me, for I limped rather prettily." He winked at her.

"You sly young fox!" Lady Jersey smacked his arm with her closed fan. "I have not seen the slightest hint of a limp as you walked in right now."

He chuckled deep in his throat. "If you would prefer me to limp. . . ."

"Oh, no you don't. After all we want to see you dance, my lord." She looked around. "Shall I introduce you to some of the young ladies?"

Troy bowed some more. "It would be my pleasure." He hesitated for a moment. Then he plunged on before an enraged Willis could come storming up the stairs. "But since Lady Lillian Abberley collapsed in a dead faint at my feet yesterday evening—as I am sure you have heard—I wish to inquire after her health first. Is she here tonight?"

Lady Jersey fiddled with her fan. "A very shocking incident, my lord," she said confidentially. "It was all over town this morning. The poor dear must have overtaxed herself at the waltz."

Troy showed her a smile full of flashing teeth. "Indeed. And imagine how shocking it was for me to find myself with Lady Lillian sprawled on the floor at my feet. So I am sure you understand how urgently I would like to see for myself that she has not taken any permanent harm from the experience. Is she not here tonight?"

"Oh yes, she is." Lady Jersey pouted prettily and airily waved her hand in the direction of the dance floor. "Dancing with Lord Shipsey."

"Thank you, madam." Troy bowed once more. "Most obliged. Would you reserve a dance for me later this evening?"

Appeased, Lady Jersey gave him a simpering smile, which she probably considered girlish, and rapped her fan on his arm again. "You *are* a sly young fox, my lord. I will see you later, then." With that she strutted away to sharpen her claws on some other unfortunate victim.

Shaking his head, Troy walked on, brushing through the throng of guests until he had a full view of the dance floor. Almost immediately, he found the woman he had come looking for, the woman whose image had been seared into his brain just like—

His right hand strayed under the lapels of his coat and splayed over his heart, his fingers clutching at his waistcoat, where underneath the cloth her lily marred his skin. Breathing became difficult as if unseen fists squeezed his lungs.

He saw her following the steps of a country dance, linking arms or hands with the poor fool of her dancing partner. A white dress billowed around her, virginal white. White as cream spread on pale skin.

His stomach heaved.

Troy closed his eyes and took a deep breath. *This will not do.* He forced himself to relax, to let his arms hang loosely at his sides.

But at the same time as air filled his lungs, wild, hot anger swept over him and washed away the last remnants of rational thought and reason. How he lusted to revenge himself, to revenge the destruction of his manhood by the brand that had seared her mark into his skin.

When he opened his eyes again, the edges of his vision seemed shrouded in a red haze. His heart beat loud and fast.

He strode forward, yet carefully so as not to break the pattern of the dance. Up the long row of dancers he marched, until he saw her head spin around, saw the color leaving her face.

He stepped between her and her dance partner, a young, young fool just like Alex. "Good evening, madam. I need to talk to you." He half turned to throw the other man a grim look. "Will you excuse us, my lord?"

Without waiting for an answer, he gripped her arm just above the elbow, digging his fingers into the silk of her long glove. Her flesh was soft under his fingers. So pliable that he would surely leave bruises on her skin.

He walked away with her, and even though the young fool behind him gaped and gaped just like Alex had done, the pattern of the dance was not destroyed. The music played on, and he marched her right through the rows of astonished people waiting at the edge of the dance floor.

At one point he thought he heard her ask: "What do you want of me?" Oh, yes, how well he remembered that voice, that cool, clipped voice.

Oui, maman.

His fingers closed tighter around her arm until he could feel the solidity of the bone beneath the flesh. He strode on into the room where the refreshments were served and out into the servants' hallway. There he propelled her into the shadows under the stairs.

She fell against the wall, but straightened quickly, rubbing her arm. "What do you want of me?" she asked again.

"As I said," he drawled. "I want to talk to you." When she would have stepped away from him, he backed her against the wall. Shoved his face into hers. His lips lifted in a snarl. "The world is a small place, is it not, *Lady* Lillian?"

"What do you want of me?" Her voice was soft. Oh, a man could be deceived by that voice alone. She stared at him, her eyes two shimmering pools in the shadows. But he remembered their color, cold and gray as steel and watching, always watching. . . .

He slapped his hand against the wall beside her face, wanting her to flinch. Wanting to break that stare. Wanting the satisfaction of her fear. *Her* fear.

Yet she neither flinched nor blinked.

She just watched and watched and watched, as if she were still the one holding the whip and he the dog on the leash.

Fury raced through his veins like molten fire. His hands closed on her shoulders, crushing the bones, and his thumbs slid to the hollow at the base of her throat. "You will stay away from my cousin!" he snarled into her face. "Stay away from Alex!"

Her pulse hammered against his fingertips, but it was not enough. Not near enough. He wanted to dominate her, just as he had been dominated. Wanted to taste her fear.

It would taste sweet on his lips.

Sweet enough to wash away the bitter taste of remembered humiliation.

He leaned forward, using his whole weight to press her against the wall. Her breasts rose and fell against his chest, and he pressed harder until they were flat and crushed.

But still she stared and stared and did not utter a word.

"You bitch!" he spat. "You will stay away from Alex!"

He slammed his knee between her legs, pushed his thigh against the juncture of her thighs, hard. He wanted to hurt

86

her as he had been hurt. His mouth crashed down on hers, squashing her lips against her teeth until he could taste blood. Sweet, coppery blood.

His fingers left her throat. Dimly he registered the sounds of ripping material before his hands filled with soft flesh and squeezed. God, so tightly.

Fury pounded against his temples, and his eyes were filled with the roaring of his own blood. Roaring for revenge. "Bitch!" he panted. "Bitch!"

More ripping material. Fabric that bit into his hand.

He pushed his knee higher, making her stand on tiptoe, helpless, while his fingers ravaged her flesh.

Oh yes, she would feel his dominance, his power, his—

"*My lord!*"

The shocked cry cut through the red haze that enshrouded his senses. Slowly, he turned his head. Slowly, his eyes focused on shocked faces.

"'Tis the one!" Willis pointed an accusatory finger at him. "'Tis the one who went up without a voucher!"

Slowly, Troy stepped away from the woman and turned his body fully toward the people who stood and stared at him. Willis wore an expression of outraged indignation. Lady Sefton, whose husband was also a member of White's, looked sincerely shocked and sad, while Lady Jersey's eyes glinted as if with secret enjoyment of the situation. The third lady present, Lord Wishart's widow, had turned pasty white.

He took a step forward. And another. Into the light.

Their eyes darted past him. Four loud gasps filled the hallway.

He threw a look over his shoulder into the shadows. To the woman's pale breasts, which bore the marks of his fingers. The blood on her lips and chin seemed almost black.

"Lillian! Oh, my dear, my dear . . ." Lady Wishart

rushed forward, shouldering past him. Lady Jersey, by contrast, produced a high-pitched yell, before she artfully fainted into Willis's waiting arms.

Troy straightened his cravat and walked away without another look. He did not retrieve either his hat or walking stick.

Chapter 6

The only sounds that filled the room were the soft clicks of silver cutlery on china as Lillian and her grandfather took their breakfast in silence. She winced slightly whenever she took a sip of tea and the hot liquid flowed over the cut in her upper lip.

Suddenly hurried steps sounded outside in the hallway. The door burst open. With heaving bosom, Aunt Louisa stood on the threshold, a newspaper clutched to her heart. "It's in the papers!" she cried. "The whole story!" She stormed into the room, wringing her hands. "Whatever shall we do now? She is ruined! *Ruined!* After all our work and efforts!" With a look of utter exhaustion she sank into the nearest chair and fanned herself with the folded newspaper. "Heavens! Heavens!"

"Calm yourself, Louisa," the Marquis of Larkmoor said sternly.

"How should I? Whatever shall we do now? That . . . that *scoundrel*! He must marry you! I shall insist on it! How very vexing this all is! Why haven't you called for help, Lillian?" She turned a baleful eye toward her niece.

Yet Nanette, who had followed Aunt Louisa into the room, shook her head. "It would not have changed the result."

"Oh well, then Papa could have shot him dead with a clear conscience. But now. . . ." Aunt Louisa groaned. She raised the hand with the newspaper and shook her fist. "That woman! Sarah Sophia Fane, all high and mighty! She is a real gossip monger, she is! Couldn't get the story into the papers quick enough! As if her family were all pure and innocent! Her own mother ran away with that Lord Westmoreland, I tell you. Got married in Gretna Green. *That* was a scandal, if I may say so. But now, she surely will be the first to cancel our invitation to her soirée next week. Oh dear, oh dear! Whatever shall we do?" She turned toward her father. "You have to call him out, naturally. You have to insist that he marry our Lillian. The scoundrel! I wouldn't have thought it of him. No, I would not."

Marry the Earl of Ravenhurst? Lillian felt all blood drain from her face. "I will not marry him," she said, and agitation made her voice quiver. "I cannot marry him." For how could she marry a man whose skin would be still blemished by the mark she had burnt into it?

"What?" Aunt Louisa eyed her with disbelief. "What nonsense you are talking, my dear! *Of course* you will marry him. We just have to make him."

Nanette had gone still. "What is it, *chou-chou?* Why can you not marry him?"

Lillian folded her hands in her lap and clutched her fingers together so they would not shake. She remembered the smell of scorched flesh, the way his body had jerked.

Her responsibility.

"Lillian?" her grandfather prompted.

Yet the only person she looked at, the only person who

would understand, was Nanette. "He was at Château du Marais."

The old woman turned pale, and shock widened her eyes.

Aunt Louisa only fluttered her hands as if to ward off a swarm of flies. "Piff-paff, of what significance shall that be? So he knows your stepmother. I cannot see how that would prevent you from marrying him."

At that moment, there was a knock on the door and the butler came in to announce a visitor.

Aunt Louisa shook her head. "A visitor? At this time of the day?"

"It is the Viscount Perrin, my lady," the butler said.

"The Viscount Perrin?" Immediately her face lit up. She straightened in her chair and made the newspaper disappear under the folds of her skirt. "What a nice surprise! He shall come in!"

Obligingly, the butler stepped aside to make room for a pale Alexander Markham, who hastened into the room. For once, his hair was not properly groomed, but in an unruly jumble. "Good morning, my ladies, my lord." He bowed first in the one direction then in the other. "Excuse my intrusion. I . . . Could I . . ." His hands fidgeted with the buttons of his coat. He gulped, but then he squared his shoulders and looked the Marquis of Larkmoor straight in the eye. "My lord, may I request a private interview with your granddaughter?"

Aunt Louisa propelled out of her chair. "But *of course!*" A beaming smile appeared on her face. She grasped the offending newspaper, which was still lying on the chair, and waved the others to leave the room. "Papa. Nanette. Come, come! And you, chick . . ." She went over to pat Lillian's cheek. "You will listen carefully to what the Viscount Perrin has to say to you. We will wait for you in the parlor. *Papa*!" Hurriedly, she ushered a bewildered Marquis of Larkmoor and Nanette out of the room.

The door was shut, their steps receded. For a moment, there was absolute silence.

Lillian had not moved during the whole exchange. She was reminded of the nights when she had sat in the box at the theater and watched the events on stage, a colorful kaleidoscope of the tragedies and comedies of life. She felt like that right now: a spectator.

Only, now she watched the Viscount Perrin pacing in her grandfather's breakfast room. She raised her chin a notch. "To what do I owe this honor, my lord?"

"Madam." Perrin stopped in front of her, his face filled with the familiar hectic blotches of red. "This morning I was shocked, truly shocked, to learn of my cousin's scandalous behavior." He held out his hand as if to halt her nonexistent protests. "I do not blame *you*, madam. I had a most disturbing discussion with my cousin yesterday morning. And this greatly impressed upon me the Earl of Ravenhurst's most worrying state of mind." A nervous tick started at his left eye. "In a word, madam, he is past all sanity." As if in pain, he pressed his fist against his mouth.

Lillian observed him in silence. Vividly, she remembered the pain of his cousin's hands on her body, the unholy fire in his cornflower-blue eyes. Wild with anger and shame. A man pushed past his endurance.

Her responsibility.

After a while Perrin continued: "I deeply regret that you had to become the unfortunate victim of . . . of this. I—" All at once, he rushed forward and dropped to his knees in front of Lillian's chair. "Madam." He took her hands. "Lady Lillian." He blew a hot, damp kiss on each of them. "As you have been brought to this through the doings of a family member of mine, I feel it is my obligation to offer you"—he gulped—"the protection of my name and my hand in marriage." He beamed at her and pressed her limp fingers. "What do you say?"

Lillian looked at him steadfastly. At the man who had offered her a way out at a great cost to himself. She cocked her head to the side. He probably did not even know the cost. "There will be a scandal," she said. "Do you not mind?"

"Scandal?" He puffed out his chest. "It will wither away in the fire of my love." He pressed two more kisses on her hands. "I love you, Lillian, dearest Lillian."

A lily for Lillian. The smell of scorched flesh. The body flinching, but helplessly bound. And the sight of the raw, burnt skin.

Her responsibility.

She gazed at Perrin, saw the hot look in his eyes, the feverish red on his pale cheeks. She remembered how she had once envisioned his body: pale, unblemished. Innocent. Much too innocent for her, though. It would be so easy to take what he offered. But how could she, now that the past had caught up with her? How could she, when his cousin was bearing her mark on his body? She would destroy Perrin's innocence with the knowledge of evil she had gained at Château du Marais.

So Lillian smiled a bit and closed her fingers around his. "Thank you for your very generous offer. I assure you I feel deeply honored by it. But I cannot accept it. I am sorry."

"But . . . but . . ." His mouth closed and opened as if he were a stranded fish.

Lillian gently drew her hands out of his grasp. "I am deeply sorry."

Painful color surged up from underneath his cravat. He staggered back to his feet and busily brushed at his coat. "Well, if that is your decision . . ." He threw his head back.

"Then I hope that you will not regret it one day." His tone clearly said that she would regret it for the rest of her life. "Good day to you, madam. I wish you all the luck you can need." With that, he marched off, and the door banged shut behind him.

Lillian closed her eyes and listened as his steps faded in the hall outside.

Troy heard her long before he saw her. The high-pitched, whinging voice settled over his butler's hoarse *basso continuo*. The volume swelled in a prolonged *crescendo*, the door opened, and Finney had just time enough to utter a croak and to flatten himself against the door before the Dowager Countess of Ravenhurst swept past into the billiards room.

"I have heard most shocking news!" she announced to the world in general and to her grandson in particular.

Troy watched the last ball roll over the baize-covered slate, only to miss the hole in the corner and bounce off the cushion. He suppressed a sigh, straightened and made the formal bow as was expected of him. "Good morning, granddame." He gave his butler a small nod. "That will be all, Finney. Thank you." He turned his attention back to his grandmother, who regarded him with obvious displeasure.

"I will not wish you a good morning, Ravenhurst, because it is *not* a good morning." She pierced him with a withering glance. "I demand to know this minute whether it is true."

He laid his cue on the billiard board. "Whether what is true?"

Stalling was not one of the best tactics to employ with the Dowager Countess, and consequently, the lines around her mouth deepened even more. "Do not pretend to be a dimwit, Ravenhurst! Did you compromise Lillian Abberley, the

94

girl your cousin plans to wed—yes or no?" Her thin nose quivered with indignation.

"If you put it like that . . ." Troy shrugged. "Yes."

"*Yes?* You shamed the girl your cousin plans to make his viscountess, the Marquis of Larkmoor's granddaughter, and all you give me is insolence?" She paused, but Troy knew better than to interrupt her. Instead, he mentally prepared himself for the thunderstorm to come.

"You behaved like the meanest blackguard, the basest scoundrel, you dishonored the family name, and this is all you can say? Oh no, Ravenhurst, this will not do! Do you want your poor father and grandfather to turn in their graves with humiliation at what their heir has done?" Bristling with anger, she approached him and poked her bony finger into his chest. "You will marry the chit, do you hear me?"

"Granddame—"

"I will have no grandson of mine put shame on the family name, oh no, not as long as there is breath in my lungs!"

"Granddame, I had reasons."

"Reasons?" One white eyebrow rose. "To bring disaster to your cousin's happiness?"

Troy gritted his teeth until his jaw hurt. "He would have brought disaster to himself had he married the girl, believe me." The girl who had branded him like an animal.

"You, Ravenhurst, are out of your mind!" The corners of the Dowager Countess's mouth turned down in an expression of utter contempt. "You have been in London but four days. How can you even attempt to judge the character of Lady Lillian Abberley?"

"Lady Lillian Abberley? *Lady* Lillian Abberley? God!" Abruptly, Troy whirled and ran both hands through his hair. With his back to his grandmother he said: "Can you not trust me in this, granddame?"

Did he deserve this? Could she not show him a bit of common human sympathy? God, how he loathed this all! His hand splayed over his chest, where his shirt hid the darkened, burnt flesh.

His grandmother's snort cut him like the lash of a whip. "You have put shame to our name, Ravenhurst." Her icy voice was a bitter reminder of how much his grandmother had changed since his grandfather died. All warmth and love seemed to have turned into bitterness and spite, until the woman he had known and loved all his childhood was no more.

Wearily, Troy closed his eyes. "When I came home from France and you oversaw the doctor tending my wounds, did you not wonder at the marks on my back?" He turned around to look at the Dowager Countess. "Did you not wonder at the brand on my chest? Did you not ask yourself where they came from?" He leaned down, his eyes never leaving her face.

A startled frown crossed her forehead. "Well . . . yes," she admitted impatiently. "But I cannot see what that has to do with the situation at hand."

Troy laughed. It was the kind of laugh he had come to learn during his years in the war, the laugh he had perfected during his time in a stinking French prison. "Because that is exactly where Lady Lillian has come from, too. So, you see, I could not let my foolish young cousin marry the woman."

For a moment, his grandmother seemed confused. "Murgatroyd . . ." Her hands reached up as if to touch his shoulders. But then, she drew her hands back and stepped away. "Whatever the reason for your most unseemly behavior last night, it might had had a somewhat contrary effect to your wishes." Her voice was cool and smooth again. "For your foolish young cousin, as you named him, plans to go off to Larkmoor's this morning." A thin brow rose as if in mockery. "To atone for your sins, I believe." With that, she left: a regal-looking old woman, who had just condemned her grandson to something worse than death.

Troy stared after her, not really seeing anything. He remembered the sounds of ripping material, the feeling of soft flesh under his hands. Most of all, he remembered the sight of blood on her lips. *Her* blood. And the triumph he had felt. To have dominated her. To have saved Alex from this woman.

He heard the front door close.

With a roar he banged his fist onto the billiard table, and the hard slate jarred his arm.

Of course, Aunt Louisa could not understand why Lillian had refused the viscount's offer of marriage. Indeed, she was horrified. She paced around the room, clucking her tongue and muttering to herself, only to stop in her tracks from time to time and moan: "The girl will go to ruins! *To ruins*, I say!"

Nanette, by contrast, sat in the corner of the drawing room and busied herself with her needlework. She always did some sort of needlework. The scarves and frocks and wraps she knitted she gave to the people of the poorhouse, Lillian knew. *Everything needs balance*, the voice of the old woman whispered in her head. *One to do the healing in a place where another does all the wounding*. One to think of the people in need while society moved from amusement to amusement, their only worry which invitation to accept, which ball to attend, which dress to wear.

Lillian looked out the window to the street below, where fashionable ladies bloomed like flowers against the gray of the city. She yearned for the silence of an overgrown garden where nobody had tread but her. She remembered how she had sat in the grass by the lake and the summer breeze had caressed her cheek.

While her thighs had still been smeared with. . . .

Lillian flinched.

She clasped her hands together in her lap to stop their trembling. Aunt Louisa's steps suddenly seemed to echo loudly in the room. Her sighs and moans rasped on Lillian's nerves, and she felt the beginning of a headache like a white hot iron behind her eyes.

"Oh dear, oh dear!" Aunt Louisa lamented. "Whatever shall we do now? Papa will have to call him out, after all. Oh dear, oh dear! He will be killed and then what shall we do? That wretched, wretched man! Oh, how I would wish to strangle him, yes I would! Put my hands around—"

The butler cleared his throat noisily. He stood in the open door and, judging from the volume of his throat clearing, he had been standing there for some time already. "My lady?"

"—his scrawny neck and—"

"My lady?"

Irritated, Aunt Louisa turned around. "Yes, what is it?"

By this time, the butler's face had taken on a delicate shade of pink. "There is a visitor."

"A visitor?" Aunt Louisa wrung her hands. "Who would want to visit us in our misery? Who?" All at once, her expression changed and she gave the butler a suspicious scowl. "It is Lady Jersey, isn't it? She has come to gloat, I am sure of it! To cancel her invitation *in person.*"

"No, my lady. It's . . . er—"

"The Earl of Ravenhurst," the Earl of Ravenhurst said as he stepped into the room, obviously having grown impatient waiting downstairs.

Aunt Louisa gasped.

Lillian's fingers clenched until her nails dug painfully into her palms. With an effort she relaxed her hands, even as his gaze settled on her like blue fire. She raised her chin and met his gaze look for look. No longer shackled and bound, he exuded danger, the play of his long, powerful muscles only half hidden by his clothes.

"*Papa!*" Aunt Louisa screamed, and Ravenhurst visibly winced. "He is here!" She pointed an accusing finger at the man she had wanted to strangle not a minute before. "How dare you to come here? This is all very annoying! Papa will have to call you out now and you will fence in our drawing room and get blood all over the floor!"

From Nanette's direction came an unintelligible mutter. Ravenhurst merely raised his brows. "I come with the most honorable of intentions, I assure you," he said smoothly.

Hasty steps were heard in the hallway and soon after Lillian's grandfather appeared in the door. When he spotted their visitor, he came to an abrupt halt. The younger man turned around and bowed slightly. "Lord Larkmoor."

"Ravenhurst."

Aunt Louisa hurried to her father's side and gripped his arm. "You have to call him out, of course." She shuddered. "Oh dear, oh dear!"

Lillian felt a most particular sensation in the region of her heart. "Grandfather...." She stood, her gaze imploringly drawn to his.

"As I just told Lady Wishart, I have come with the most honorable intentions." The Earl of Ravenhurst's voice was filled with subtle mockery. Yet he bowed again. "May I ask you most humbly for the hand of your granddaughter in marriage, my lord?"

Aunt Louisa, momentarily robbed of speech, gaped at him, while Lillian's grandfather looked him up and down. "Your methods of courtship are most uncommon, my lord," the Marquis of Larkmoor finally said in a hard voice.

"You can always call me out, of course."

At the earl's challenge, Aunt Louisa shrieked and made as if to faint in her father's arms. This particular farce, Lillian decided, had gone far enough. "*Quelle bêtise!*" she said firmly and stepped forward, ignoring her aunt's shocked gasps. "My lord, I would suggest that you go home now. I will not have my grandfather call you out, and I will not have *you.*" *Even though you're bearing my mark on your skin.*

He stared at her, his eyes as blue as the summer sky. Then his lips turned up into a humorless smile and he gave her a mocking little bow. "I beg to differ. It seems that I have compromised you, so my honor"—his eyes flashed—"demands that I rectify the wrong done to you." As if by belated thought, he added: "My lady."

"No." Lillian shook her head. Why would he want to do such a thing? When the wrong she had done him was so much greater?

Her grandfather left Aunt Louisa standing with her mouth slightly open. He went to Lillian and took her hand to pat it lightly. "My dear, this seems to be the only solution."

"No."

"My dear." There was compassion and sympathy in her grandfather's eyes. "You have no other choice."

"No." She looked over his shoulder to the tall man who was watching her intently, a small, derisive smile curling his lips.

He stood with his arms crossed in front of his chest, and Lillian saw how broad his shoulders were. She remembered how, at another time and place, his body had been so lean that the ribs had seemed to be poking through skin, how his shaved skull had gleamed in the candlelight. Most of all, she remembered the brand, the angry red brand, the flesh puckered and raw, and the blood marring his pale skin.

He was no longer so pale, and his shock of auburn hair had a healthy glow. He was no longer a prisoner, and no dogs had torn his body to pieces. Only the eyes, Lillian saw, the eyes were still the same, always the same: an intense cornflower-blue that seemed to burn her very soul with anger and hatred.

"Grandfather." She looked back to the Marquis of Larkmoor, whose kind eyes reflected worry and concern. "I would like to speak with Lord Ravenhurst in private."

He searched her face. "Very well, my dear," he finally said and released her hand. "But it will not change anything." He turned around to face the younger man. "This time, you will behave."

The Earl of Ravenhurst bowed. "I assure you, I will."

"Oh, my lord!" Nanette left her needlework and rushed to Lillian. Her arms fluttered through the air like the frail wings of a small bird. "Please, my lord, you have already heard Lillian's reasons. Please." She glanced at the earl with something approaching dread in her eyes. "Don't do this."

The Marquis of Larkmoor gave her a sad smile. "I am afraid we have run out of choices, Nanette. Come." He beckoned to her to leave the room. "We will leave these two alone for a while."

Not one muscle moved in Lillian's face as she watched them go out of the room. When the door closed, she turned and went back to the window, looking onto the street below, where people ambled by and life whirled past, uncaring.

"I will not marry you," she said quietly. "I *cannot* marry you."

"Why?"

"You know why." *Because I pressed the hot brand against your skin and witnessed what she did to you.*

"Oh." Sarcasm dripped from that one small sound. "You mean, because of our—how shall we put it—*history*?" She heard his steps behind her, and she remembered the iron grip of his hands as he grasped her shoulders and wrenched her around. And his scent. She remembered his scent, that dark, beguiling mixture of sandalwood and oak-moss, so different from the stench of prison and of fear. "Well, that's just too bad, *Lady* Lillian. Because I will be damned if I stand aside and watch you marry that young fool of my cousin!"

She stared at his face, saw how the clear lines of politeness had shifted to reveal the burning anger below. His eyes seemed to spray blue hatred. The corners of his mouth were drawn back into a feral snarl.

"*Do you hear me?*" He shook her.

How easy it was to spark his anger. "I will not marry you." She wrenched out of his grip and slipped past him.

It is yours, so you will have the honor of setting the mark, the echo of Camille's voice whispered in her head.

Mine.

My responsibility.

"So?" he growled. "And what do you think your family will do? Your grandfather is too old to call me out; I would never fight against an old man. And your reputation is now ruined in any case. The only chance you have got to avoid social death is to marry me. *Me*, do you hear me? Not Alexander!"

At that, Lillian had to fight against hysterical laughter. Did he not know that she had already turned his cousin down? And did he really think she cared about what society did or thought? But then, he would not want to hear any of this, and in the end, it did not matter. Only one thing did—

"I will not marry you," she repeated. She turned and looked at him. "I will not." She clasped her hands together, so he would not see them shaking, and took a deep breath. "And I am no longer a virgin. Surely you must care about that."

A sneer distorted his face. "Did you really think I expected anything else?" he spat. "Surely not! But I have got the honor of my family to protect. And I would do much worse than marry you in order to keep my cousin safe."

When she did not react to his barely veiled threat, he strode toward her until their bodies nearly touched. "And you?" Effortlessly he towered over her. "Have you ever spared a thought of your family? Your ruin will be theirs. Society will not just cut you. *They* will suffer, too."

Lillian went very still. She recalled her aunt's fear that Lady Jersey might cancel their invitation. That the other woman had come to gloat.

"But perhaps you are so cold that this does not matter to you. That they will keep to the country, exiles in their own land. And you one of them. All your clever scheming will be for naught."

Lillian felt light, floating almost. She had not really thought about how the scandal would affect her aunt and her grandfather. She had not known that it would affect them.

Everything needs balance . . .

She almost laughed then. She had not wanted to ruin Alexander Markham's life by marrying him. And now it seemed as if she had to marry his cousin so as not to ruin the lives of her family.

Everything needs balance . . .

She looked at him.

Camille liked her men attractive. Even shackled and clumsily shaved and much too lean, this man had been beautifully made, his body finely proportioned. With his health restored, his body would be even more beautiful now—but his back still would be marred by the scars of the whip lashes, and his chest . . . on his chest would bloom a lily forevermore.

A lily for Lillian.

Her mark on him.

Her guilt.

Her responsibility.

Everything needs balance . . .

April was a cold month. Cool drafts found their way through the slits under doors and windows. And now, Lillian reached for the chill and cloaked herself in the coldness. It seeped through her skin to the place where her heart was beating.

It did not matter.

Nothing did.

Ever.

Subtly, she straightened her shoulders and looked him straight into the eyes. "I accept your offer, my lord," she said.

Chapter 7

On the morning of Lillian's wedding day the skies of London were weeping. She was married barely a week after the engagement had been announced to the public in the *Morning Post*, the *Gazette*, and *The Times*. Aunt Louisa had wrinkled her nose and had sniffled a bit. At least he did something in style, she had said while cutting the articles out to put them into the box that already held the announcements of her own children's engagements. But she did not like the fact that there would be no reading of the banns for her niece. The groom had insisted on a marriage by special license. He had insisted on quite a lot of things Aunt Louisa had not liked—to leave for his country estate directly after the ceremony was probably the worst. There would be no wedding breakfast for her to organize, which she considered a scandal, a scandal indeed.

Their steps echoed loudly in the wide, empty cathedral as Lillian walked on the arm of her grandfather up to the altar. Under the high arches to their right and left hovered shadows that the faint light of the morning was not able to dispel. The thick, solid walls of stone kept the air inside to an icy chill. With each step Lillian let the coldness seep deep into her flesh and bones until it seemed to her as if her white and silver dress had turned to woven snow on her skin.

She looked down on the posy she was holding, a cheerful assortment of red and *rosé* flowers whose names she had forgotten.

There were no roses, though. She had not wanted roses.

Her grandfather put his hand over her fingers on his arm and squeezed them lightly. When she glanced up, she saw that his eyes were dark with concern. Lillian gave him a slight smile.

The altar was so much nearer now.

Behind her she heard Nanette's tripping steps, her worries almost palpable, and Aunt Louisa's angry mutters at the empty church, the unholy hour of the ceremony, the lack of joyful spirit. As if it mattered.

Lillian's gaze was drawn to the tall angels on the golden frieze above. They smiled, untouched by what happened below, and they would still smile a hundred years from now. Above them the dome rose up as if it wanted to compete with the sky itself. Below, the air grew even chillier as cold drafts from the transepts gathered in to cloak her in ice.

So it did not matter when the groomsman turned and stared at her. He was handsome, the groomsman, his dark hair cropped short to his head and his superbly fitting uniform accentuating the powerful physique of his body. But most of all, Lillian noticed that the tip of his nose was red with cold.

The groom, by contrast, was wearing what looked like a casual riding outfit with highshafted boots, caramel-colored trousers and a gray coat. He did not turn around, did not spare her a glance even as she stepped beside him. Lillian felt her grandfather start, yet she smiled at him and gave her posy to Aunt Louisa. Smiling, she was good at smiling; and she smiled at the priest, too, when he cleared his throat to begin the ceremony.

"Dearly beloved . . ."

The man at her side could have been a statue carved out of stone.

It had stopped raining when they came out of the cathedral. The Earl of Ravenhurst's coach was already waiting for them. Not one crack or scratch showed on the gleaming black, and the colors of the coat of arms looked as fresh as if they had been painted on not a minute before. One of the footmen hastened to open the side door, his stylish livery spotless.

"Oh, my dear child . . ." Aunt Louisa burst into tears. "How we shall miss you!" She tried to muffle her sobs behind a white, lacy handkerchief.

"It is all right, Aunt Louisa," Lillian murmured and watched as her husband shook hands with his groomsman. He had avoided as much as possible touching her during the ceremony. The priest might have thought it strange. But then, he might have heard of the scandal at Almack's. Lillian did not know.

The groomsman took leave of her aunt and grandfather, even bowed to her and was the first to call her "Lady Ravenhurst." He did not offer his felicitations.

"Oh dear, oh dear!" Aunt Louisa sobbed. "How horrid this all is! No wedding party, no wedding breakfast. And where is Ravenhurst's family, I ask you? No one there to see our poor child off. Oh dear, oh dear!"

Lillian's grandfather cleared his throat and patted her back awkwardly. "Calm yourself, Louisa. Nanette will accompany Lillian. Everything will be fine."

"And no wedding breakfast!" Aunt Louisa wailed. "Our

poor, poor child! Not even a honeymoon. How very dreadful, oh, it is perfectly horrid."

The groom watched the spectacle with a bored expression. Behind him, the six horses in harness stomped their hooves and snorted, and the sweet smell of damp horse-flesh mingled with the sharper scent of horse dung. A servant was holding the reins of a seventh horse, dressed for riding.

The Marquis of Larkmoor cleared his throat some more. "It will be time, Louisa," he said gently. "Calm yourself, my dear."

"How horrid this all is!" his daughter sniffed. She shot the groom a dark look. "You should have called him out, after all, Papa."

"Now, now, my dear. . . ."

"The scoundrel," she muttered before she enfolded Lillian in a tearful, violet-scented embrace. "Oh, my poor, dear child! Do not take it too hard. Bair Hall is supposed to be very stylish, or so I have heard. Oh dear, oh dear. I am so glad Papa insisted that Nanette accompany you. It is a consolation, a consolation indeed. All alone with that horrid man! Oh, it would not bear thinking of!"

"Yes, Aunt Louisa," Lillian murmured.

"Good-bye, my dear, good-bye. Oh, how I shall miss you!" Upon the Marquis of Larkmoor's gentle insistence, Aunt Louisa finally broke the embrace with a last: "Oh dear, oh dear!"

The marquis merely pressed Lillian's hand, but his green eyes, she saw, sparkled with unshed tears. His throat worked. "My dear child . . ."

"I will be fine," Lillian reassured him. "Truly." *There are worse things. So much more worse things.* She smiled a bit. "Thank you . . . grandfather."

His lips trembled, but then they lifted in an answering

smile. "Take good care of our girl, Nanette," he said to the old nanny.

Nanette in her dark traveling dress gave the resemblance of a small, frail sparrow. "I always have, my lord," she said softly. Then she took Lillian's arm, and together they went toward the waiting carriage.

Fashionable society was still asleep when they left London, two women all alone in a big, wide coach. The groom preferred to ride his own horse. When Lillian put her forehead against the glass of the window, she could sometimes catch a glimpse of him, far ahead, the shock of his auburn hair a beacon for them to follow. After a while, though, rain veiled him from view.

Rain continued to fall all day and washed out the colors of the landscape until it became dreary and gray. Tucked under one of the benches, Nanette found a basket with cold meat and bread for their lunch, but Lillian was not hungry. She remembered another journey through the rain and wondered what would await them this time.

When darkness fell, they stopped at an inn for the night. The coach rattled into the big yard, where cobblestones glittered wetly and people were waiting with umbrellas. The door of the carriage was opened and a footman offered his hand to Lillian. His livery, which had looked so stylish this morning, was now hidden beneath a rain-soaked, mud-bespeckled coat.

Lillian put her hand in his, felt, for just one fleeting moment, the strength in his. Then she stood on solid ground, and a servant hurried to hold a dark umbrella over her head while the rain plastered his shirt to his skin.

The smells of wet wood and horse and the sweat of men tickled her nose. Slowly, Lillian looked around the yard, three galleries high. Fairy lights twinkled in the windows, danced on the glistening cobblestones and cast shadows over the huge wooden board over the entrance to the yard. They flickered over the form of a coiled dragon and the man standing above him with a bloodied lance.

Lillian remembered black dragons curling over lampshades and on red walls, flanking the man who bore her mark on his skin. But most of all she remembered the song of Camille's dogs when they cornered their prey.

With a small shudder she turned away.

Busy activity filled the yard, and the clutter of hooves and the shouts of men dimmed out the sounds of the rain. Servants hurried by to take inside the carpetbags from the box of the carriage.

A frail hand touched her arm. "Lillian?" Nanette said behind her.

"Yes. I'll come," Lillian murmured and followed the servant with the umbrella to the door, where the Earl of Ravenhurst stood and talked to the innkeeper and the innkeeper's wife. The couple bowed and curtsied at her approach, while the earl shot her a dark look. The lines of his face seemed more deeply etched into his skin, and his stance was slightly awkward as if his left leg was giving him pain. His lips tightened. He went inside, limping.

Lillian stared after him, remembering the sounds of his shuffling steps behind her on a garden path.

"Lillian," Nanette prompted again.

"Yes," Lillian said.

Inside, a servant took their redingotes, and they were led to a private parlor where hot soup and a platter of cold meat awaited them. The table was laid out for two. There was no sign of the earl.

"He might be eating downstairs," Nanette said as they sat down to eat. "You should not worry, *chou-chou.*" When, in truth, it was Nanette who worried.

Lillian smiled a bit and ate her soup and the meat, without tasting any of it. Strange this. Before, she had come to learn to enjoy some meals. She had liked Yorkshire pudding and ratafia ice cream. Now, all food again turned to sand in her mouth.

After the meal a maid led them to another room. In the gallery the song of the rain greeted them, and the coldness of the water rose to reach for Lillian. She would have liked to stand in the yard below and let the rain soak her clothes. Instead, she stepped into the waiting bedroom brightly lit by candles, the four-poster bed huge, with white linen. Fragrant steam rose from a tub, and on the chest in front of the bed stood her carpetbag, filled with a few clothes for the journey. A thin, white nightgown. A new dress for tomorrow.

"If this is all, my lady?" The girl curtsied. "The maid's room"—she shot a curious glance to Nanette—"is through here." She pointed to another door.

"Thank you," Nanette said. "We shan't need anything else." When the maid left, Nanette bustled around the room, opening the bag, plumping up the pillows. "It's not too bad."

"No," Lillian agreed. But, in truth, it did not matter.

"You should go and take a bath, *chou-chou*, as long as the water is still warm." The old woman ran a finger over the towels and the soap on the stool beside the tub.

"*Oui*," Lillian murmured. Slowly, she pried the buttons of her dark dress open.

Nanette brushed her hands away. "Let me, child." Intent on her task, the woman hummed under her breath, an old song with which she had soothed and hushed Lillian when Lillian was a little girl.

Lillian closed her eyes and inhaled the faint, soft scent of lavender, which still clung to Nanette's clothes even after a day's journey. As the familiar hands of the old woman gently stripped her of her clothes, Lillian felt like a little girl again. Like a golden bubble, the memory of security, her mother's laughter in a sun-warmed garden, rose inside her.

It warmed her when she sat in the cooling water and washed the soap off her body. It warmed her more when Nanette helped her into the thin nightgown and the matching robe. Lillian sat on a chair and let the old woman comb out her curls.

And then, the door banged against the wall. An icy gust of wind swept into the room, made the candles flicker and gooseflesh rise on Lillian's skin. The soothing movements of the hairbrush stopped. Nanette gasped. On the threshold, with wild hair and burning eyes, loomed the Earl of Ravenhurst. His coat and waistcoat were gone and with them the last veneer of civility.

The old woman fluttered around his wife like an agitated mother bird. Troy squinted against the light of the candles. He knew that he had drunk too much. *Celebrating his wedding.* He bared his teeth in a silent snarl.

"You." At his glance, the old woman froze. "Get out!" he growled. He barely recognized his own voice. It resembled the sounds of a feral animal. Harsh. Ferocious.

He watched as the old woman scurried away into the servant's room. The door closed behind her, and he was alone with his blushing bride.

His bride. Who had branded him like an animal.

He sauntered into the room, looking his fill.

She was sitting on a chair, hands folded in her lap. Where her robe gaped open her skin shone through the thin material of her nightgown. He could see the curve of a pale breast, a tightly puckered nipple the color of caramel cream. A hot shaft of lust surged into his loins. He wanted to bite that nipple, to make her cry out. To use her pain to ease the churning of remembered humiliation and fear in the pit of his stomach.

Riding all day, though, had taken its toll. And so, when he kicked the door to the room closed, his bad leg nearly made him stumble.

She just watched. As she had done all those months ago. *Oui, maman.*

Lust was joined by anger.

His fingers twitched with the urge to bury his hands in the mass of her brown curls, to wind all that hair around his fist, around and around.

So he did.

Her eyes were gray, cold and gray.

He forced her to her feet. Then he pressed his mouth on hers and a heady feeling of power coursed through him. Her lips did not move, so he bit them. Afterwards, he watched how they darkened until they were red and ripe.

He remembered the feeling of her breast in his hand. It had felt like a ripe fruit, too. All soft flesh. . . . He pushed the robe off her shoulders. Beneath the delicate embroidery on the nightgown circled two lush globes. He pinched the nipples, felt them pebble against his fingers.

He pressed himself against her, hardened.

"Touch me," he growled and lifted his pelvis against her. "Touch me."

Obligingly, her hand crept upward, brushed against his cock, before her fingers closed around him through the material of his trousers. He groaned, and with his hands still full of her hair, he pulled her head back and kissed her, hard.

"*Touch me.*" Her hair smelled of flowers.

She stroked him and fire ran through his body. His hips jerked forward.

Her hair smelled fresh and sweet, of flowers, yes, flowers. Yet their perfume could not banish the stench of the prison. It rose and enveloped Troy, the stench of sweat and blood and excretions. The smell that had soaked his skin until all the water and soap in the world could not wash it away. The end of Gratien's whip pressed against Troy's windpipe, cutting off the air.

Troy gasped. Bile rose in his throat.

"Enough," he croaked. He forced his eyes to open, to focus on the girl before him.

She watched him, unmoved.

Watching . . . watching . . . watching . . .

"Enough!" This time, he would not be subdued. He was stronger.

The rattling of the chains sounded loud in his ears.

"No!" he roared. "Damn it, *no!*"

He gave her a shove, which had her staggering backwards toward the bed.

Her legs bumped against the hard edge of the bed, and the force of his push sent her sprawling across the white linen. His face, she saw, gleamed with sweat, and his chest heaved as if he had run a mile.

How curious that he should sweat, when her own skin seemed encrusted with ice. She did not move. There was no knowing what might set another person off. She had come to learn that at a very early age.

So she just watched as he raised trembling hands to the buttons of his shirt. "No," he murmured. "*No!*" With another roar, he ripped his shirt. Unnoticed, the material dropped to the floor.

He looked different.

For one thing, his skin was darker and covered with hair.

And he was no longer painfully thin, either. Instead, muscles bounced and rippled, rounded his arms and shoulders.

But all of that dimmed to insignificance as Lillian's gaze fastened on the mark that was half hidden by the damp, curly hair. No longer angry red, it had faded to a dark brown. A dark brown lily.

A lily for Lillian.

His chest gleamed with sweat. It ran in tiny rivulets over his skin and soaked the waistband of his trousers. When he followed her onto the bed, he limped badly.

"Bitch!" he rasped.

Even his scent was no longer civilized, all lingering traces of sandalwood and oakmoss washed away by the sharpness of his sweat.

His hands fastened around the collar of her nightdress. His fingers trembled, then he ripped the flimsy material apart. Cold air whispered over Lillian's skin, before the weight of his body pressed her into the mattress.

Yet his body gave off no heat. Astonished, she noticed the clamminess of his flesh. Fine tremors raced through him, and the breath hitched in his throat.

There was no evidence of arousal.

He stared at her.

"Bitch," he whispered. "Bitch!"

The tremors intensified.

He gasped.

His face took on a pasty color. For a moment he looked as if he was going to be sick.

"God . . . dear God . . ." Breathing heavily, he rolled off her and swung his legs over the side of the bed.

For a while he just sat there, elbows on his knees and hands buried in his hair, which had turned dark with perspiration. Finally, he stood, and as he turned to look down on her, his face was devoid of all expression. It was a granite mask of human flesh and bone. His eyes were still intensely blue, but instead of burning with anger or hatred, they were flat and dead.

"You disgust me," he said. "God, how you disgust me."

And then he turned and walked out of the room. With a loud bang, the door slammed shut behind him.

Alone in the wide bed on the stainless, white linen, Lillian closed her eyes.

PART III

When will the hundred summers die,
And thought and time be born again,
And newer knowledge, drawing nigh,
Bring truth that sways the soul of men?

—Tennyson, The Day Dream

Chapter 8

From the distance, Bair Hall seemed a jumble of oriels and turrets and chimneys. Lots of chimneys. The bricks blurred into a single rusty-brown, the shades of red, orange and apricot lost just like the delicate blue pattern among them, a diamond-shaped tattoo on the thick hide of the Hall. Due to the fact that the first Earl of Ravenhurst had preferred a good view above a weather-sheltered home, the Hall sat comfortably on its green hill like a fat brown hen on her eggs.

Hill, the butler, had told them all about the first Earl of Ravenhurst's liking for a good view from his bedroom window. Sometimes it seemed to Lillian that Hill must have been there from the time the house had been erected. He knew all its stories and secrets, how it had once been "Bear Hall," as on his first hunt in the area the first Earl of Ravenhurst had killed a mighty brown bear, which now adorned the entrance hall in all its fearful, dead glory.

Indeed, all of the earls of Ravenhurst had been fond of collecting trophies of one sort or another. For the first earl it had been hunting trophies. The second had brought home exotic plants from all over the world to fill his garden and conservatory. The third had liked paintings and stuffed two galleries with them. And the fourth earl, who had died when his son had just been out of his leading strings, had a fondness for ludicrous books and filled his library with them.

Or so Hill said.

He had not told them, Lillian and Nanette, what the current earl liked to collect. His master, Hill had remarked, had spent most of his adult years fighting for his king and country. A most valiant man, Murgatroyd Sacheverell, fifth Earl of Ravenhurst.

And he was Lillian's husband, whom she had not seen ever since they had arrived at the Hall all those weeks ago. But then, she did not spend much time in the house. Each morning, almost as soon as the sun rose and painted the eastern sky in shades of pink, Lillian went out into the gardens of Bair Hall.

There was nothing wild or unkempt about these gardens. Around the house, paths of gravel or of thick green grass led through luscious flower beds, under pergolas, which dropped Golden Rain, by banks of rhododendron and by ponds filled with white water lilies.

The rose garden Lillian did not like, even though the flowers filled the air with their sweet scent. On some days it was enough to coat her body in cold sweat.

So she preferred to walk on, to the landscaped garden where groups of deciduous trees evoked a small forest. One of the softly rolling hills harbored the ice house, another displayed a set of artificial ruins: the fourth Earl of Ravenhurst had not just had a fondness for silly books, but also for any other oddities that touched his sense of humor.

Lillian liked wandering through the orchards filled with row after row of apple trees and cherry trees and peach trees, divided by hedgerows of blueberries and raspberries, all hinting at delights to come. Sometimes it seemed to her that she could already taste the sweet fruits on her tongue—round, sun-warmed treats. One bite would be enough to fill her mouth with sticky juice.

She loved to be out in the garden when the first dew still glittered on grass and petals, when the only sounds were the jubilant songs of the birds and the croaks of the frogs. She would take bread to the ducks on the lake by the small forest and would admire the swans' loving displays of affection. Then she appeared to be the only human in that world where sunshine reigned over brimming life.

And when the sun stood high in the sky, she would walk on, all the way to the wall on which stone animals stood guard. She followed the wall past the lion, the unicorn and the eagle, until she reached the raven with its widespread wings and the little gate beside it. That led out into the fields and meadows that surrounded the family estate.

Here, the scents of high grass and young corn mingled with the dust that rose from the path. Sometimes Lillian would see the people who worked the fields, or she would pass by a meadow of brown cows, which regarded her with soft, long-lashed eyes. They smelled of warmth and hay. Sometimes they would let Lillian caress their heads or their soft flanks, and their warmth would seep deep into her skin. She also saw woolly sheep, which filled the air with their bleating. They would nibble on her fingers, and she would watch the lambs grow strong and sturdy, while the sun shone on her face and the soft breeze played with her hair and the memories slowly faded.

From the distance, Bair Hall with its turrets and the two towers of the side wings always reminded Troy of a proud castle, warding off all peril. He smiled fondly while he wiped the sweat off his brow. He had spent the day with his steward, riding up and down the Ravenhurst lands and taking stock of things that needed to be done. In the late afternoon he had sent the man home, so he could spend an hour or two enjoying a brisk gallop through the green meadows and woods of his home. In the wild joy of the ride, almost like flying, he had been able to forget, had been able to exist just for the moment, pains and worries all gone.

Troy sighed.

Now that the fine lawn shirt under his rumpled riding habit was plastered to his skin and a dull throbbing had started in his thigh, common sense had returned with the familiar weight of responsibility.

He patted the warm neck of his brown hunter. "Come on, old boy, time to go home." Nudging Brueberry's side with the heel of his boot, Troy guided the horse toward the high stone arch that marked the entrance to the family estate. When he rode through the open gate, a soft wind lifted the sweaty locks on his forehead and ruffled the white blossoms of the rowan tree that grew just behind the entrance.

"Afternoon, Master Troy." The gatekeeper's cheerful voice cut through his reverie, and with a smile, Troy turned to nod at the old man. His greeting for Nolan, however, died on his lips as he saw the woman who sat beside the gatekeeper on the bench in front of his house. He felt new sweat form on his upper lip and he resisted the urge to wipe it dry.

"Mistress Nanette here," continued Nolan, "has just told me what a lucky choice a rowan is as a gate tree. Isn't that so, Mistress Nanette?"

"Indeed it is." The old woman nodded and smiled, and even more wrinkles appeared around her eyes and mouth.

Small and frail, with her white bonnet she looked like one of the old women in fairy tales who, at the blink of an eye, would transform herself into a mighty fairy godmother or such.

Troy blinked.

Brueberry, his horse, snorted.

The old woman rose and ambled toward him. "A useful tree to guard one's home, the rowan is." She reached out and patted Brueberry's nose.

Troy's eyes widened. Brueberry, the Holy Terror of the stablehands; Brueberry the Horrible, who was known to have once bitten off a man's finger—the Fearsome Brueberry now stood meek and soft like a lamb under the old woman's touch.

And then Troy remembered.

A shaft of pain sliced his heart, for Brueberry, his companion of so many years, had been shot under him on the battlefield, had been hacked to pieces all those months ago. The hunter he sat on was just a nameless horse from his stables, brown like Brueberry, but no replacement at all for his old friend.

Troy shook his head and willed the pain to recede so he could concentrate on the old woman smiling up at him.

"For no evil shall come to a house that is guarded by a rowan tree," she said. When she ceased patting its nose, the horse began nibbling on her shoulder, spreading spittle over her woolen shawl.

Troy blinked. "I see," he murmured faintly. "Er . . . I . . . a good day to you, Mistress Nanette, Nolan."

Nolan waved good-bye. "And a good day to you, Master Troy."

Feeling more than slightly dazed, Troy nudged his horse on to a comfortable walk. After a moment, he looked back over his shoulder. "Mistress Nanette, shall I have somebody fetch you with a cart . . . or something?" After all, she was an old woman and might be too frail and too tired to walk all the way back to the main house.

Her face again crinkled into a smile. "That will not be necessary, my lord. Thank you. And a good day to you."

"Ah yes, yes," he murmured and turned around. The old oak trees on either side of the path formed a natural green roof, which held off the heat of the sun. A spring-scented breeze cooled his face, and after a while the dazed feeling faded. He shook his head. He now seemed to remember that his steward had told him about Mistress Nanette constantly ambling around the village, bringing old Widow Gobar a new blanket and Maggie Smith, whose son was ill with fever, herbs and chicken soup.

So Mistress Nanette obviously had a kind heart.

Troy allowed himself a cynical smile.

At least somebody had one.

As always these days, the decreasing distance to the Hall inevitably blackened his mood. It was back to home and hearth, back to a wife whom he did not want, whose existence he yearned to forget, whose gray eyes followed him even into his dreams and turned them into nightmares.

Warily, Troy rubbed his chest where the stain of scorched flesh would never fade.

"I have seen his lordship today," Nanette said as Lillian entered the bedroom. "I must say he looked extremely dashing on top of his big brown horse."

"Did he?" Lillian unfastened the ribbons of her straw hat and threw it on her bed. She and Nanette used the bedroom in the tower as morning room, drawing room and dining room all in one, since it had not been indicated that they were allowed to make use of any other room in Bair Hall. Not that Lillian would complain. It was a lovely, sunny room with windows on three sides, a big, comfortable bed, a table, a few upholstered chairs and two old chests for her wardrobe. Not that she needed them. She had left all her fine dresses in the trunks just as they had come from London in the extra carriage. These days she only wore simple cotton dresses with floral prints, a pair of sturdy boots and her curry-colored spencer jacket. Oh, and how relieved she was that she no longer had to deal with tight, long gloves or bust-improvers, or with hairstyles that made her scalp hurt. Now only a single ribbon held her brown curls in place, and sometimes she would let them fall down her back in all their unruly abundance so that the wind could lift single strands and play with them. She liked to stand on one of the small hills, the sun warm on her face, and turn around and around and feel her hair swirling about her like a thick cloak.

Nanette looked up from the sock she was knitting. "Soon you will be brown as a nut and have freckles all over your face. This will not do for a fashionable lady."

At that, Lillian could not help smiling. "But I am not a fashionable lady."

"You are a countess."

"Who lives on her absent husband's estate like—what is the term—a wild hoyden?" Lillian's smile deepened. "I have visited the lambs today. They bounced all over the grass and nudged my thigh as if they wanted me to bounce around with them."

Nanette's knitting needles once more took up their cheerful rattle. "I am worried about you, *chou-chou*. You should spend your time with people and not with lambs. Now that we are far from the château and that horrid woman." She glanced at Lillian, and suddenly her expression became wistful. "I would wish a normal life for you," she said softly. "A good life just like your mama had."

Lillian sat down on the bed and twiddled the ribbons of her hat through her fingers. The joyful memory of the bouncing lambs slowly dimmed and faded, only to be replaced by other memories. Memories of cold and misty places. Of the song of the hunting pack when it cornered its prey. Memories of her father's coffin slowly being lowered into the damp brown earth, leaving her all alone in the world.

"But then she married Papa. And after her death he went to Camille." Lillian let go of the ribbons and folded her hands in her lap. "Sometimes I think that he was not a very good man."

The old woman put her knitting on the table at her side. "Oh, *chou-chou*, your father was a good man. A weak man, perhaps, but a good man."

Lillian arched her brows. "Can you be truly a good person when you are weak?" She turned her head to gaze out of the window to the gardens beyond. "I was weak, too." Vividly she remembered the smell of scorched flesh and the sounds of a whip on naked skin, the dark lily underneath damp body hair. "I let things happen. That is why Ravenhurst cannot bear the sight of me." She shook her head, then turned to cast a sad smile at Nanette.

Her old nanny stood and walked over to grasp Lillian's cold hands in hers. "What really happened, *chou-chou*? You only said he was there at the château. Was he . . . ?"

Lillian felt her hands grow even more chilled. Coldness seeped through her whole body, chasing off all remains of warmth and sunshine. She drew her hands from Nanette's loose grip. "She got him out of the prison," she said tightly and looked away. How would it help if Nanette knew the whole truth? That he was to be Lillian's own toy, that she herself had marked him?

A lily for Lillian.

"It is not your fault, *chou-chou*."

"Maybe." Lillian forced her lips into a smile. "I am just out of sorts today. Forgive me."

"Lillian?"

"It is quite all right." She saw the worry in the old woman's face and wished she could somehow wipe it away. Nanette deserved some rest. Abruptly, Lillian stood. "Do you mind if I take another stroll in the garden? It is so beautiful out there today."

"Your aunt has written again," Nanette said plaintively, and pointed to the small pile of unopened letters that grew steadily each week. "Isn't it well past time that you write a reply? Surely she must worry."

Moving backwards toward the door, Lillian lifted her shoulders. Aunt Louisa belonged to the bustle of London, all so very removed from her right now it seemed her aunt and grandfather belonged to a different life altogether. "You write her every week," she said, and wanted to flee from the room.

"It would reassure her to hear from *you*, *chou-chou*."

One hand on the latch, Lillian shook her head. "What shall I tell her? About the lambs and the green grass or the crooked tower of the little church in the village? Don't be cross, Nanette. You can tell her so much more than I." With a last apologetic smile, she left the room.

Chapter 9

Troy blinked. The figures and columns in the account book danced before his eyes, blurred, only to form new shapes and lines. Wearily, he rubbed a hand over his face.

Tiredness lent weight to his bones until his whole body ached, until he walked like an old man, bent over by life. Around him, all was silent. These days the spacious study on the second floor felt like a tomb, with the walls pressing down on him, squeezing the breath from his lungs.

Troy dug the heels of his hands against his eye sockets. His fingers clenched on the flesh of his face. How he longed to mold these bones and blood into a new form. How he longed to wipe away all traces of the last few years.

Sometimes his throat was still raw from the acrid smoke of gunfire; his ears still rang from the roar of the cannons; sometimes his nose still quivered from the smell of sweat and fear, leather and horses, from the smell of death and of gunpowder, threatening to choke him. And then there were the other memories. Of the stench of that prison, the shuffling of bodies, the crack of a whip and the sting on his skin. Memories of humiliation and pain and utter helplessness. He did not dwell long on those memories, for they made his hands shake with anger. They made him want to roar and drive his fist against the wall.

And they made him fear to break down as he had on his wedding night.

He drew in a shuddering breath. He had buried himself in his work to forget. Yet it seemed that the memories would never leave, would never cease to torment him. They were there, night and day, each hour and each minute. There was no escape.

A shudder wracked his body. God, how tired he was. So tired.

In the distance a dog barked. Troy lifted his head.

He had not owned a dog since he was sixteen and buried Luned. At first, he had not wanted a new dog after Luned. And later, on the battlefields of Europe, he had not needed a dog. There had only been Brueberry the Horrible.

Troy sighed and ran his hands through his hair. Linking his fingers at his neck, he leaned his head back. On top of everything else, he was now suffering from hallucinations— ghosts of the past calling for him, a dog, a friend long dead. "What a mess," he muttered. "What a bloody, bloody mess."

Another bark sounded, closer this time, and now it seemed to him that he could also hear the distant pounding of hooves. He shook his head, then stood and leaned forward to open the window. His study overlooked the drive and the entrance to the Hall, yet the thick foliage of the old oak trees prevented him from discerning anything on the path beneath. However, the thunder of hooves carried clearly up to the house, and soon it was joined by the crunch of carriage wheels on gravel and joyful canine barks once more.

Obviously, he was about to have visitors.

Troy sighed.

You would expect that the north of England was far enough removed from London to prevent anybody from getting it into his head to come for an impromptu country house party.

He scratched his left eyebrow.

At least it was not his grandmother. She detested animals. And it could not be his aunt and uncle either, for even though the Marquis of Waldron kept a few pointers at his country estate, the Marchioness was mortally afraid of dogs. She was mortally afraid of quite a lot of things. One time, when Troy had still been a boy, she had nearly screamed the house down upon finding a teeny-weeny spider in her chamberpot.

Troy grinned at the memory.

He had been twelve, and it had taken him hours to find and catch that particular spider. And his seven-year-old cousin, trying to outshine him, had fallen into the fishpond the next day in an effort to catch a frog.

Troy's grin faded. Alex had been a featherbrain even at that young age.

Troy sighed and rubbed his hands over his face. Of course, he was doing Alex an injustice. His cousin was no worse than the other young bucks around town— irresponsible, vain, and generally scatterbrained.

He looked back out the window just as the first pair of dusty black horses came into view. Now he could also discern male laughter among the excited barks. Soon the black barouche, drawn by six horses and looking a bit the worse for wear, pulled up into the forecourt. The top of the barouche was folded back so that the three sleek, silver gray dogs with floppy ears could thrust their heads over the side of the carriage and herald their excitement to the world. The rims of dusty high hats screened the faces of the two men lounging on the seats of the carriage, yet Troy knew the timbre of their voices and the coat of arms painted on the side of the barouche, and his knees went weak with relief.

Leaning forward and supporting his weight with one hand on the windowpane, he put two fingers into his mouth and gave a shrill whistle.

Coachman, dogs, barouche-drivers, and footmen—his and theirs—all looked up.

"Hey, you pair of rascals," he shouted, "have you lost your way, or what?"

The dogs jumped out of the carriage, wildly barking, and chased each other around the vehicle, causing the horses to neigh and snort in disdain. One of the men in the carriage, his white teeth flashing in a grin, nudged his companion and hollered over the din: "Look, Justin, the rumors have been quite wrong: He has *not* gone and moved to a cave in the woods."

"A cave in the woods?" Troy infused his voice with mock dismay before he laughed. "Hold on, boys. I'll be with you in a minute."

He gladly abandoned his desk and hurried through his study to throw the door to the hallway open. As he dashed toward the main staircase, he could already hear the jumble in the hall below, and it seemed to him that his heart must surely start to sing in his chest. He skipped down the stairs, taking two at a time, and rushed through the big hall, past his butler, who attempted to straighten tufty gray hair and direct the footmen at the same time. In truth, they needed little direction, for they had already begun to carry the luggage inside and upstairs.

Troy pressed past them outside, where next to the carriage curious canine noses and outstretched arms awaited him.

"Troy, my boy!" Drake, tall, athletic and with an ever-merry twinkle in his green eyes, pulled him into a tight embrace. "God, it's good to see you!" His voice wavered slightly. As if to make up for it, he thumped Troy's back a few times before he pulled back in order to have a better look at him. His hand gripped the back of Troy's neck and shook him lightly. "Look at you! *Look* at you!" Suddenly there were tears in his eyes and once again, he enveloped Troy in a tight hug.

"Sweeting," a nasal drawl was to be heard, "it will not really do to crush the poor fellow to death, you know."

"Jus, you can be a pest at times," Drake mumbled into Troy's shoulder.

"Shut up and give him to me," came the affectionate reply, and then Troy found himself within the circle of another pair of strong arms. "Hello, my boy." Troy was rocked from side to side in a slow motion. "I see you've gained a bit of flesh on your ribs in the past few months."

"I have." Troy smiled against Justin's dusty greatcoat.

"Good. Good." After a last tightening of his arms, Justin finally released him. "And here we are." He threw his arms wide. "Tweedledee and Tweedledum, complete with bag and baggage."

"And dogs." Drake grinned. "Sit, girls." Three silver-gray doggie bottoms hit the gravel with a crunch. "Troy, meet Anna, Sophie and Marie, our wonderfully wicked Weimaraners, a present from our dear friend Ludwig von Müffert."

"Our wonderfully wicked Weimaraners, which are finally and thankfully free of worms and fleas and thus fit for civilized company," Justin added. Even though his voice did not lose its normal nasal twang, the softening of his features betrayed his affection for the dogs.

Troy smiled. A hard nut, Justin de la Mere, at least on

the outside, with his façade of polite boredom, but all mushy and soft inside.

He watched how Justin's eyes lifted from the dogs to Drake and how the man's features softened even more. Troy's smile widened. He had known these two since his first week at Eton, when the three of them had banded together to prevent being bullied by the older boys. They were not really like the twins from the old song, Justin and Drake, more like night and day in coloring. Where Drake Bainbridge, Viscount Allenbright, was all pale English skin, sparkling green eyes and shiny, golden hair, Justin de la Mere had inherited the olive-hued skin of his South-French ancestors, Huguenot immigrants of two centuries past, as well as the chocolate brown eyes and the black curls, which he kept cropped short. He was of slighter build than Drake, yet his agility and his wiry strength made him a deadly opponent with both *épée* and rapier.

Troy slung his arms over Drake's and Justin's shoulders. "I am damn glad to see you and to have you here. You, too, girls." Grinning, he inclined his head toward the three dogs. "Let's go inside. You must want to freshen up, and if I'm not mistaken there's a mighty good old port hidden somewhere in my cellars."

"Indeed." Justin whistled to the dogs to follow them. Tails wagging and floppy ears flying, Anna, Sophie and Marie scrambled off and darted past the men. "I guess we've got some catching up to do, too."

"Do we?" Troy raised his brows.

"London news might take a while to reach the outposts of civilization in Cornwall," Drake remarked dryly, "but even there we eventually heard that you've gone and got yourself a wife."

His friend's last words acted like a needle to Troy's bubble of joy. He gave a harsh laugh and let go of their shoulders. "So you've come all the way from Cornwall to find out whether it's true?" He could not prevent his voice from taking on a bitter tone.

He noticed how his two friends exchanged a look.

"No," Drake said lightly. "In fact we've come to drink the cellars of Bair Hall dry since you haven't invited us to the wedding."

Troy's answer came out harsher than he intended. "That might be because there was no wedding feast."

"No wedding feast?" Justin's brows rose high. "My dear chap, this sounds as if you've got yourself into a bloody scrape."

Sighing, Troy rubbed his temple. "I apologize for sounding clipped. I . . ." He rolled his shoulders, then shrugged.

Drake reached up to grab Troy's shoulder. He searched Troy's face, undoubtedly noticing the dark rings under his friend's eyes. "Never mind, old chum," he said softly. "We're here now and we're here to stay for a while. As Jus has said, we're here with bag and baggage." His teeth flashed in a quick smile.

"And dogs." Troy smiled back. "And I'm glad for it. Really. Let's meet in the library after you two have restored your natural beauty."

Drake lightly nudged Troy's chin with his fist. "That's my boy."

"My lord!" An agitated Hill descended the stairs to the entrance of the Hall. "My lord!" His face beet red, he came to a skittering halt in front of his master. "My lord . . ." He took a deep breath.

Troy raised his brows. "Yes?"

"My lord," Hill informed him in his best butler-voice, "the dogs have hunted down the Bear."

Troy blinked. "The bear," he echoed.

"No, no, my lord, *the* Bear." Hill looked at him expectantly, then obviously felt compelled to elaborate: "The first Earl of Ravenhurst's bear, my lord. It fell down."

"Oh dear," Drake said. "Weimaraners are bred to hunt bears and deer."

"Then they'll probably enjoy their stay at the Hall." Troy felt his lips twitch. "Let's hope they'll leave great-great-grandfather's deer heads on the wall." The weariness lifted from his shoulders.

It was good to have friends.

The chill of the evening had settled on the land by the time Lillian slipped into the Hall through a side entrance. Her curls, liberally dotted with wilting daisies, whirled around her head like a cloud made of sunshine and the perfume of flowers. Smiling, Lillian twirled a brown lock around her finger. After a day spent out in the open, she felt strong and healthy as if all darkness had been wiped away from her world. Her feet hardly touched the stone stairs as she danced up to the little room under the roof. But when she threw open the door, she skittered to an abrupt halt, nearly colliding with the imposing figure of Mrs. Fitzpatrick, the housekeeper, fists on her rounded hips.

"There you are!" Mrs. Fitzpatrick's nose quivered with indignation. "My Lord Ravenhurst has enquired for you."

Lillian's eyes darted past the housekeeper to the corner where Nanette sat with her knitting needles. The old woman gave her a reassuring smile.

"... scandalous behavior! You are awaited in the drawing room. Well, in the dining room, now, more likely. Where have you been? Have you any idea what you look like? Is that a grass stain there on your skirt? And what's that? Daisies?"

Lillian stood very still. She felt the warmth of happiness fade, while the outside world pressed into her little haven, reality intruding into her happy dream.

"Really, this is no fit behavior for the Countess of Ravenhurst! And no proper dress, no proper wardrobe at hand! Everything packed away! I had Millie go through the trunks and iron that green dress over there." Mrs. Fitzpatrick waved her hand, pointing in the general direction of the bed, where a pale green evening gown was laid out. "As if the maids didn't have enough to do with all the excitement and the guests."

"Guests?" Lillian asked.

"Of course, guests. That's why his lordship wishes for your presence in the dining room. Immediately!" Mrs. Fitzpatrick's small, pale-lashed eyes narrowed. "And no proper dress ready! A shame this! A—"

"Mrs. Fitzpatrick, I think this is quite enough," Nanette's soft voice interrupted.

"Enough? *Enough?*" The housekeeper rounded on her. "The family is going to ruins. I wonder what the Dowager Countess would have to say to the behavior of your ward. Ashamed, she would be. I—"

"Leave." Her hands curled into fists at her sides, Lillian interrupted the tirade in an icy-quiet voice. How dare this woman talk to Nanette like that? This woman would *not* bring back the darkness into their lives.

"What?" Mrs. Fitzpatrick turned to gape at her, her thin lips slightly opened.

Standing straight, her head raised, Lillian looked at the woman while anger flowed through her veins. She reveled in its heady power. "If I remember correctly, it was you, Mrs. Fitzpatrick, who assigned this room to me after Lord Ravenhurst made it clear that he does not want me in the family apartments." Her lips lifted to form a chilly little smile. At Château du Marais she had had opportunity enough to study the fine art of demanding respect from the servants. "You must have known that the room lacks a proper wardrobe for my clothes. So it would appear this is entirely *your* fault."

A mottled color rose in the woman's face. "Well, I say!" she huffed.

Lillian took a tiny step toward her, all the while smiling down in that chilly, chilly way she had come to learn so well. "And in the future you will call me 'my lady.'" Lillian deliberately intensified the smile. "For I *am* the countess. Your *mistress*. And you would do well to remember that." Abruptly, she clapped her hands together and had the satisfaction of seeing the housekeeper flinch. "Now go."

Mrs. Fitzpatrick scurried past her, a fat old goose with ruffled feathers. Lillian waited until the sound of footsteps receded down the stairs before she raised her eyes to look at her old nanny.

"Well done, *chou-chou*. Well done." Chuckling, Nanette rose from her chair. "I really cannot stand the old bat." Yet then she turned a worried eye toward the bed. "She is right, however—Lord Ravenhurst has demanded your presence downstairs. You should get ready."

At the mention of her husband, Lillian's anger drained away. "He has guests?"

"Friends of his, Hill said." Nanette went over to Lillian and helped her with the buttons at the back of her dress. "The kitchen is in upheaval." She gently tugged at a strand of Lillian's hair. "Daisies?"

Hearing the amusement in the old woman's voice, Lillian could not help smiling. She put her foot on one of the chests and started to undo the lacings of her muddied boot. "I am afraid I won't have time to comb out my hair." She straightened and wriggled her foot free of the boot.

Another tug at her curls made her look back over her shoulder.

"It looks very pretty, I think," Nanette said, a mischievous twinkle in her eyes. "In any case, they are bound to have never seen anything like it ever before." Her lips twitched. "My Lady Lillian of the Hundred Daisies."

A short while later Lillian emerged from her room, clad in her pale green evening dress with the tiny, floral embroidering down the skirt. The white satin slippers as well as the long kid gloves were slightly rumpled, but then, Lillian detested the gloves anyway. Even now, her fingers itched and her skin felt uncomfortably damp. Impatiently, she tugged at the gloves while she was walking down the corridor to the main tract of the house and the main staircase. She did not want to go down the tower stairs and through the servants' hallway and thereby risk running into the housekeeper once more.

Lillian sighed, and finally let the gloves be. Clasping her hands firmly behind her back, she walked down the big staircase with its intricately carved banisters. From golden frames against salmon-colored French wallpaper, stately men peered down on her, while the blue Persian carpet swallowed up the sounds of her steps. The further she went, the taller and more imposing the paintings became until at the bottom of the stairs they covered nearly the whole height of the hall, showing larger than life men in old-fashioned high wigs and proud poses, large golden chains on their chests.

Lillian's hand flew up to cover the golden cross, which hung on a thin chain around her neck. The small Maltese cross had been a present from Aunt Louisa, who had insisted that Maltese crosses were all the fashion for demure, young maidens.

138

"My lady!"

At the sound of the butler's voice, Lillian let her hand drop to her side. Her lips lifted automatically into the little smile she had perfected for social functions. "Good evening, Hill."

"Oh, my lady." He hurried toward her, a horse brush in hand. His hair was ruffled, and a hint of ruddiness stained his cheeks as if he had been exerting himself. "They have been looking for you all over the place, my lady." He blinked rapidly several times. "Are these daisies?"

Lillian rubbed the tip of one satin slipper over the pale blue floor tiles. "I have been out in the gardens." The color of the tiles reminded her of the delicate shell of a robin's egg.

"I see." Hill cleared his throat, then looked back over his shoulder at the first earl's bear in the far corner of the hall. "I . . ." His eyes darted back to Lillian. "Shall I show you to the dining room, my lady? I believe Lord Ravenhurst is awaiting you there."

"That would be very kind. Thank you." Lillian followed him through the hall. When they approached the brown bear, its nose appeared to be slightly flatter than usual. And when they got even closer, Lillian noticed that one fluffy ear had a decidedly munched-on look to it.

She frowned. "Has something happened to the bear?"

"Yes, my lady," Hill answered in dignified tones and held up the brush. "It has been hunted down." He heaved a deep sigh, which seemed to indicate that all the weight of the world rested on his shoulders alone. Puzzled, Lillian followed him down the corridor. However, before she could question him further, he stopped and swung open one of the mahagony-colored doors with a flourish. "My lady." He made a small bow.

". . . married her in *St. Paul's?*"

In the ensuing silence after her entrance, the echo of the unfamiliar male voice hovered in the air for several tense moments. Then two chairs scraped over the polished wooden floor, and the two strangers at the table scrambled to their feet.

Lillian's eyes skimmed past them to the figure at the head of the table. The candlelight sparkled on his auburn hair, lent it a fiery life of its own. Her husband, the man who bore her mark on his chest, remained firmly seated. While she looked at him, he saluted her with his glass. "Ah, there you are, my dear. Have you finally managed to find your way to dinner?"

Lillian was only dimly aware of the two other men, who had turned to stare at Ravenhurst with twin expressions of faint shock on their faces. She cocked her head to the right, all the while watching her husband sip his expensive red wine.

He was good, yet not anywhere near good enough. The words "my dear" had nearly choked him, and the skin around his mouth was stretched tight. Whatever charade he intended to play for the benefit of his friends, it would cost him dear.

A swift stab of compassion made her heart clench.

"Oh, my lady, never mind," the handsome sandy-haired man hurried to say. "We came here unannounced, so the mistake is all ours."

A mocking smile crossed her husband's lips. "A fair St. George come to aid the damsel in distress."

"Troy!" his friend protested.

Yet Ravenhurst continued, unperturbed. "My dear, your champion here is Drake Bainbridge, Viscount Allenbright. And on my left you have Justin de la Mere."

"My lady."

The two men bowed, and Lillian dropped into a curtsy.

The second man was as dark and sleek as a big cat. "It is a pleasure to meet you," Lillian murmured.

"The pleasure is ours," Lord Allenbright said smoothly. As if to show his agreement, Mr. de la Mere bowed again.

Lillian found them utterly charming. She gave them a shy smile before she glanced back to her husband. He still sipped at his wine, yet when their eyes met, he lifted a sardonic brow. Putting his glass back on the table, he gestured to the plates before them. "I hope you do not mind, my dear, that we proceeded to dine when your presence proved so elusive," he drawled. "We will have another place set immediately."

"That is very kind of you." Lillian walked around the table to Lord Allenbright's side to take the chair next to his. Officiously, he pulled it out for her. Yet when he did not help her being seated, Lillian turned her head to look at him.

He was staring at her hair.

She had forgotten about her hair.

A quick glance confirmed that all the men were staring at her. Even the servant who had chosen this moment to enter the room with a clean plate and cutlery, undoubtedly sent for by Hill, stopped and stared in wonder.

"My, my," Ravenhurst purred. However, a catch in his voice rather spoilt the effect.

Lillian could have wept for him, but she had learned to act well. So she raised her brows, her face a careful mask of innocence. "Have you not heard? It is all the cry now, the look *au naturelle*."

Justin de la Mere gave a polite little cough. "It looks rather . . . unusual," he said after casting a quick glance at Ravenhurst.

"A flower-fairy," Lord Allenbright murmured behind her.

Lillian's husband in turn looked as if he had just sunk his teeth into a particularly sour lemon.

"Ah . . . well . . ." Lord Allenbright fiddled with his chair and sat down, a faint flush covering his high cheekbones.

All through the awkward dinner that followed, Lillian kept the smile glued to her face. While the two visitors made heroic attempts at stilted conversation, Ravenhurst assumed an air of aloofness and polite boredom. The untouched food on his plate, however, belied his pretense.

He did not look at her again.

Lillian, by contrast, repeatedly peered at him from the corner of her eyes. She noticed the whiteness around his mouth and the dark circles under his eyes, which, as the evening lengthened, became even darker, the color of rotten apples. It reminded Lillian of the testimonies of beatings and worse on his smooth skin, of the thin lines of blood, of the deeper gashes where the whip had ripped off pieces of his flesh.

The blood pounded in her head, but still she smiled and smiled and gave no indication that the food crumbled to dust in her mouth.

She heaved a small sigh of relief when finally, *finally* the servants cleared the table. She knew propriety and convention demanded she retire to the drawing room and sip some tea while waiting for the men to finish their port and cheroots. All the same, she did not think that she would be able to stand another minute of desperate attempts at normality. So she stood, smiling—of course, smiling, all the time smiling—and said, "I am afraid I am rather exhausted this evening. . . ."

Lord Allenbright and Mr. de la Mere stumbled to their feet while her husband again remained seated. He reached for his glass and took a sip of his dark red wine. "Tired, my dear? Then perhaps you should not exert yourself so much." He glanced up at her, the wineglass nonchalantly balanced on his fingertips. He raised one brow in an attempt at mockery.

But it was a sad attempt, Lillian thought. The circles under his overbright eyes were like bruises, and they were the only color on his pale skin except for the feverish slashes of red across his cheeks.

Lillian's smile never wavered. "Will you excuse me? I would prefer to retire for the night. I should think this is in accordance with your wishes, as well."

To their credit, Lord Allenbright and Mr. de la Mere uttered some weak protestations. Ravenhurst just stared into his glass and frowned. "So obliging, my dear?" he murmured a little hoarsely. His eyes darted back to hers. They were very blue. So blue it made her heart hurt.

"Always," she said softly. "Good night."

She walked out of the room with graceful strides, for she had learned how to move gracefully even when she was weeping inside. Yet just when she closed the door, she heard the violent scraping of a chair against the floor. Before she had even reached the hall, the door banged against the wall, steps sounded on the corridor behind her, and then a large hand closed around her elbow like a band of steel.

"A word with you," her husband rasped, and wrenched her around. He towered over her, his eyes a little wild, his body so hot it might sear her skin. The scent of sandalwood and oakmoss rose to envelop her.

Calmly, Lillian looked up at him.

His fingers around her arm tightened. "My friends, they are used to being themselves at the Hall. My servants are discreet. I expect the same thing from. . . ." He stumbled over the last words. ". . . my wife." A muscle in his jaw jumped. "Do I make myself clear?"

"I do not understand—"

He shook her. "Do not pretend ignorance with me, do you hear? Not one word will pass your lips, or else. . . ."

The muscle in his jaw jumped again. As threats went, his was not one of the best or the most inventive. She searched his face. It seemed to her that a slight tremor ran through his body, a quiver of muscles that had his fingers vibrating on her skin.

Perhaps he realized it for himself, since he shoved her away with an expression of disgust. "Another thing," he said, and his contemptuous gaze swept over her curls. "I expect my wife to behave with decency. I will not have you run around like a whore."

"Of course not," Lillian said blandly. "My lord."

She turned and walked away.

This time, he did not hold her back.

Chapter 10

The midday heat forced Lillian back into the garden to seek the shadows of the grove at the lake. The buzz of insects sounded in her ears, the symphony of summer, while the air was heavy with the smell of dusty earth and drying grass.

She was grateful for the hint of coolness that welcomed her when she stepped through the small gate by the stone raven. Tendrils of her brown hair lay damply against her cheeks and throat, and tiny droplets of sweat trickled down the valley between her breasts.

The cows had all huddled in the shadow of the single tree on their meadow today, and the lambs had been standing listlessly around. In fact, they were no longer lambs, no longer small, woolly bundles of energy. They had grown into little sheep, strong and sturdy.

Lillian smiled a bit while she walked down the band of grass adjacent to the gravel garden path. The green stalks tickled the soles of her bare feet, and sometimes a small flower got caught between her toes.

Yet when she neared the assembly of trees around the

lake and the grassy spot on the shore where she liked to sit and dangle her feet in the water, the sound of male voices hovered in the lazy summer air. A carefree cadence they had, both voices. Speech was interwoven with low chuckles.

Lillian stopped.

There on her spot of soft grass, her husband's friends had settled down on a big checkered blanket, a basket beside them. They had shed their jackets and waistcoats, their necks were free of the restraints of cravats, and the sleeves of their white shirts were rolled up to reveal muscular forearms sprinkled with dark and golden fuzz.

Lillian put her hand to the bark of the tree beside her.

Lord Allenbright's pale head rested on Mr. de la Mere's lap, and he looked so comfortable, as if the muscular, nankeen-clad thigh had transformed into the softest pillow. While Allenbright read aloud from a book lying propped upon his belly, de la Mere lovingly played with his sandy-colored hair, letting the short strands run through his dark brown fingers again and again. Sometimes, though, his fingers would stray, carressing forehead or temple, or playfully tapping against a cheek. Very carefully, he traced a golden eyebrow with his forefinger, only to bend forward afterwards and place a kiss on Lord Allenbright's forehead.

Lillian blinked.

A stray sunbeam created bluish lights in Justin de la Mere's short black curls. Allenbright laughed, his eyes darting up to his friend's face. The book, momentarily forgotten, fell flat on his belly when he reached up to wind a hand around the other's neck. With a little tug, he drew de la Mere's head downward, his fingers caressing the short hair at the man's nape.

Their lips met and parted, nibbled and teased each other, until husky chuckles rumbled in the men's chests.

Allenbright's hand glided from de la Mere's nape to his face, cupped his cheek, and finally their mouths met and clung, and the kiss went on and on.

Lillian could see the underside of Lord Allenbright's chin, a bit of de la Mere's cheek where his shoulder did not block the view, and her heart missed a beat. They were a statue come alive, a statue from another garden, overgrown and long forgotten, the limbs of marble lovers intertwining, a memento of bygone ages and bygone love.

I did not know . . . Lillian's finger spasmed against the rough bark of the tree. *I did not know such love exists for real. So beautiful it hurts* . . . The wonder of it, and the beauty, made her eyes sting.

The men changed the angle of their kiss; a smile dimpled Justin de la Mere's cheek. Then they broke apart, smiling, both of them, until Lord Allenbright looked up and noticed Lillian standing between the trees. Abruptly, he sat up, his radiant smile momentarily dimmed. He murmured something, and de la Mere's head whipped around and he also stared at her. A dark frown settled on de la Mere's features. Lillian saw his lips move, a curse maybe, and Allenbright reached over to grip his friend's thigh.

Lillian tilted her head to the side.

It looked very much like reassurance, this gesture, intimate reassurance, a large hand curved over a thigh.

Then Lord Allenbright turned back to her, all smiles again, and waved. "A good day to you, Lady Ravenhurst." His voice was strong and clear, yet with a hint of defiance.

Why he should feel defensive, though, was beyond her. So much beauty after all the ugliness she had seen. . . . She felt herself ~~herself~~ irresistibly drawn to these men, as if the unadulaterated joy she had just witnessed could rub off on her. *Just a little bit* . . . Her feet whispered through the grass as she approached them. "A good day to you, too. My lord. Mr. de la Mere."

She saw how their gazes wandered from her hardly tamed curls over the grass-stained dress to her flower-bedecked feet. When he looked up, Justin de la Mere's frown was gone. Instead, a smile tugged at the corners of his mouth.

Allenbright chuckled. "I see you really do prefer the look *au naturelle*, my lady."

"Indeed I do." She stopped a few feet from their blanket.

"And the gardens of Bair Hall are indeed a magical place." Allenbright's voice was laced with soft amusement, inviting her to share the joke. "Not only do elusive flower fairies tread there—no, one can also meet some . . . fauns."

To her own surprise, Lillian found herself laughing. "If you say so, my lord."

He nodded earnestly. "They meet in the garden—"

"For lunch," de la Mere broke in, his lazy, nasal twang at odds with his twitching mouth. "Would you not like to join us, Lady Ravenhurst? We have some cold meat and chicken and Cornish pastries."

"Oh yes, do join us." Allenbright scrambled to his feet and offered her his hand. "Flower fairies and fauns simply must have lunch together. One of the time-honored rules of Bair Hall."

Lillian hesitated, the joy of the moment dissolving. "I would not want . . . to intrude," she said awkwardly. She took a step back. "I—"

De la Mere stood, too. "I hope you do not begrudge us our lack of manners, my lady. It would be a pleasure to talk to you awhile."

"To get to know our best friend's wife some better," Allenbright added with a smile. Smiles seemed to come easily to Lord Allenbright. Charm, as well. "We would be delighted."

Lillian twisted her hands together. "You were reading."

"Rereading only." One corner of de la Mere's mouth twisted briefly.

"I see."

"Perhaps we might discuss the joys of Mrs. Radcliffe's literary fancies?" Allenbright coaxed. "Would you like that?"

"I . . ." Lillian's gaze darted from one man to the other. They seemed genuinely friendly, these two. She dabbed at the dampness on her throat. "I am afraid I do not know any of Mrs. Radcliffe's works."

"Not know any novel by Mrs. Radcliffe?" Allenbright's brows darted up. "Then you simply must join us, my lady." Again, he offered his hand.

Lillian waited a moment more, searched his eyes. They were green and clear, without shadows lurking in their depths. Though she did not understand the powerful lure of the joy she had witnessed, she finally gave in to it. With a little sigh, she took his hand and allowed him to seat her on the blanket.

De la Mere flopped down beside her and started to rummage through the contents of the basket. "Are you hungry? With which delicacy might we tempt you?"

"Hm." Lord Allenbright still stood, hands on his lean hips, the sunlight creating a halo of his golden hair. "Do we have delicacies that might tempt a flower fairy, Jus?" He turned to Lillian. "What do flower fairies normally eat?"

Lillian lifted her shoulders, unsure how to take their clowning. Never before had she met men like them. "Fruit," she murmured.

"Fruit?" Golden and raven brows shot up as the men exchanged a look. Abruptly, Allenbright sat down on the blanket. "Fruit?" he repeated.

Lillian felt the hot flush of embarrassment stain her cheeks. "Fruit." She made a vague movement with her hand in the direction of the orchards. "The raspberries have ripened. And the black currants. . . ." Her voice trailed off. Again, she lifted her shoulders.

The men exchanged another quick look. Justin de la Mere was the first to regain his composure. "Ahh!" he exclaimed and dived into the basket once more. "Then we have got *exactly* the right thing to tempt a flower fairy." Triumphantly he produced a peach from the depths of the basket. "A peach!" He rummaged around some more and came up with a piece of folded white linen. "And a napkin." With a flourish he presented fruit and cloth to Lillian.

"Thank you," she said softly and took both.

"A Bair Hall peach." Lord Allenbright shifted his weight and leaned back on his hands. "It's a shame that its owner seems so reluctant to take delight in the joys of the Hall." His voice sounded wistful.

Lillian kept her eyes downcast and watched how her hands played with the velvety soft peach. Around and around it turned, in shades of darkest red, of orange and bright yellow.

"He's grown into a recluse, after all," Justin de la Mere muttered darkly. "Shuts himself up in his study all day. Works himself to death."

Lillian suppressed a shudder. The atmosphere had changed; the clowning was gone, replaced by an almost angry intensity. She wished she had stayed in the fields and the heat. Gardens, as she should have known, provided only a false haven.

"That damned war!" Allenbright swore, but he hastened to add: "I beg your pardon, my lady."

"It was not just the war," his friend argued. "The war only completed what had started before. There was nothing to hold him at home."

There was one spot on the peach where its skin was so dark that it reminded Lillian of dark, red wine. "He had his family," she said, so softly she was surprised they heard her at all.

Justin de la Mere's laugh held no humor. "His family, my lady? Have you not met his family? His grandmother is a heartless cold bitch, his uncle a fat pompous ass, and his cousin a foppish young fool, more concerned with the cut of his waistcoat than the welfare of Murgatroyd."

In London, Alexander Markham had seemed to like his cousin well enough. But then, Lillian remembered the bouts of jealousy that had surged up from time to time, when the Viscount Perrin spoke of war and manliness and the ableness of a man with his weapon.

"Jus," Lord Allenbright chided gently. "You must excuse our language, my lady. We are no longer used to a lady's company or to refined London manners. We spend too much of our time on the wild coast of Cornwall." There was a rueful note to his voice. "I am afraid we have spoilt our picnic party with all this talk of war and such. We planned to speak of the merits of Mrs. Radcliffe's works, did we not?"

Lillian looked up and met his earnest green eyes with her own. "It does not matter, my lord."

"We know that you have not wed him because of any tender feelings," Allenbright continued gently. "But you should know that Troy is a good man. The war and his imprisonment have changed him."

The war, the imprisonment and the brand that had seared his skin.

A lily for Lillian.

Despite the warm summer day, a sliver of ice seemed to touch Lillian's heart. Hastily, she scrambled to her feet. "I am sure you are right, my lord. Please excuse me now. I need to. . . ." Her gaze darted past the men, even past the trees; she envisioned the small gate guarded by the stone raven, the fields and meadows that stretched far and wide. "Thank you for the . . . for the peach."

Surprise registered on their faces. It did not matter. Nothing did.

Lillian felt how coldness drifted up from the earth, reached for her, seeped through her skin and chilled the blood beneath.

"Perhaps you might want to join us again tomorrow?" Allenbright coaxed.

"Perhaps." Her smile was fleeting, a careful show of politeness. She took a step back.

Yet her husband's golden-haired friend was persistent. "And if you would like to read some of Mrs. Radcliffe's novels, you should check the library at the Hall." He held up the book from which he had been reading aloud before. "This one is from the library as well. Troy knows how much we enjoy Radcliffe." He gave her one of his friendly smiles. He reminded Lillian of a puppy, all eager to please.

Suddenly, a wave of anger washed over her, anger that he could smile while for her the coldness had returned, had invaded even this garden, which she had thought safe.

"The library?" She lifted her chin. "I am afraid I do not know where the library is, my lord."

That wiped the smile off his face.

* * *

Angrily, Lillian stomped past the fields and meadows and sought the coolness of the forest beyond. She did not mind the stones and gnarled roots that bit into the soles of her feet—indeed, the sharp little pains perfectly accompanied the bitterness inside her. The peace of her garden was disturbed, her haven destroyed.

Did they have to intrude into my world? They already have so much . . . The recollection of the kiss she had witnessed twisted her heart. The miracle and beauty of their love made her long for things that were not for her, had never been for her.

Lillian drew in an unsteady breath.

She felt shaken. As if her world had been turned upside-down because of one little glimpse of a love so wonderful. And she, in contrast, had . . .

. . . a husband who bore her mark seared into his flesh.

No! Sick to her heart, Lillian put her hands over her ears. Squeezing her eyes shut, she crouched low to ground. *Stop! Oh please, stop!*

She willed the memories away, yet unbidden they rose, a nightmarish parade: His body, still beautiful, though shackled to Camille's construction. The blood running down the curve of the broad back. And the mark itself, puckered and raw but the design piercingly clear.

A lily for Lillian.

A sob rose in her throat.

She remembered how she had pressed the brand against his skin, how the smell of burnt skin had filled the room.

Oh God, please, no . . . no . . .

Tears streaming down her face, Lillian scrambled to her feet and ran deeper into the forest. She did not care whether thorny branches reached for her dress or cobwebs caught in her hair. Like a small, injured animal, she sought the solitude of the dark, green shadows.

Farther and farther she ran, reaching for the silence of the forest, far, far away from human society. The heart of the forest, known only to badger and fox. And then she slipped and fell, her elbow scraping over the bark of a tall tree, her face buried in old leaves.

Her breath hitched in her throat as she inhaled the musty smell of decay, underlaid with the fresh tang of earth. Her heart pounded in her ears like a drum, drowning out all other sounds. Lillian drew her knees against her chest and rolled herself up into a ball. There she lay, an unborn child in the womb of the forest.

Little by little, the hammering of her heart subsided and her breathing evened. Gradually she became aware of the sounds around her, the rustling of a small animal and sometimes the hoarse call of a jay.

She rolled herself onto her back and stared up to the roof of leaves above her, the brilliant green interwoven with twirling specks of dust and sunshine. Her arm tickled where a few ants scrambled across her skin. Between the twigs of a tree, a spider had spun her web and, touched by a lone sunbeam, the threads glittered like spun silver.

Lillian's chest rose with a deep breath.

As the light slowly faded, a breeze stirred the lazy stillness among the trees. Leaves rustled, changing the play of light and shadow on the ground below. The little breeze ruffled Lillian's hair and brought with it the faint, sweet smell of faded woodruff.

Lillian sat up.

This time, she did not fight the memories that rose inside her. Memories of summers gone by when she had walked through other forests with Nanette. Together they had collected the delicate stalks of blooming woodruff in wide baskets, to be bundled and dried. Woodruff to soothe nerves and fight headaches. Woodruff tea to waken the tired heart in late spring.

Lillian's heart gave a painful thud.

Everything needs balance, she heard Nanette's voice say. *One to do the healing. . . .* But this year, Lillian had let the time to collect woodruff pass by. It had bloomed unnoticed, tiny white stars in the shadows of the forest. So many chances missed—chances to heal, to help—all wasted. . . .

As if awakening from a deep dream, Lillian rubbed her eyes and looked around.

One to do the healing. . . .

Pictures of bloodied flesh and puckered skin passed again before Lillian's inner eye. A lily burnt into a man's chest.

A lily for Lillian.

Her responsibility.

Her heart squeezed with remembered pain and guilt.

She had fled, had lost herself in a dream of lush flowers and frolicking lambs, while in the past few weeks Nanette had done all the healing on Ravenhurst lands.

Her responsibility.

Lillian took a deep breath. Now the lambs were grown and the flowers nearly faded; it was time to step out of the dream. The woodruff might have wilted, yet there were still other plants to collect, other remedies against sickness and disease, against pain and illness. They were waiting for her, in the fields and meadows and in the expanses of the forest. They were waiting to be picked, dried, made into salves or filled into small muslin bags for tea. It was the least she could do.

Lillian squared her shoulders. Determinedly, she walked away and left the faded woodruff behind.

* * *

On the same evening, Troy allowed himself the luxury of sitting in one of the deep leather chairs in the library and enjoying a glass of brandy with his friends. The smoke of cheroots hovered in the air, a bluish veil filling the room with the familiar smells of male company. How he had missed these quiet evenings spent with his friends, how he had longed for the sight of their faces, the sound of their voices, all these weeks and months.

How he had feared he would never see them again.

Troy suppressed a shudder.

He'd had friends in the military, too. Friends whose deaths he had witnessed. Their young, clean-shaved faces had been burnt by the Spanish sun and then lost all ruddiness in the winter that was to follow. He remembered the hollow cheeks of the men when their rations had barely kept them alive, the over-bright eyes of those who had been swept away by the fever. He remembered the faces of the men who had been ripped apart by cannonballs or gouged open by bayonets. He recalled the scrawny drummerboy who had accompanied them to foreign lands, his sightless eyes turned up to the smoke-darkened sky, his thin body shapeless and bloodied in death. Troy remembered the screaming of horses, the screaming of men, the roar of the cannon, and for a long moment he was lost in his memories, thrown back into his own private hell.

"—flowers all over. Have you heard a word of what I've said, Troy?" Drake sighed and muttered something unintelligible.

"I'm sorry." Troy took a large swallow from his glass of brandy. The alcohol burnt its way down his throat, all the way into his belly. Yet as cauterizing fires went, this one provided only a temporary refuge. To drown memories in alcohol was not a method Troy preferred.

He grimaced.

Besides, it was not very effective. Especially since some of the memories were embedded in his flesh forevermore.

His hand rose and splayed over his chest. Quickly, though, he let it fall.

"You were saying?" he asked. He looked up in time to catch one of Drake and Justin's silent exchanges. Over the years the two of them had brought this wordless communication to perfection. Troy himself had never known such closeness with another living being.

For a moment, Drake looked almost bashful. In his cheeks color came and went. Then he raised his glass in a silent toast. "I was saying"—he drank—"that Bair Hall has taken on disturbing similarities to Bedlam."

"Due to your precious dogs," Troy tried to joke, and he nudged one of the silver-brown creatures lounging about on his Persian carpet with the tip of his boot. Anna, Sophie or Marie, whichever it was, grunted sleepily and continued to snore, paws up in the air. And no wonder it was, since the dogs had spent the afternoon jumping at his great-great-grandfather's hunting trophies and erupting into loud excited barks whenever one of the deer-heads had dropped to the floor with a dull thud. The splendid fourteen-pointer, the centerpiece of the trophy room downstairs, had been transformed into a twelve-and-a-half pointer with a missing eye. With an eye patch, it might look a proper would-be pirate deer.

Grinning, Troy took another sip of brandy.

Drake sighed. "I told you, we would compensate you for the damage."

Troy raised an eyebrow. "And I told you that it is not necessary. Great-great-grandfather made sure that the attics are filled with hunting trophies. Why, he once brought home an elephant foot. What do I need an elephant foot for, I ask you?" He shrugged.

Drake heaved another sigh, his face remaining serious.

Troy grimaced wryly. He dreaded what was to come. His friends certainly saw too much.

"I was talking about the fact," Drake said slowly and carefully, as if talking to an especially dense person, "that day after day you shut yourself up in your study as if it were a monk's cell and you in the application line for holiness."

"Drake," Troy groaned.

"And about the fact," his friend overrode him, "that the Countess of Ravenhurst, your *wife*, is running around the garden like a fey maiden straight from a gothic novel."

Justin nodded in agreement. "Barefoot and all bedecked in flowers—a fair Ophelia she would make."

"And what is more"—Drake leaned forward, his beseeching gaze on Troy— "she has not taken any meals with us since that first evening, nor does she sleep in the family apartments."

"Don't try to deny it," Justin drawled. "We were curious and looked into the countess's rooms. Unless your wife prefers white sheets over all her furniture. . . ." His voice trailed away suggestively.

"There is no proof of her existence in this house, Troy," Drake continued. "No proof at all that she lives here. It is as if she were a ghost haunting your gardens. Heavens, Troy, the girl doesn't even know where the library is. She practically told us she's living on fruit."

That finally got his attention. "She *told* you?" It came out sharper than he intended.

Drake rolled his eyes. "We talked to her this afternoon. We had a picnic in the garden—"

"In the garden?" Troy surged to his feet in an attempt to

evade the icy fear that clutched his heart for his friends. "She *saw* you? Together?"

"Blast it, Troy! You told us that you've talked to her about it." Drake shook his head, incomprehension written on his features. "She did not seem shocked, if that's what you are thinking. What is the matter with you? She is a sweet girl, your wife, yet you behave as if . . . as if. . . ." His hands waved through the air.

"As if she were the devil incarnate?" Troy laughed harshly, the sound grating on his ears. "A sweet girl, you say? *God!*" He turned around, his back to them, so they would not see his face, would not see. . . . He ran both hands through his hair.

"Troy," Drake said, his voice gentle, "whatever misunderstanding there is between the two of you, I am sure—"

Troy felt as if he were suffocating. "A misunderstanding?" he choked. "*Merde*, Drake, you are a blathering innocent. A misunderstanding? A sweet girl?" He shrugged out of his frock coat and let it drop to the floor. With shaking fingers he started to unbutton his waistcoat. He did not heed the rustling behind him, nor the sound of Drake's worried voice.

"Troy, what are you doing?"

In his haste he ripped off some of the buttons of his shirt, and they fell to the floor like pearls, tears of a long-forgotten deity nobody cared about any longer. When he was finished, not only his hands shook, his whole body trembled. His skin was slick with sweat.

He turned around to face his friends. "A sweet girl, you say?" he repeated. "A misunderstanding?" He parted the lapels of his shirt, exposed his chest to their gazes. With something akin to satisfaction he watched how Justin's nostrils flared, how Drake's eyes widened with shock. "Do you call this a misunderstanding? *She* held the brand that seared my skin. Your 'sweet girl' did this." He dropped his hands to his sides, suddenly bone-weary. "The Countess of Ravenhurst, my friends, is a cold-hearted, evil little bitch, a cunning schemer. . . . I would have done anything to prevent her from marrying Alex."

Justin drew on his cheroot, then leaned his head back to puff out perfect circles. "Even ruin her," he remarked, his nose still in the air.

"And even marry her yourself," Drake added softly.

"Should I have stood by and watched her destroy my foolish, besotted cousin?" Troy snorted. "Better to let my family think me the villain in that particular farce than. . . ." His fingers clenched into fists.

Drake rubbed his forehead. "Yet the girl we've met, she doesn't give the appearance of being . . . evil." He and Justin exchanged another one of their unfathomable glances.

Tiredly, Troy lowered himself onto his chair. His bones seemed to have suddenly gained added weight, dragging his body down. "Well, she *is*." He grimaced. "My family, of course, adores her. She would have made the perfect viscountess. And now. . . ." Unsteadily, he reached for his glass. "And now. . . ." The brandy felt good on his tongue, the liquid a burning distraction from the aches of his body. Or perhaps it was just his soul that hurt. Who knew? "And now we have to keep face and the family honor and all that, so my grandmother has ordered me . . . *us* back to London for the little season." He took a deep breath, and finally he looked at his friends once more.

Thoughtfully, Justin munched on his cheroot. "You hate London."

"I detest London."

"You could always say no to her," Drake said carefully.

Troy sighed. "She raised me. You know that I—"

"Feel honorbound to jump whenever she snaps an or-

160

der. Yes, we know." Justin's drawl had a sarcastic timbre.

"She raised me. She took me in after the death of my parents."

Justin just rolled his eyes. "Heavens, Troy, you were the *heir*. They could have hardly sent you to an orphanage."

"Nevertheless—"

"I know, I know." As if in surrender, Justin raised his hands. "So, come September, we'll just flock to London, one and all." When Troy opened his mouth, he lifted one of his elegant black brows. "You did not really think we would leave you alone, did you?"

In the following weeks, Lillian roamed the fields and meadows with a purpose. In the shadow of a boulder on a forest clearing she found milkwort and, at the bank of a small river, she picked some late elder blossoms. She found a meadow with blooming fennel and even some hedge-hyssop. It was too late to harvest the knotted figwort, yet she knew where to find some the next year if some of the younger people from the village would want a cure for bad skin.

And so, she brought Nanette basket after basket of delicate blossoms, cut-off stems or carefully dug-up roots. In the evenings, they would wash the roots in Mrs. Blake's kitchen and dry them between layers of linen cloths. The rest of the plants they would bundle or spread onto a kiln and leave them in the attic above Lillian's bedroom to dry.

"'Tis the only place old Fitzpatrick isn't goin' to find 'em," Mrs. Blake had sniffed. She held no fondness for the housekeeper, as Mrs. Fitzpatrick repeatedly tried to tyrannize the female servants and even rapped the chambermaids' fingers if she found a speck of dust on a cupboard or a chest of drawers.

"That woman's a pest," Mrs. Blake would mutter, and

then Lillian would imagine how she would do things differently if she were the mistress, the *real* mistress of Bair Hall. She would hire a new housekeeper and would make sure that the lower servants were treated well. She would put small, potted trees in the bare inner court where only the gurgling of a little fountain disrupted the silence. She would put pots of flowers in the entrance hall, would put flowers on small tables in the long hallways so their fragrance would fill the emptiness and bring the Hall to life. For Bair Hall, Lillian now realized, was in the grip of paralysis, another enchanted castle where a curse had put all life to sleep.

The Hall was a big house, built to fill with family and friends. Yet when she had finally started to explore the mansion, she found that dustcovers shrouded most rooms, that they were settled on the furniture like numbing layers of snow.

But it would take more than the kiss of a prince to break the spell. So much more; and despite all Lillian knew about healing herbs, she did not have the remedy to battle the demons of her husband's past. Anger and remoteness seemed to have become so much part of him that she could not even imagine him without the deeply etched grooves bracketing his mouth, or without the circles under his eyes that bespoke his weariness.

Sometimes, in the evenings, she would hide in the shadowy dimness of the gallery in the library, while below her husband and his friends sat around the fire, smoking and talking. His voice would lift then and he looked relaxed. Yet the shadows under his eyes never waned, Lillian saw.

She would curl up in one of the wide, comfortable leather chairs and listen to the blend of male voices. There, in the darkening library, when the conversation lazily moved from one topic to the next, she learned that her husband was a well-read, highly intelligent man. He displayed open affection for his friends' dogs, and Lillian wondered why he did not have dogs of his own.

And another thing she noticed: While Lord Allenbright and Mr. de la Mere would frequently laugh when alone, there was never any laughter to be heard during those evenings in the library. They would just talk about Latin literature or Greek sculpture, about horses and pointers, about London politics and the riots in the countryside. They would talk and talk, lost in earnest discussion. Sometimes the sound of their voices would lull Lillian to sleep, curled up on her chair like a stray kitten.

Yet, what made her husband who he was?

Despite all the evenings Lillian spent in the library, the answer to that question remained elusive. She witnessed her husband's reserve even with his best friends, even when he lost the veneer of social politeness. It seemed to her that Ravenhurst resembled a tiny snail that never really left his protective shell. It was understandable, under the circumstances, yet she suspected that such a life would prevent him from ever healing properly.

Everything needs balance.

Nanette had taught her to heal, and still . . . still, the enchanted castle would forever remain locked within its spell; the sleeping prince would never wake up, and the beast would never be transformed. For how could her husband forgive what had happened to him? How could he forgive the theft of his soul?

Lillian sighed.

When depression threatened to weigh her down, she went outside to wander alongside fields, through meadows and below trees, to harvest what nature offered freely. Day after day, week after week, she would come back to the

Hall, her basket full of flowers, herbs and blossoms so the supply would last over the winter.

Until one day, when the corn on the fields was golden and almost ripe and the rose hips were almost ready to be picked, Lillian came home and found Nanette earnest-faced. "Lord Ravenhurst wants to return to London," the old woman said. "And you are to go with him."

Lillian schooled her features into nonchalance. "I see. And when does he want to set off? Next week?"

There was pity in Nanette's kind eyes. "Tomorrow, *chou-chou*."

Lillian swallowed. "I see."

"It was to happen sooner or later, you know."

"Yes. Yes, of course." Lillian turned away. She would have thought he'd prefer to spend the autumn and winter in the country, and only return to Town in spring. She had thought to see the apples ripen, to watch the harvest on the fields, to wave the birds good-bye when they started their journey to the south. But it was not to be.

Lillian closed her eyes.

The summer idyll was over.

PART IV

All precious things, discover'd late,
To those that seek them issue forth;
For love in sequel works with fate,
And draws the veil from hidden worth.

—*Tennyson*, The Day Dream

Chapter 11

After the lush green of the countryside, London seemed gray and dreary. The smells of the streets, the smoke that stung one's eyes and nose, the noise of the carts and carriages, of the people and the animals, came together in a shrill symphony of discord and made Lillian yearn for the peace and quiet of the gardens of Bair Hall.

She missed not just the gardens, but the house, too, that vast, empty building where she had not met her husband for days or even weeks. In London, however, they lived in a narrow town house, too small for her to keep out of his way, to stay hidden in shadows. Time and again she was thrust into his presence, was confronted with the signs of strain and weariness on his face. As tall and dark as he was, always impeccably groomed, Lillian still saw traces of the man in the prison cell, the man chained to Camille's construction.

Every time she met him on the stairs or entered the breakfast room when he was still taking his coffee, her heart would constrict in her breast, a funny, little pain, which for a moment would cut off her breath. He would look up, his eyes so blue, those same eyes she had seen clouded with pain, and then he would pretend to look through her as if she were not there. Yet he never succeeded very well. His eyes would become all stormy, his lips compress into a thin, tight line, deepening the grooves that bracketed his mouth. He looked old and haggard then, and the pain inside Lillian would intensify until she wanted to cry and scream.

Of course, she never did.

Instead, she witnessed his pain in silence, a penance for the hurt she had inflicted upon him all those months ago. *Her responsibility.* . . . Where at the Hall she had been able to flee into the gardens and the fields, here in London she had nowhere to go. She could not roam the streets on her own; she had no friends to visit; she was stuck in the house, was stuck in the churning of shame and guilt.

How she missed the easy chatter of Aunt Louisa and the quiet presence of her grandfather! Nanette urged her to sit down and write a letter to her family. "You should have done so weeks ago," the old woman said. "But, of course—"

"Yes," Lillian said quickly. She did not want Nanette to worry more than necessary. Nanette had taken up again her work for the sick and the poor, sewing blankets, knitting socks and scarves. In the afternoons that dragged so endlessly along, Lillian would sit down with her in the morning room to knit, to sew, to create things that would keep other people warm in the winter to come.

But she also wrote the letters to her family. Her grandfather would spend the autumn and winter at Abberley House before he would return to London for the opening of Parliament. Aunt Louisa stayed with her eldest daughter, who was coming down with her fourth child, and asked Lillian to light a candle in church for mother and babe. So Nanette went with Lillian to a small church nearby, a

Catholic one, where they lit a candle at the feet of a smiling Mother Mary and her chubby baby son.

During their second week in London, the Dowager Countess Ravenhurst honored Lillian and her grandson with a visit. Clad all in black, she sat enthroned on the only chair in the drawing room and watched with eagle eyes as Lillian poured tea. Calmly, Lillian passed her a cup and tried not to notice the proximity of her husband's body beside her upon the settee. He sat near enough, though, for her to feel the heat radiating from him and to be enveloped in the alluring scent of sandalwood and oakmoss. *Such a lovely smell.*

He cleared his throat. "We are very happy, granddame, that you found the time to call."

The old woman sniffed disdainfully. "It is a disgrace, Ravenhurst, that you chose to return to your bachelor lodgings instead of moving into Ravenhurst House." She pierced her grandson with a withering glance. "I told you I would move out if need be."

"And I told you that this would not be necessary."

"Do not talk rubbish, Ravenhurst!" Her thin nose quivered. "Not necessary? How do you plan to entertain in this . . . this *house?*"

Tension radiated from his body, and Lillian felt her own muscles stiffen in sympathy. "I did not realize that entertaining would be part of the obligation," he said through gritted teeth.

Obligation? From underneath lowered lashes, Lillian risked a glance at him. His face was granite, his jaw set; in fact, he did not look happy at all to see his grandmother—and small wonder, if all she did was round up on him. Could she not see how desperately he needed her support and understanding?

"I do not know what has come over you, Ravenhurst!" the old woman snapped. "The way you behave I could almost believe that your cousin is right and that you have truly lost your mind!"

It was only for her years of exercising self-control that Lillian managed not to flinch. How could the Dowager Countess speak in such a way to her grandson? Lillian's heart ached for her husband, who did not deserve such cruelty. Had he not been hurt enough in the past? The tip of that brand pressing against his skin, the smell of scorched flesh. . . .

Her responsibility.

"Granddame—"

"Be quiet, Ravenhurst! I have not brought you up to bring shame over the family name time and time again!" The corner of her mouth turned down, making the woman look even older, like the witch in the fairy tale. "After you destroyed your cousin's happiness and after all the scandal, the least you could do is to make some sort of effort. You have lived as a recluse long enough."

Lillian looked up. In the past few months she had seen enough hurt inflicted upon this man, and now she'd had enough. "But Lady Ravenhurst, do you not think that after all the years at war, Lord Ravenhurst has deserved some months of rest?" Her voice rang loud and clear in the sudden silence of the room. She made herself smile at the old woman, whom she would have happily thrown out of the house. *If I were the real mistress. . . .*

Her outburst earned her a look of contempt. "And what would you know about it, young miss? Years at war? He went and got himself imprisoned in some nameless village in France. It is time now that he acted like a man instead of—"

"Lady Ravenhurst." Lillian stood, her back straight, her

hands clenched into fists to keep them from trembling with anger. "I have just remembered that I have urgent business with my dressmaker to attend. I am sure you know how it is." Her smile sweet, she looked the old woman straight in the eye.

The Dowager Countess raised one white brow. "Well, what is this? This is most unusual, young woman. I am not used to such rash behavior." Her eyes narrowed. "But then, what can one expect from a young miss who encouraged one cousin and had her merry way with the other? In any case," she turned to her grandson, "you will have to throw a ball for her so that there won't be any talking. And she needs a carriage. People will wonder if she does not go out for a drive."

Lillian lifted her chin. "You can rest assured, my lady, that I have no wish for either a carriage or a ball."

"Your wishes, young woman, are of no concern here. I will not sit by and see how the family goes to ruins because of a flimsy young miss."

"Granddame, this is quite enough," Ravenhurst said stiffly. "You were in favor of this marriage."

"In order to curb the scandal!" The old woman rounded on him. "Have you any idea how your poor cousin suffered? I would not have thought you so selfish as this, Ravenhurst. I am *displeased*, very much displeased." With that, she stood and swept out of the room.

They heard how she hailed the butler on the stairs to bring her pelisse and call the coach. The high-pitched voice echoing in the hallway made Lillian shiver.

"That was not very clever," Ravenhurst said. Lillian turned to look at him. He had crossed his arms in front of his chest, his face dark and brooding. "She would have supported you in society."

Lillian squared her shoulders. "I do not need her support."

"You could have used it." His mouth curled into an ugly sneer. "It was not wise to rouse her enmity."

Lillian calmly held his gaze. "I have lived with worse," she said. "As you well know." And with that, she left, before the feelings of guilt and shame engulfed her wholly.

The next afternoon, while Lillian and Nanette sat in the small drawing room, both of them knitting, the door opened to reveal the rather red face of the butler. "My lady, the carriage," he said in dignified though slightly breathless tones.

"The carriage? Which carriage?"

"Why, your carriage, of course, my lady."

Nanette's needles kept clicking merrily, even when she looked up to glance at Finney. "Now, don't talk in riddles, Fred."

At the butler's longsuffering expression, Lillian had to bite her lip to prevent it from twitching betrayingly. Some days ago, Nanette had cured Finney of his aching back, and since then he had been putty in the old woman's hands.

"My Lady Ravenhurst's new carriage is waiting in front of the door," he elaborated. "Please, my lady, you have to drive through the park in it, else the Dowager Countess will hear and then we'll all be well and truly cooked." A fleeting look of despair crossed his kind, blotchy face.

"A drive in the park. What a lovely idea. Don't you agree, *chou-chou?*" Nanette gave Lillian a wide smile, obviously all in favor of the new carriage.

Of course she would be. Lillian suppressed a sigh. Time and time again, her old nanny had implied how much she wished for Lillian to have a "normal" life. Yet after the delights of the Ravenhurst lands, a drive through a park seemed very tame. Nevertheless, Lillian forced herself to smile and say: "Very nice, indeed."

"Good, good." Finney gave an audible sigh of relief. "The carriage can depart whenever you are ready, my lady."

"You should change into something more stylish, *chou-chou*." It seemed to Lillian that even Nanette's knitting needles had taken on a merrier sound. "And don't forget your parasol!"

Fifteen minutes later, Lillian walked down the stairs to the town house entry. She had not changed her muslin dress with the floral print, which she liked very much, yet she had taken great pains to tame her wild curls so that only a few would fall from underneath her bonnet and tickle her cheeks. A reddish brown spencer jacket and gloves completed her outfit. Her frilly white parasol dangled from her arm and slapped annoyingly against her legs with each step she took.

How she wished she were back at Bair Hall.

Yet for the butler's sake, Lillian plastered a smile on her face and stepped out of the door as if the prospect of a drive through a park was the most exciting thing in the world.

Officiously, Finney handed her into the shining black landaulet. "Be careful, my lady, the print of the coat of arms on the doors is still wet, I understand. We have put the back down as it is such a beautiful day today. I hope this meets with your approval, my lady."

"Yes, thank you." Lillian made herself comfortable on the soft, sandy-colored leather seat.

"And this, my lady, is Ronan, your driver."

The tall, pale man on the driver's seat turned around to bow. "At your service, my lady."

"Lovely," Lillian said.

"May I suggest a ride through Hyde Park, my lady?" Finney went on. "It is quite beautiful and safe—if you beware of the duelists and the deer." He threw a look at her driver. "And as I am sure Ronan will beware of the duelists and the deer, there is no need for disquiet, my lady."

"I am sure there is not," Lillian agreed. *Duelists and deer?*

Finney's worried eyes swiveled back to her. "Are you quite comfortable, my lady? Will you need a pillow or a blanket for your legs?" Now that he finally had her inside the carriage, the butler seemed reluctant to let her go.

"I am fine. Thank you."

"Fine, fine." The man nodded. "Well, then, off you go, Ronan. To Hyde Park Corner. And drive carefully."

An expert crack of the whip above the backs of the two dun horses, and the landaulet jerked into motion. To the left and right, elegant town houses rolled by. When Ronan clicked his tongue at the horses, the landaulet gained speed and soon the gates of Hyde Park Corner rose in front of them. As it was still early in the afternoon, there were not yet many people and carriages crowding to get into the park. They passed through the gates, by a great stately house, and immediately the clean, fresh smell of grass met Lillian. Gratefully, she leaned back in her seat and took a deep breath. This was so much better than being shut inside Ravenhurst's dreary house all day.

Lillian frowned.

It was not that she disliked the house; the rooms were sunny and snug. Nevertheless, she felt as if for a short and precious time she had escaped from prison.

Her frown deepened.

It had nothing to do with the interior of the house. It had nothing to do with the servants, either; they could not have been nicer or more attentive to her wishes. Still, the overall atmosphere was oppressive, stifling.

She recalled how uncomfortable she had felt the day before, when Ravenhurst's grandmother had called. How the walls had seemed to draw in on her until Lillian had been ready to scream. How Ravenhurst's grandmother had ranted at him, had taken him to task as if he were a stupid little boy instead of a grown man who had risked life and limb in service of king and country. How the old woman had scorned him for having fallen into the hands of the French before Waterloo. Lillian remembered that Perrin had frequently rambled on about the glories of the battlefield. Clearly, the grandmother cherished similar views of the war.

Lillian doubted her husband did.

No, there were still shadows under his eyes, weariness written in the lines of his face. She could only imagine how much the Dowager Countess must have hurt him yesterday. If not even his family gave him its support. . . .

Lillian knew what it felt to be lonely, lost in a world that had stopped making sense. There was no one her husband connected to, except, of course—

"Lady Ravenhurst!"

Lillian looked up.

—his friends?

The men rode matching brown horses that shone with health and care. They even wore matching riding outfits, long beige coats over dark brown jackets and caramel-colored trousers. While Mr. de la Mere's face showed merely the faintest hint of a smile, Lord Allenbright positively beamed at her. "What a lovely surprise," Allenbright said when he came level with the carriage.

"Be careful, the paint is still wet." Lillian leaned over the side of the landaulet to glimpse the drying coat of arms.

"My, my," murmured de la Mere, "if that isn't a nice little demi-landau. I could've sworn that I saw a similar—"

Whatever else he wanted to say was lost as Lord Allenbright waved impatiently. "Don't be a pest, Jus! My lady, it is a pleasure to meet you here. Would you allow us to accompany you for a while?"

Surprised, Lillian blinked. "Yes, of course," she murmured. Yet she could not imagine why they wanted to further the acquaintance.

"Is this not a most beautiful day?" Allenbright continued, his voice as cheerful as his smile. "Normally, London is quite dreadful in autumn, of course, but this year—"

"You *generally* dislike London, Drake," de la Mere cut in, his brows raised.

"Ah well, all that hustle and bustle and all these odious balls and dinner parties and matchmaking mamas." Allenbright rolled his eyes, making Lillian giggle. Quickly, she stifled the sound with a hand over her mouth, but to no avail. Allenbright's green eyes had already alighted on her face. "Ah, that lovely laugh is back!" His pleased appearance grew. "You should laugh more often, my lady," he said gently. "It becomes you."

To her consternation, Lillian felt a flush stain her cheeks. She lowered her face and mumbled something unintelligible.

"The next season is going to be a very dull one, I believe," de la Mere smoothly interjected. "With both Brummell and Byron gone."

Allenbright gave him a wry grin. "I am sure the Prince Regent will be happy to provide society with a scandal or two."

Lillian could not interpret the look the two men exchanged. Their gazes locked and held for a few heartbeats until Allenbright's eyes fastened on some new marvel.

"Oh, look at that!" he cried, then burst out laughing and nearly fell off his horse.

Mr. de la Mere glanced heavenwards. "Really, Drake!

One should think that this is your first visit to London. Remind me next year to keep you locked up at home."

Still chuckling, Allenbright wiped tears of mirth from his eyes. "Don't be such a spoilsport." He grinned. "It's not every day that I see the Red Dove holding court." He pointed at the strange assembly on the path to their right.

In the middle of the group, a dark-haired woman sat in her chic little phaeton like a queen, all cast in ruby red to match the upholstery of her equipage. A small red hat was balanced high on her carefully arranged curls, and in the lobes of her ears diamonds glinted in the sunlight. Flitting all around her carriage like bees around honey, several men on horse or foot tried to catch her attention. There were men in their forties or fifties, their hair thinned and gray, men in their thirties, of portly inclination, and young men with fresh, flushed faces, their curls as artfully arranged as the woman's.

"Ah," Lord Allenbright sighed. "Reminds me of the old days when the Three Graces used to grace the green of this park with their presence."

"Yes," his friend agreed, his drawl even more pronounced than usual. "It was great fun to watch all those fellows make complete fools of themselves. Even our great national hero, the Iron Duke himself, became all sappy near Miss Harriette Wilson."

"Gone, too. Left for France or wherever." Allenbright heaved another big sigh.

"And how our friends would brag whenever they got an *audience* with Miss Wilson." De la Mere rolled his eyes.

Allenbright winced. "Goodness, you might have thought she was the queen herself!"

"On the other hand, it's not very likely they would have wanted to lock lips with the *queen*. . . ."

The two men looked at each other and then dissolved into fits of laughter. Even Ronan the landaulet-driver allowed himself a quiet cackle. These men were really the strangest of creatures! Her hands primly folded in her lap, Lillian sat and waited for the merriment to subside.

"Oh dear," giggled Lord Allenbright. "I am sorry, my lady. We probably shouldn't be talking like this with you present and all . . . and talking about the goddesses of the demimonde, on top of that." He had to stop to overcome another burst of gaiety. "Oh dear. Oh-dear-oh-dear. Troy would take us to task for this. . . ." He shook his head, obviously trying to restore his control.

Mr. de la Mere, by now all suave impassiveness again, raised one brow and commented dryly: "In that case, we would blame it all on the Cornish wilderness and lack of civilization. At least dear Troy was not one of the chaps swarming around Miss Wilson's carriage. So, my lady, you can rest assured that your husband's foolishness has certain limits." He gave her a strangely unfathomable smile.

Lillian wondered what he was getting at, yet Lord Allenbright's restless gaze had already bounced to another object of curiosity. "Oh, look at that!" he cried, as excited as a small boy in a candy shop.

Over the next hour, the two men took turns pointing out the more interesting members of society enjoying outings in the park. There was Lady Bumbleham, who not only had a queer name, but also a tendency to adorn herself with the strangest of hats—hats with generous, wide brims and opulent flower arrangements. On that particular day she even had a stuffed bird nestled among the wilting blossoms. Then there was the Green Man, a gentleman who went around dressed in shades of green. Even his hair had been dyed green, a fate that had also befallen his unfortunate poodle.

"He looks like a wandering fir tree," Allenbright muttered.

The Honorable Mr. Beran, by contrast, sported the most enormous moustache of London, carefully groomed and twirled. A bit further down the path, surrounded by her liveried footmen, her driver and her pale companion, the old Dowager Duchess of Deary sat in her carriage and peered at the world through an overdimensional monocle, which made her look like a strange insect.

Ravenhurst's friends were charming and courteous, and apparently eager to please Lillian and to make her smile. They enchanted her with their witty humor, their obvious affection for each other and the constant cheerful banter they so much enjoyed. They enquired after the dinner parties she had visited, the balls she had attended. When she told them that she only had been presented at court a second time since returning—this time, not as the granddaughter of the Marquis of Larkmoor but as the wife of the Earl of Ravenhurst—they appeared scandalized.

"What!" Allenbright exclaimed, his clear green eyes round as saucers. "You have spent all these weeks in that town house? But surely you've been shopping at least?"

Lillian shook her head. She would not know what to buy anyway, even if she could.

Mr. de la Mere frowned, his gaze far too sharp for her liking, as his next words revealed. "He forgot to give you money."

"Who? *Troy?* Surely he would not—" Allenbright shot a glance at Lillian's hot face. "Oh." All at once, his expression darkened. "Sometimes I truly believe he needs a good thump on the head so he stops behaving like a ninnybrain!"

It would be horrible, if even his friends criticized him. "Oh please," Lillian said quickly, "promise me you will not say anything to him about this. It is nothing, I assure you. I am"—she swallowed—"quite happy. . . ."

"And a terrible liar," de la Mere sighed. "But if you prefer to play the role of the martyr . . ."

Lillian felt her cheeks grow even hotter. "I beg you, do not say anything to him." She only could imagine how devastating it would be for him to lose the support of his friends. "The Dowager Countess called yesterday. My husband's family is . . . very hostile, I believe. He needs you."

De la Mere stared at her, his dark eyes inscrutable. Then he leaned over and took her hand where it rested on the rim of the carriage. "Your husband, my lady, is a blind fool," he said quietly, and then he bowed low to kiss her hand. Straightening, he said, "But in return, you must allow us to accompany you on your drives through the park."

"I will gladly promise you that." Lillian smiled.

"Very well, my lady, then we've got a pact." De la Mere winked at her and released her hand.

"We don't need to seal it with blood, though, do we?" his friend asked innocently. It promptly got the desired effect.

"Don't be *absurd*, Drake!"

Lord Allenbright chuckled. "You're such an easy nut to crack, Jus!" His eyes twinkled mischievously.

Lillian looked from one man to the other. Their moods were so changeable and erratic in many ways. "But you will look out for my husband," she pressed.

"Of course. We always do." For a few moments Allenbright managed to give himself an extremely dignified air. "Just like Achilles and Patrokolos."

He held the pose until de la Mere dryly pointed out, "They were just two. We're three. I'm afraid your simile is inappropriate."

And as easily as that they were diverted; they happily threw themselves into a heated discussion of Greek mythology. Lillian listened quietly, marveling not only at their knowledge, but also at the fact that they could argue in such a merry way.

What was more, they remained true to their word: Each day, they waited for Lillian beyond the gates of Hyde Park and took their rounds with her. So perhaps it was due to their presence that no wounded duelist dared to come close to the Ravenhurst landaulet. When they met early, though—and soon they made a habit of meeting early— she could catch a glimpse of the deer and sometimes a rabbit lollopping across the lawn or munching on a flower.

Meanwhile, though, Lillian saw less and less of her husband. He left the house early and stayed out late, on some days never coming home in between. She knew that his behavior worried the servants; the housekeeper had talked to Nanette about it, perhaps in the vain hope that Lillian might have some influence over the earl.

Nothing could have been further from the truth.

Lord Allenbright and Mr. de la Mere sometimes met him at White's, they said. He did not gamble, they were quick to assure her, at least not excessively. Mostly he sat in an armchair in the corner and looked all moody and distant. Yet Lillian got the impression that Allenbright and de la Mere did not visit the club that often anyway; something in the atmosphere seemed to make them uncomfortable.

Lord Allenbright, however, obviously enjoyed shopping. He could tell Lillian where to find the best snuffboxes—as if she needed a snuffbox—the best and most beautiful cloths, the sturdiest walking sticks, the shiniest hats, the most delicate jewelry and the most delicious cakes.

One day, he came to the house before they were due to meet in the park and gave Finney a parcel for her. It contained the most beautiful paisley scarf Lillian had ever seen. When she tried to explain to him later that day that she could not possibly accept his present, he just grinned and waved her objections aside. "It's all the rage at the moment, I assure you. And if Ravenhurst is stupid enough to call me out over this, I will just tell him that in the future he should buy the presents for his wife himself. Do not worry so, my lady. Nobody needs to know, do they?"

Chapter 12

One morning, just as Lillian prepared for her daily drive in the park, Finney came panting up the stairs and knocked on her door. "My lady," he gasped through the wood, "you've got a visitor."

"If it is Lord Allenbright—"

"No, my lady, it is the Viscount Perrin."

Lillian laid down her gloves and opened the door. "Viscount Perrin, you said?"

"Yes, my lady." Finney's face resembled a large strawberry without the seeds. "Shall I tell him you've gone out?"

Resolutely, Lillian shook her head. "No, it is all right. Bring him to the drawing room, if you please."

A worried expression rose in Finney's brown puppy-dog eyes. "Do you think this is right, my lady? Would it not be better to wait for my lord—"

"No, Finney." She reached out and gently patted his forearm. "Do as I say. Bring him to the drawing room." For a while she listened to the butler's mutterings and laborious breaths as he went downstairs. Then she hurried to get her gloves in order to reach the designated room be-

183

fore the men. She wondered what Alexander Markham, the Viscount Perrin, would want from her. Her husband would probably be furious when he found out that his cousin had called.

Lillian lifted her chin a notch higher.

Well, it was his own fault for spending his days and nights all over town rather than at his house.

So she sat, her back straight, her hands demurely folded in her lap, and waited for the arrival of her husband's relative. She did not have long to wait. Soon she heard Finney's deep voice; then the door was flung open with a flourish and the butler announced in a dignified manner, "The Viscount Perrin, my lady."

Lillian rose from her seat to greet her visitor properly, but he just strolled in, looking around the room with interest. His clothes were just a bit too rumpled, his cheeks just a bit too ruddy. He did not acknowledge her.

Neither his appearance nor his manner boded well.

Finney's brows rose high, yet Lillian gave the butler a small nod to indicate he should leave. He threw her another of his worried glances and left, but without closing the door. Apparently he did not like the viscount's behavior, either.

"My lord," Lillian firmly said.

At that, Perrin turned his head toward her, his face registering artificial surprise as if he had just now noticed her presence. "My dear cousin." He approached her, arms outstretched.

Lillian stepped aside to evade his embrace.

"So shy?" He smirked. "There have been times, I seem to remember, when my touch was not so abhorrent to your sensibilities. In fact, I seem to remember that you liked my hands on you exceedingly well."

Lillian chose against dignifying this with an answer. If

he had come in order to provoke her, he would fail. After all, she had learned the game from a true master.

Or rather, a mistress.

So she just gave him a stony look.

Unperturbed, he grinned and took up idly pacing around the room. "Where is my dear Cousin Ravenhurst? Gone out? A shame that, quite a shame. First he becomes a recluse on his own estate, and now I have heard he has gone even more mad. Is that so?" His spurs clicked on the wooden floor. "Of course, we all know that he was struck by the battle madness. It is quite natural, I have heard, for the *vétérans de la guerre*. Perhaps the family should send him to Bedlam so the crowds can suitably admire him." He threw Lillian a sly smile.

With studied indifference, she sank down on the little settee. "Have you just come to heap insult on my husband?" she inquired in bored tones, while inside she felt her anger rise. How dare this fledgling boy talk like that about her husband, a man who had endured so much more than Perrin could possibly fathom!

"Ah, your husband." Perrin stopped his wandering and waggled his finger at her. "Whose title is, of course, so much nobler than a mere viscount's. And his fortune is quite something, too. How much does he have these days? Twenty thousand a year? Thirty?"

"Ah, I see, now you are insulting *me*." Lillian gave him back smile for smile. "I will have you know that I do not know my husband's fortune. Nor was this the reason I married him—as you well know."

"The public ravishment. The baring of a pair of pale breasts at Almack's." His lips became thin as his face twisted into an ugly sneer. His eyes dropped to the swell of her bosom, all properly covered by her walking dress. "But tell me, did he ravish you for real before the vows were exchanged?" Perrin's voice rose in synchronicity with the color in his face. "Did the two of you enjoy a romp in a secluded alcove? On this very couch, perhaps? Did he properly hump you? Did he?"

Lillian's brows rose. She wondered how she could have ever considered marriage to this immature dandiprat. He reminded her of a small boy throwing a tantrum because his sweets had been taken away. "Are you drunk? I do not see how any of this would be any of your business."

He took up his pacing again, but now his strides were short, and his spurs sounded an angry staccato on the polished floor. "I made some discreet inquiries, if you must know," he informed her loftily. "At the inn where you spent the first night of wedded bliss." With an almost triumphant expression he turned to face her. "And lo and behold, the next morning there was not the slightest trace of virgin blood on the sheets."

"So we did not spend that night together." Lillian's voice remained cool and uncaring. Yet she did not like where this conversation was headed. He might behave like a small boy, but still he might present a danger.

"Oh, my pet, but he was seen leaving your room in a— how shall I put it—rather delicious state of undress." Perrin smirked. "The maid was much taken with the sight of my cousin's naked torso. So, of course, I now wonder, did he tail you even when I was courting you? Did you consent to let him shag you even when you accepted my presents?"

"My lord, you are forgetting yourself."

"But then," he mused as if he had not heard her, "perhaps there is quite another reason for the absence of your virgin blood on those sheets. Perhaps my cousin's madness has affected him in other areas as well. Perhaps he could not perform. . . ." His voice trailed off suggestively, while his eyes glittered with some wild emotion Lillian did not care to guess at. She had had quite enough of Viscount Perrin's insolence.

She rose to her feet, head held high. "This is quite enough, my lord." She made her voice icy cold. "I will not have you slighting your cousin in his own house any longer."

"Do you threaten me? Do you really dare threaten me, you little doxy?" Quick like a snake to strike, he advanced and gripped her upper arms. His eyes, Lillian saw, were bloodshot, and his breath, when he opened his mouth, stank of mixed alcohols. "But perhaps the absence of the virgin blood has even other reasons. Tell me, how does my coz like it that his wife is carrying on with his best friend?"

"What do you mean?" Lillian asked, for the first time honestly puzzled.

"Why, my dear," he smirked. "Your affair with Lord Allenbright. Quite the little hussy, are you not?"

Lillian blinked. Dazedly, she realized that Ravenhurst had not entrusted him with his friends' secret. But Perrin was not through yet.

"Shall I tell you what I have also found out? Interesting things, really, about your stepmother. Have you learnt your trade from her? All these gruesome things could quite ruin even the wife of the Earl of Ravenhurst." The Viscount's lips lifted in a feral smile, exposing his sharp, little ferret teeth.

A freezing coldness came over Lillian. She remained quite still in his grip. "I would take care, my lord," she whispered. "I have seen much worse things than you ever could imagine. Do you really think I would let you threaten my husband and my family? You, my lord, are an innocent. A glaring, glaring innocent. You know *nothing* of my stepmother. And you should pray that I will never teach you any of it."

At her words, his color rose even higher. A vein pumped across his forehead. Then he gave a bark that might have been a laugh, shoved and threw her across the settee. "Oh, you will teach me some, my pet." He put both hands on either side of her and leaned down, leering. "If you don't want to be ostracized by society, you will let me shag you— until you bleed, if need be."

Lillian's hands clenched into fists. "My lord, get off me," she warned him softly. A pup like him would not threaten her. And she would not let him drag her back into the darkness. Never again.

His fingers closed around her throat. "You will let me use you for my pleasure and—"

Quick as lightning she struck, raking her nails over his cheek. Howling, he reared back, holding his cheek, while blood dropped through his fingers. "What have you done? You little hussy!" And he burst into tears.

Lillian stood and straightened her skirts before she advanced on him. Nonchalantly she leaned near and whispered into his ear, "Take heed, my lord. Do not meddle with me or my kin. It would cost you dearly. I know a hundred ways and more to bring pain to a man, and I could make you rue the day you were born. So leave my family and me alone." She stepped back and forced her lips to curve in a satisfied smile. "Now go."

Still blubbering and bleeding and holding his cheek, the Viscount Perrin hastened out of the room like a little boy who'd been scolded. She heard him clomping down the stairs, the click of his spurs mingling with his sobs.

When the front door closed behind him, the tremors started in Lillian's hands and knees and legs until they shook her whole body. She staggered to the settee and sank down. Wearily, she buried her face in her hands. *Dear God*, she thought. *Dear God.*

A moment later she heard Finney's hesitant steps. "My lady? Are you all right, my lady?"

Lillian lifted her head and gave the butler a smile. "Quite all right, Finney." And, with a start, she realized she was. It would have been so easy to let Perrin victimize her. But she had not. Instead, she had made a stand.

"You have another visitor, my lady." Finney's voice was still tentative, as if he feared she might shatter if he spoke too harshly. "Lord Allenbright. He asks whether you are ready for the afternoon drive."

Lillian took a deep breath, then she reached for her gloves. "Quite ready. Tell him I shall be with him in an instant."

"Yes, my lady." With a last worried look, the butler left.

Lillian stood. "Quite ready," she whispered. "Quite, quite ready." Then she straightened and walked out of the room.

Troy liked to spend the mornings at his club, which at that time of day was wonderfully quiet and almost deserted. He would lounge in one of the comfortable armchairs, just like a young buck new to town, and would smoke one expensive cheroot after the other until he felt quite dizzy with all the smoke.

Quite sick, in fact. Troy coughed and coughed until his eyes watered. Dear God, how long had he been sitting here, staring into empty space like a bacon-brained dimwit? Too long, surely, too—

"Ah, good, here you are." Drake Bainbridge erupted into the room in a whirlwind of silver-gray dogflesh and excited barks. "Quiet, girls. Sit! *Sit!* Oh, never mind." He strode forward, only to stop and be seized by a coughing fit. "Jeez, Troy, what are you planning? Turning this room into a smokehouse with you as the salmon?" He hurried to one of the tall, white-framed windows and fumbled with the latch.

"And a good morning to you, too," Troy said dryly. "Where's Justin?"

"Jus?" Drake finally managed to lift the latch. With a relieved sigh he flung the window open and thrust his head outside. "God, this is better." After taking several audible gulps of air, he turned. "He had some business to attend to, Jus had."

Troy lifted a brow. "Is this the reason why you're up so early? I thought the two of you preferred a nice, long sleep-in."

"Sleep-in?" His friend grinned, mischief making his eyes sparkle. "I like the sound of that." Yet abruptly, his expression turned serious. "Really, Troy, what do you think of, whiling your time away and smoking yourself to death?"

At these words, irritation flared up in Troy. "Don't lecture me," he warned. "I don't need this."

"No, you need a good thump on your thick head, that's what you need. And that's what I told your wife. Yes, your wife—and don't make such a grumpy face, it doesn't become you." Drake glowered at him. Mischief had fled from his eyes; instead, they now glittered with what looked like very real anger.

Troy reared back in his seat.

Whenever had he last seen Drake glowering?

"Have you seen that cousin of yours lately?" his friend asked in clipped tones.

"Alex?"

"Heavens, don't be so dense! Of course, *Alex*. Have you got any other pea-brained cousin hidden in a closet somewhere or what?" The glower intensified. "Well, have you seen him?"

"Not since I've come to London, no."

Drake rolled his eyes. "But you've heard that he has gained a certain reputation over the last few months, haven't you?"

The old feeling of responsibility reared its head, making Troy spring readily to his cousin's defense. "It surely must have been a shock for him. After all, he considered himself in love—"

"In *love!*" Drake snorted. "The only person Alexander Markham is damn well in love with is his bloody self! Good God, Troy, open your eyes to the facts: He's known to gamble excessively, to drink excessively, to run through the *filles* of Covent Garden. A bit of a rough sport, is oh-so-wonderful, lovely Alexander Markham, Viscount Perrin."

"He's still young!" Troy protested.

Shaking his head, Drake came over and perched on the arm of the chair nearest to Troy. "He is older than you were when you went to war. Don't you think it's time he shows a bit of responsibility and maturity instead of sulking around like a spoilt brat? He bloody *is* a spoilt brat! Do you know that he runs around dragging your name through the mud? Claiming you're a bit soft in the head, to put it nicely?"

Wearily, Troy rubbed his hand over his eyes. "Well . . . I. . . ." He looked up. "Can't you let this drop, Drake?" he pleaded.

For a moment, his friend's expression softened. "I know you don't feel like yourself these days. I cannot even start to imagine what you've been through, and I know all this is difficult for you. But, Troy, you cannot walk around wearing blinders for the rest of your life." Drake's face hardened once more. "Your precious cousin is an impertinent little sod, my boy, who's trying his best to sully your name. Do you know that he called on your wife yesterday?"

"Yes. Finney told me."

"Do you know that he's been seen sporting a couple of nice, bloody scratches on his cheek?"

Troy sighed. "What are you getting at, Drake?"

"He did not have the scratches when he came to your house yesterday."

"So?" Impatient and more than slightly irritated, Troy fidgeted on his seat. Really, he loved his friends, but sometimes they could be a real pain in the neck.

Drake leaned forward, gazing at him intently. "But he had the scratches when he left your house," he said slowly, emphasizing each word.

Troy stilled. "What exactly do you want to say?"

"Do I have to spell it out for you, then?" Drake gave a long-suffering sigh. "Our precious, precious boy was apparently a bit peeved that his big cousin went and snatched his toy from underneath his nose. Especially since, back in spring, said toy gracefully declined the honor to become the possession of the wonderful Viscount Perrin."

"What?" Troy's heart constricted. "What do you mean?" he spluttered.

His friend raised his brows. "Are you acting this dim on purpose? What do you think I mean? He offered for her hand, of course—"

"He did *not!*"

"—and she declined."

"The hell she did!"

"Shows her good taste, if you ask me." Drake positively smirked.

Feeling as if he might burst at any moment, Troy jumped to his feet. "You stupid bastard, Drake! Alex did not offer for her. I prevented it, do you hear me? *I prevented it!*" he shouted.

"Dearie me." Drake wiggled a finger in his ear. "Caught

a sore spot, didn't we?" But then the smirk vanished, and something like compassion showed in his eyes. "He offered for her, Troy. He must have offered for her before you did."

"*No!*" Troy turned away from him, ran his fingers through his hair. "No, I cannot believe this. She would have—"

"Would she?" his friend interrupted gently. "Apparently she did not. It's not something a fellow admits to easily, making a very generous offer, casting himself in the role of the knight in shining armor and all that, and being jilted. But since our precious boy here gets somewhat talkative when in his cups. . . ." Drake raised his shoulders in an eloquent shrug.

Dazed, Troy fell back into his chair. "But I thought. . . ." He shook his head. "Why did she not accept him?" Feeling suddenly utterly lost, he raised his eyes to Drake, who just shrugged once more.

"This, my friend, is something you should ask your wife. To come back to the matter at hand . . ." Drake squatted down so his face was level with Troy's. "Fact is, your lovely cousin went into your house with his cheeks unblemished and went out of your house with a few bloody scratches. Ask Finney. Ask him about that rude attitude your cousin displayed toward your wife."

"So . . ."

"So, we believe that our chap Alex Markham *accosted* your wife. Thankfully, he got more on his plate than he could swallow. In a manner of speaking." Drake's smile was tight and unpleasant.

Troy digested this for a moment, until a new thought occurred to him. He frowned. "And how do you know about all this?"

"Oh. I was wondering when you would catch up with

that." Drake stood, hands clasped behind his back. "According to your cousin, I'm having an affair with your wife."

Troy's mouth went slack. "You're fibbing."

"I'm afraid not, my friend. It's all about town." Looking at him expectantly, Drake bobbed up and down on his feet.

Troy shook his head in a vain attempt to clear the haze that seemed to have befallen his brain. The world at large appeared to have turned into a madhouse. "And what do you suggest I should do now? Call you out?"

"I wouldn't advise it, Troy, my boy," Drake said, his usual cheerfulness returning with full force. "For one thing, if you so much as harm a single hair on my head, Jus would happily run you through with whatever pointy thing he comes across first."

"Yes, let's not forget Justin," Troy muttered and started when his friend gave an unexpected laugh.

"He would, you know," Drake said brightly. "Run you through." He grinned. "Why don't you just silence all these gossipmongers instead? Take your wife and go out, let them see you in public. *Together*." He raised his brows in silent question.

"Charming."

Drake chuckled. "I knew you'd like that. Here." He took an envelope out of his breast pocket and threw it into Troy's lap.

Troy cast a suspicious look at the piece of paper. "What's that?"

"An invitation, of course." Drake gave him his most charming smile. "To Lady Holland's dinner party on Saturday."

"Lady Holland?" Troy groaned. "You can't be serious!"

"She squeezed you in at my special request, so don't you dare to wriggle out of this!"

"But . . ." At a loss for words, Troy shook his head.

Drake's lips twitched betrayingly. "Just look at it like this: If we have to attend one of these boring, boring dinner parties, we can at least go to the best London has to offer. And now . . ." He glanced around the room, obviously trying to locate his dogs. "I should bring the girls home. And don't forget: We are counting on you." With a wave and a smile and three bundles of joyfully quivering dogflesh, Lord Allenbright swept out of the room.

That evening, when Lillian by chance met her husband on the stairs, he said: "I have heard that my cousin called yesterday morning."

"Yes."

"I see." Cornflower-blue eyes searched her face. It surprised her that he did not show any signs of anger.

"He will not come again," she said.

"I have heard that he has turned worse for the drink." Now his eyes scanned her body before they rose to her face once more. "Are you quite all right?"

Lillian smiled airily. "Is there not a saying, 'right as a trivet'—"

"I see," her husband said and started to walk down the stairs. "I am glad," he said over his shoulder.

Lillian stared after him. She remembered how the skin of his back had gleamed in the candlelight. Now his jacket fit snugly, and she realized how much his shoulders and back had filled out in the last few months. What she now beheld was a man back in his full power.

"I am glad, too," she whispered.

He halted at the foot of the stairs and turned. "By the way . . . we will be attending a dinner party on Saturday night. Just so you know."

Lillian blinked. "Yes, my lord."

He nodded and bowed. "Then I wish you a good evening, my lady." One last time his blue eyes flashed up at her before he veered and slipped out of her sight. All that remained was a hint of sandalwood and oakmoss lingering in the air.

Chapter 13

The carriage rumbled along the road for quite some time, but it finally turned and passed beneath a high iron arch between two solemn stone pillars and open gates. Flickering torches showed the way up the avenue of elm trees, which stretched to form a natural dome of greenery, creating a false sense of countryside peace and quietness. In truth, the big gray beast—the city—was waiting just beyond.

Lillian would have liked to draw her velvet pelisse tighter around herself, but instead, she forced herself to remain sitting straight and unmoving. After all, her husband lounged in the opposite corner of the dimlit coach, a dark, silent presence. In his formal evening wear he blended into the shadows until he seemed to become part of them; a creature of the darkness, of the night, unfathomable.

A shiver slithered down Lillian's spine.

She concentrated on looking out of the carriage windows, on the glimpses of Holland House that the foliage now and then revealed. Dusk-darkened greenery framed the red-brick walls, cloisters and balconies. All the windows blazed with light, a cheerful, twinkling welcome.

Lillian did not feel cheerful.

She did not know why Ravenhurst had insisted on this outing. It worried her. A change in attitude, she had learned at high cost, did not necessarily bode well. However, when the carriage came to a crunching halt on the gravel, she plastered a smile on her face. The door was opened; a footman in dark livery helped her out. Taking a deep breath, she looked up at the famed house, at the turrets and oriels, at the weathervanes high above. "The northwind doth blow," she whispered and, once again, suppressed a shiver.

"Ho there!" The cheery call from behind snatched her out of her reveries. She started and turned around, just in time to see Justin de la Mere alighting from the Allenbright coach.

Lord Allenbright, already standing on the gravel, waved his gloves through the air in blithe disregard of social etiquette. "Hello, Troy, my boy. And Lady Ravenhurst." He bowed, nearly losing his shiny black hat in the process. "Drat," he muttered.

Mr. de la Mere tsked and pointedly wiped nonexistent specks of dust from the sleeves of his coat.

Lillian felt a smile tugging at the corners of her mouth. When she glanced at her husband to gauge his reaction, she was surprised to see his lips curl upward. All at once, the sternness vanished from his face, the hard lines around his mouth disappeared to make way for a boyish grin and mischievous twinkle in his eyes. The transformation was so startling, so *breathtaking*, that for a moment all Lillian could do was stand and stare, hardly believing.

Never before had she seen Ravenhurst smile, really smile; never before had she seen the burden of the past lifted off his shoulders, if only for a few moments. She let out her breath in a deep sigh. When she went toward her husband's friends she did not have to fake the smile that bloomed on her face. "Lord Allenbright, Mr. de la Mere. A pleasure to meet you here."

"Indeed, my lady, indeed. The pleasure is all ours." Lord Allenbright beamed at her, his eyes all sparkling green. "May I offer you my arm up the stairs to the entrance? Troy, my boy, you might want to talk to Jus about that new pistol of his." He fought with his gloves, trying to wriggle his fingers into them. Noisily exhaling, he looked up. "Do I *have* to wear these?"

Ravenhurst barked a laugh, a deep sound that rumbled in his broad chest, and slapped his friend's shoulder. "And you accuse *me* of being a recluse? In all that Cornish wilderness you've grown into a perfect barbarian."

"Civilization would be much better off without these ridiculous things. White silk gloves? *Please!*" Lord Allenbright rolled his eyes in a rather dramatic fashion.

A giggle escaped Lillian's lips. Quickly, she tried to stifle the sound with her hand, yet Ravenhurst heard her nonetheless. Frowning, he turned and looked her up and down.

She felt a blush creeping into her cheeks, not used to such scrutiny.

"Ha!" Lord Allenbright exclaimed, triumphantly holding up his gloved hands and thereby diverting her husband's attention. "I won!"

Mr. de la Mere only shook his head. "I blame it on all that Cornish brigand blood that runs through his veins." Tolerant amusement laced his light drawl, and for a short moment his love for Drake Bainbridge lit up his eyes as he exchanged a look with his friend.

Ravenhurst cleared his throat. "Well, I suppose we should go, else our hostess shall assume we got lost in her Dutch gardens."

De la Mere raised one perfectly trimmed brow. "And heaven forbid that Lady Bess's wrath descend upon our heads."

"We would get rapped with fans," Lord Allenbright muttered darkly.

De la Mere's other brow shot up. "We will get rapped with fans anyway," he complained. He made a sweeping movement with his hand. "Shall we?"

"Oh yes, yes. Let's." Lord Allenbright hurried toward the flight of stairs to the entrance of the house. Then he seemed to remember that earlier he had offered to escort Lillian inside, for he stopped and turned back. "My lady." Gallantly, he held out one arm. "You wanted to talk to Jus about that pistol, didn't you, Troy?"

Ravenhurst shrugged, amusement written on his face. "If you say so." With a courteous wave of his hand, he let Lillian pass by to take Lord Allenbright's arm.

They proceeded up the stairs, Lillian's hand securely tucked into the crook of Allenbright's arm. Behind them she heard de la Mere enthusing over his new pocket pistol—four barrels, two shots. "So small that it would fit nicely in your wife's reticule," he said.

Her husband's voice was dry when he answered. "I do not think my wife is in need of a pocket pistol. Or any other weapon, come to that."

Lillian gulped. The skin on the back of her neck tingled, and it seemed to her that she could feel his eyes burning into her. She recalled the feeling of the riding crop in her hand, the wooden handle slick with sweat, the scents of an overgrown garden. . . .

Her steps faltered.

"Are you all right, my lady?" Lord Allenbright inquired worriedly.

"I am fine," she murmured. "Just fine."

The front door was opened wide, and a butler in stately black greeted them. "Good evening, my lady, my lords."

A round-faced, middle-aged man peered around his shoulder. "Whom have we here?" His lips shone like the skin of a polished red apple. "Lord Allenbright!" His shaggy black brows lifted in recognition. "Good evening, good evening."

Allenbright bowed. "Lord Holland, may I introduce Lady Ravenhurst."

The clear, intelligent eyes fastened on Lillian. "Delighted, my lady." He bowed.

Lillian curtsied. "Thank you for the invitation, my lord."

Yet he waved all thanks aside. "Oh, do not thank *me*. It is my wife who is mistress of our guest lists. Or rather, John and my wife." He winked. "She worries that should she give me free rein, I would go and invite everybody I meet in the course of the day."

"And so you would, my lord," said the deep voice of Lillian's husband.

Lord Holland grinned. "Good evening, Lord Ravenhurst, Mr. de la Mere."

Once they stepped into the entrance hall, servants came and took the men's coats and hats as well as Lillian's pelisse. Carefully, she shook the folds of her dress of white Indian muslin. It was adorned with silver stitchings and pink silk roses along the hem, in color matching the satin ribbon under her breasts and the roses in her hair.

She had not wanted the roses.

"Flowers become you, my lady," Lord Allenbright whispered teasingly.

With a forced smile, Lillian looked up, a polite answer hovering on her lips, when she detected the mischievous twinkle in his eyes. She found it utterly enchanting. "You are incorrigible, my lord," she whispered back, and tried to suppress the twitching of her lips. "I do not think it is quite fitting to tease a lady like this."

"Ahh, well . . ." He cleared his throat and made a sweeping gesture with his hand. "Have you noticed the Arazzi along the walls? They are superb," he said more loudly. "There's Vulcan presenting Jupiter with the thunderbolts, Apollo with the Muses, and over there Bacchus and the Bacchantes. Now, *that* is something I consider naughty!"

Lillian laughed, yet the tapestries against the silk and velvet brocade of the walls were indeed beautiful, with gay colors and frolicking figures.

"Should you wish to admire all of Lord Holland's treasures, my dear, it would take you the better part of a month." Ravenhurst reached for her hand and placed it on his forearm. Even through the material of his clothes she could feel the hard muscle beneath. His flesh was unyielding, and its heat drifted up to warm her fingers. "Shall we? We don't want to keep everybody waiting."

"Of course." Lillian lowered her eyes. Even though she realized he was only playing the considerate husband for society's sake, she felt his touch to the marrow. Tingles shot up her arm, and her fingers almost twitched with the urge to explore the strength of his arms. Yet her hand remained stiff, for she felt the tension coiled within his big body. She risked a quick glance at him from the corner of her eyes. The sternness had returned to his face, the lines etched into his skin deeper than ever.

Inwardly, she sighed.

A thick, red carpet swallowed the sound of their steps as a footman guided them through a silk-hung doorway on their right to a large staircase and up to the first floor. Here they stepped through a door into a wainscoted chamber, large enough to count as a ballroom. Arrangements of upholstered chairs and delicate-looking settees were grouped around two fireplaces. Tall, graceful figures looked down from the paintings above each chimneypiece, and beneath, some lightly clad nymphs danced on a ground of gold.

"Most decidedly naughty," came Lord Allenbright's dramatic murmur from behind, and Lillian had to bite her lip in order to suppress another giggle.

"Through here, my lady, my lords, sir." The footman bowed and showed them into an adjoining room where sounds of conversation and laughter resonated. A company of maybe twelve people stood around in small groups, talking and gesticulating, all apparently in high spirits. Against the crimson walls they looked like an artfully arranged tableau, a study in polite parlor conversation. A middle-aged, ample-bosomed woman broke off from one of the groups and approached, her tight brown curls bouncing up and down with each step.

"Lord Ravenhurst!" she exclaimed. "Good evening, good evening. And this delightful creature must be Lady Ravenhurst." She took Lillian's hands. "Delighted, my dear, delighted." Her gaze honed in on Lillian's hairdo, and immediately the smile vanished from her face to be replaced by a frown. "But what have we here? Five roses? *Five?* Decidedly *beaucoup trop*, my dear. Five roses! Heavens!" She reached out and plucked two flowers from Lillian's hair. "Much better, this. Don't you think so, too, Lord Ravenhurst? Mr. Allen? Mr. Allen! Do get rid of these roses, will you?" She thrust the offending blossoms at a tall man with graying hair and enormous spectacles balancing on his nose.

"Shall I proceed to eat them, my lady?" he asked courteously, a Scottish accent lengthening his vowels.

"Oh, don't be silly, Mr. Allen." She rapped his arm with her fan. However, her attention was immediately drawn to something else. "My dear Lord Allenbright!" she exclaimed, all smiles again. Enthusiastically she reached out as if to clasp him in a hearty embrace. "What a pleasure to have you here. And Mr. de la Mere, too."

Mr. Allen issued a polite snort. "Ye are so seldom in London that yer stay caused quite a sensation. Of course, Lady Holland *must* be one of the first to have ye for dinner. Isn't that so, my lady?" For that, he felt the rapping of her fan a second time.

"The roses, Mr. Allen, the roses." She threw him a pointed look before she turned back to Allenbright and de la Mere. "Quite the inseparables you two are. Like the Dioscuri, Castor and Pollux, twinkling among the field of stars." She blinked. "Doesn't Lady Nicolai have some parrots that are inseparable, too? General Luttrell?" Her fan hit the arm of the man who was just trying to squeeze past them. "You are late, Luttrell."

"My lady, I am devastated." Grinning, he bowed, hand on his heart.

"Yes, yes." Lady Holland poked her fan into his chest. "Lady Nicolai?" she prompted.

"No. Not any longer. One of the parrots died while trying to lay an egg."

Lady Holland lifted her eyebrows. "How perfectly shocking. Whatever is she going to do now?"

"I am sure Lord Nicolai is already on his way to Africa in order to catch a new parrot for her," the man said with a perfectly straight face. Half turning, he spotted Mr. Allen. "Allen! What are you doing with the roses?"

The other cleared his throat, lifting his hand as if to point, then scratched the side of his face. Surprised, Luttrell looked back, then coughed politely as he noticed Lillian. "Your locks are slightly askew, my lady."

"Oh." Lillian's hands flew up to her hair.

"Hmph." Lady Holland thrust her chin forward. "It looks much better than before. *Five* roses! *Beaucoup trop!*" She glared at Luttrell, daring him to contradict her.

Lillian lowered her hands to her sides. "You are quite right, my lady," she agreed softly. She was a bit overwhelmed by the woman's vivacity.

Lady Holland's face lit up. Cheerfully she patted Lillian's cheek. "And you are a perfect dear, Lady Ravenhurst. Now run along and have some fun." She turned to continue poking her fan into Mr. Allen. "You are still here? Tsh, tsh, go!"

Luttrell lifted an eyebrow. "Dearie me, you got promoted to pet chicken, Allen. What a lucky devil you are!" He slung a friendly arm around the other man's shoulder, and together they marched off, Lady Holland and her fan in tow.

Behind her, Lillian heard Lord Allenbright's light chuckle. "Poor Allen," he murmured.

"Lady Holland's very own Nubian slave," de la Mere added in an amused drawl. "I suggest that we make the rounds before the procession begins. Shall we?"

"By all means." In a show of apparent solicitousness, Ravenhurst once more reached out to place Lillian's hand in the crook of his elbow, putting his large fingers over her much smaller ones.

Perhaps he is afraid I will run away. . . . In silent reassurance, Lillian curled her fingers over his arm and gently squeezed the hard muscles. Whatever charade he intended to play for their hosts, they were in this together. So she lifted her chin a notch and let him guide her around the room to do the introductions.

She soon found that many different sets of people made up the Hollands' dinner party. Beside the titled, she also met writers and actors, the famous John Kemble even, whom she had seen doing Shakespeare in Covent Garden. She was introduced to high-ranking people of the middle-class as well as commoners from abroad, like the short Italian, Mr. Foscolo, whose English was almost unintelligible, but who made up for it by talking with his hands and feet instead. At one time, lost in a convoluted narrative of his adventures in St. Omer, he almost knocked off Mr. Allen's silver eyeglasses.

The tall, bespectacled Scot happily took on the obligation to introduce them to the people Ravenhurst did not know, like Mr. Prestwood Smith, Esquire, a lawyer whose waistcoat stretched so tight over his enormous belly that Lillian feared the buttons might pop off at any moment. The man eyed Lillian speculatively before he turned to Ravenhurst with a sly smile on his face. "I am surprised you have brought your wife here, my lord."

Ravenhurst lifted his brows. "Whyever should I not?"

"Well, you know how it is. . . ." The lawyer, all fake innocence, lifted his shoulders. "Mrs. Prestwood Smith would rather drop dead than cross the threshold to Holland House."

Angry color rose in Mr. Allen's face, but before he could say anything, Lord Allenbright beat him to it. "I fail to see why." To Lillian's shock, his voice oozed icy disdain.

Mr. Prestwood Smith failed to read the warning signs, for he continued blithely. "Why? Because of Lady Holland's rather—how shall I put it—dubious past, of course!" Because of the fact that Lady Holland divorced her first husband in order to be with Lord Holland, that their first son had been born out of wedlock.

Aunt Louisa, of course, had known all about it and about the terrible scandal that followed. But how heavy weighed that old scandal against the friendliness Lady Holland had shown Lillian? She thought she understood, though, why a man like Mr. Prestwood Smith would slight a higher-born woman in her own home.

From under lowered lashes Lillian watched the men around her. Mr. Allen looked ready to explode. Allenbright's and de la Mere's faces mirrored their open contempt, while Ravenhurst's expression had frozen to stone.

Mr. Prestwood Smith's dart had hit true.

Lillian frowned.

Prestwood Smith. The name seemed to tickle a memory, one of Aunt Louisa's anecdotes of Seasons past, of—"Mr. Prestwood Smith," she said softly.

"Yes, my lady?" Smirking, the lawyer turned to her.

Lillian cocked her head to the side. "Are you the same Prestwood Smith who in the winter of 1810 fell into the Thames while in pursuit of—how shall I put this—a bit of muslin?" She smiled politely, as if the question were the most natural in the world. Next to her, Allenbright broke into guffaws of laughter.

Very slowly, a mottled color covered Mr. Prestwood Smith's face. "Well . . . I dare say!" He huffed and puffed. "This is—"

"The ice broke, did it not?" Lillian went on sympathetically. "Oh dear, that must have been *quelque pen déplaisant* for you, *non?*"

"A little bit unpleasant?" Mr. de la Mere echoed, then erupted into a coughing fit.

She would not have been surprised to see foam emit from Mr. Prestwood Smith's mouth. Clenching his fists until the knuckles showed white, he threw his head back and marched off, an image of injured dignity.

"Oh dear." Mr. Allen allowed himself a small chortle before he became serious again. "My dear Lady Ravenhurst, you are a true Penelope." Obviously deeply moved, he shook her hand.

Feeling that he was paying her a compliment, Lillian gave him a shy smile. "Think nothing of it, Mr. Allen," she said softly. When she risked a quick glance at her husband, she saw that he was looking at her with a most peculiar expression on his face. Quickly Lillian averted her eyes.

Some short time later Lady Holland clapped her hands, and Mr. Allen immediately hastened to arrange the assembled guests in rows of two, according to their rank and importance. Then they all marched into the adjoining dining room in a festive procession. The room blazed with lights, which were reflected in the great glass above the chimney-piece and lent a luxurious sparkle to the crimson damask walls. Golden-framed portraits looked down on the party as the guests tried to find their places according to Lady Holland's wishes.

"Ibby? Ibby, do change your seat with Lord Allenbright. We do not want to separate the inseparables, do we?"

Obligingly Miss Fox, a small, middle-aged woman with a shy smile, stood.

"Mr. White, do not make such a horrid face." Lady Holland rapped her fan against the table. "Lest anybody think we give you poison to drink."

"The champagne is enough to poison any man's soul," the so-chided White muttered rebelliously, if a bit quietly. He raised soulful eyes to look at Lillian. "I am a practicer of asceticism," he explained with great dignity.

"Stuff and nonsense, asceticism," Lady Holland cut in, omniscient of all that went on at her table. "Holland House is not a monastery, Mr. White. Make sure that you do not stuff poor Henry's head with such rubbish. Lord Ravenhurst, I see with pleasure that you have found a seat next to your wife. We would not want to separate newly-weds any more than the Dioscuri."

"Especially when they are so *happily* wed," murmured

Mr. Prestwood Smith. Those sitting nearest him tittered and threw arched looks at Lillian and her husband.

Beside her, she could feel Ravenhurst growing tense, yet before his fury could erupt, his friend leaned back in his chair, apparently all ease and polite boredom. "My dear Smith, is it?" Justin de la Mere drawled. "If you had seen the paradisical environs of Bair Hall, where Lord and Lady Ravenhurst spent their honeymoon—a fair Garden Eden it is, with them as Adam and Eve in all their beauty and innocence. . . ." He threw Ravenhurst a look.

Lillian felt color rise in her cheeks. Surely he must be thinking of their encounter in the garden, when she had run around bedecked with flowers.

Strangely, though, her blush seemed to help to defuse the situation, for Miss Fox sighed and said, "Ahh," and Lady Holland looked much touched.

"Indeed." Ravenhurst's voice betrayed none of the agitation Lillian still felt in his tightly coiled muscles. With apparent ease and familiarity he took up one of her gloved hands to lift it to his lips. At the last moment, he turned her hand around and placed a slow, lingering kiss on her palm. Even through the material of her glove his hot breath warmed Lillian's skin, and a tingle of awareness raced up her arm.

"We are the most happily wedded couple you can imagine," he said. The lie fell lightly from his lips, but when he raised his head to meet Lillian's gaze, she saw that his eyes were curiously flat and dead.

Icy apprehension replaced the pleasant tingle of before. In an unconscious move, Lillian turned her hand and curled her fingers around his.

The corners of his mouth lifted into a sarcastic smile, and with great care, he put Lillian's hand back on the table before he faced the potbellied lawyer. "You see, Mr. Prestwood Smith," he said, his voice deadly soft, "there is no need for concern. Absolutely none."

Coldness reached for Lillian, clamping around her heart like a painful vise. Dear God, did none of them see that his smiles were all façade? That beneath the cool veneer he was hurt and suffering the torments of the damned?

She looked around the table, yet all faces reflected delight at his romantic display. Only when her frantic gaze reached de la Mere and Allenbright did she find any who had seen beneath his charade, who had noticed his emotional pain.

Lillian closed her eyes and thought, *I wish I had drowned that night on the Channel. I wish the waves had reached up and closed over my head.*

The damask-covered table could have safely held nine people. It was laid out for sixteen, forcing the guests to squeeze together while course after course of food appeared. Lillian was still unused enough to the opulence of London dinner parties to marvel at the many dishes that the footmen brought for each course—sometimes as many as twenty different delicacies. Lillian tasted mutton roast with thyme butter, pistachio cream, duckling with apple and chestnuts, stewed mushrooms, little fish cakes, roast beef and rosemary sauce, woodcock, boiled potatoes, lobster cream, guinea fowl with asparagus, duck and orange salad, green peas in a white sauce.

During the fifth course—Mr. Allen was busy carving the roast pheasant—Mr. Foscolo got into a heated argument with Lord Eckersley. They leaned forward and backward or stretched up to talk around or over Lady Eckersley, who sat between them. In the height of his agitation, Mr. Foscolo's English got mixed with more and more languages.

In between, Mr. White's mournful murmurings reached

Lillian's ear. Obviously he was keeping track of each new language Mr. Foscolo brought in. "French . . . Portuguese . . . Latin . . . German . . ."

"*Diabolo!*"

Lady Eckersley visibly winced when Mr. Foscolo's fork missed her nose by scant inches.

"Spanish!" Mr. White said almost triumphantly.

His eyes wide with disbelief, Ravenhurst stuck his nose into his wineglass. "This is worse than Bedlam," he muttered.

"*Gentlemen!*" Lady Holland rapped her fan against the table in a vain effort to stop the heated discussion. All she achieved was knocking over her husband's glass.

"No! I do not agree, sir!" Mr. Foscolo jumped up, knife still in hand, and proceeded to march around the room, all the while talking rapidly. Important points he emphasized by slashing his knife through the air.

"Oh dear," Lady Holland sighed. But there was nothing to be done.

After the main courses, the footmen removed the table-cloth and afterward carried up the desserts and champagne wines. Full of wonder Lillian eyed the assortment of exotic fruits, and the cremes and puddings that were spread out on the table before her. She tried a bit of the baked Jamaican bananas and the candied pineapple and orange slices. The chocolate cream, however, she liked best of all.

Eventually, the women left the gentlemen to their port and cheroots and ambled back into the crimson drawing room. Here the footmen went around with trays of coffee and tea. Lillian sipped her bitter tea, undiluted by either milk or sugar, while Lady Eckersley discussed with Miss Fox the merits of watercolor. On the settee, meanwhile, Lady Holland told the ladies Swanscott and Holroyd all about Holland House's priest hole, which was hidden behind a panel in one of the rooms. Apparently, the mistress of the house liked a good, bloody tale, for she launched herself with enthusiasm into a long, gory story of how the Roundheads once searched the house, dragged the poor priest off, and how afterward all came to a horrible, horrible end.

Lillian hid her smile behind her teacup.

She looked up when the door opened and the butler appeared. To her surprise, he strode toward her, bowed, and then leaned down to whisper discreetly, "I beg your pardon, my lady, there is a lady waiting for you downstairs. She says she has important business to discuss with you, but I could not show her up. Lady Holland does not like surprise additions to her dinner parties." He stood back.

"I quite understand," Lillian hastened to assure him. Who could this mysterious lady be? Hesitantly, she put her cup on a side table and stood.

"Is everything all right, my dear?" inquired Lady Holland from the settee.

Lillian forced herself to smile. "Everything is fine, my lady. Thank you. If you will excuse me? I will be right back." She nodded at the butler, who led her out of the room and back to the great staircase.

"This lady, did she not give you her name?" Lillian asked.

The servant shook his head. "She did not. I am sorry, my lady. Yet she has the manner and looks of one of high rank."

"I see." The oaken banister felt slippery under Lillian's hand.

They reached the landing and rounded the bend in the stairs, allowing Lillian a clear view of the woman who was waiting for her at the foot of the stairs. A tall, sleek man hovered behind her.

When the woman caught sight of Lillian, her ruby red lips lifted into a smile. "*Bon soir, chérie*," she said.

Chapter 14

It was, Troy had to admit, the sneakiest, most perfect revenge possible. Mr. Prestwood Smith, Esquire, did not stand a chance. First Allen drank with him, soon to be joined by Luttrell. Even Mr. White broke his vow of asceticism for the good cause, sidling up and regaling the stout lawyer with numerous toasts, some in Spanish, some in Irish-Gaelic, some in Latin and Greek. As soon as Drake and Justin had smelt the rat, they cheerfully raided Holland's drinking cabinet and armed themselves with bottles of whiskey and brandy.

"Look at that!" Drake whistled appreciatively. "Jamaican rum!"

"And Austrian gentian schnapps!" Justin grinned.

"And kirsch! Have you ever had kirsch? No?" Drake had problems balancing all the bottles in his arm. "My dear Prestwood Smith, you simply *must* have some kirsch. I insist on it. It is *delicious*, I tell you, delicious!"

The two friends joined the group around the lawyer, and less than half an hour later, Mr. Prestwood Smith, Esquire, slowly slid off his chair and landed on the floor with a dull thud.

"Dearie me," said Luttrell.

Mr. Allen took a handkerchief out of his pocket and started to wipe his glasses. "The poor fellow—"

"Will have such a dreadful headache come tomorrow morning," Justin finished. He shook his head.

"*Sláinte!*" Mr. White added, his expression slightly less mournful than several minutes before.

"Whatever has happened to poor Mr. Prestwood Smith?" inquired Lord Holland from the other side of the room where he had been absorbed in a discussion with Lord Swanscott about the assets of ancient Greek literature.

With great care, Mr. Allen put his spectacles back on his nose. "I am afraid he feels rather indisposed at the moment. In fact, it appears that the food and drinks at Holland House do not quite agree with him." He peered at his friend. "My lord."

"I see." Lord Holland cleared his throat. "Gentlemen, I suggest we join the ladies next door lest anybody else should start feeling . . . um . . . indisposed."

"As you wish, my lord." Mr. Allen bowed courteously.

Grinning, Troy emptied his glass and left it on the table. As they were all walking toward the door, he sauntered over to his friends. "You two are quite incorrigible," he said with amusement.

"Troy, my boy, I am devastated." Drake's eyes sparkled with devilment. "You do realize that you've begun echoing your wife."

Troy frowned.

"Besides," Justin said, poking one long finger into his arm. "You have to admit that it was great fun. That odious man only got what was his due. Regard it as a form of . . . well . . . higher justice." He raised his hands in a Gallic shrug.

"Higher justice." Troy stared at him. "You mean, Drake

Bainbridge and Justin de la Mere are the helpers of the gods?"

Drake shrugged. "You heard what Lady Holland said. We are the Dioscuri. Ahh, Lady Holland, we were just talking about you." Smiling, he went to the settee where the mistress of the house reclined.

Idly, Troy went to the sideboard and poured himself some coffee. Cup in hand, he turned and scanned the room. Luttrell and Kemble helped Lord Holland, who, after all the sitting, apparently could walk only with great pain, to one of the upholstered chairs. Mr. Foscolo had decided to join Lady Eckersley and Miss Fox in order to regale them with some more of his Italian adventures. Lady Holland was busy ordering Mr. Allen around, while Mr. White had started a conversation with Lady Swanscott.

Troy took a sip from his cup. The bitter coffee hit his tongue in a scalding wave, nearly causing him to drop the delicate china. "*Damn!*" he muttered.

"You were saying?" asked Luttrell, who had come up to the sideboard to pour two cups of tea.

"Nothing." Troy coughed. "General Luttrell, you haven't by any chance seen my wife?"

"Your wife?" The other turned, brows lifted quizzically. "Have you misplaced her?"

Troy frowned and let his eyes glide over the assembled party again. "It would seem so."

"Oh dear." Luttrell glanced around the room. "You should ask one of the footmen. John?" He snapped his fingers. Immediately, one of the livery-clad figures hurried toward him.

"Sir?"

"Have you any idea where Lady Ravenhurst has gone?"

"Sir?" Hesitantly, the man looked from Luttrell to Troy and back again. "Mr. Lund—the butler—he said there was a lady who demanded to speak to my lady. But he could not let her up, of course. So—"

"Yes?" Troy prompted, growing impatient. He could not imagine what kind of scheme his precious wife was spinning here, but he found it rather annoying. Especially since he had almost, *almost* been prepared to believe his friends were not totally wrong about her.

"So Lady Ravenhurst went downstairs to meet her."

"And this mysterious lady," Luttrell drawled. "Does she have a name?"

"No, sir," said the footman. "I mean, sir, she did not give Mr. Lund one."

"I see." Troy put his cup back on the sideboard. "Are they still downstairs?"

"I do not know, my lord."

"Never mind, I'll have a look. No," Troy halted the man. "There's no need to accompany me. You have got enough work here. I shall find the way by myself." Giving Luttrell a tight smile, he strode off.

He went through the short passageway into the wainscoted room and through there to the main staircase. From below the sound of murmuring drifted up, too quiet to distinguish the voices, too quiet really to say whether the speakers were male or female. It might be servants talking.

Troy hesitated.

Outside night had long ago fallen, and the staircase was brightly illuminated by several candles. Through the doorway at the far end of it, however, Troy caught a glimpse of another, much smaller and more dimly lit staircase, the servants' passage most likely. If he was lucky, it would take him to the back of the main staircase, from whence he could observe the speakers unnoticed. Without further ado, he walked to the back stairs and down into darkness. A beam of flickering light showed him another doorway, on level with the first landing of the main staircase.

The voices were much clearer now, much, much clearer.

Cautiously, he approached the archway, making sure that he kept to the shadows all the time. He could already see the head of his wife. Just a little bit nearer now and the second speaker would be visible. Just a little bit . . .

Troy stopped dead.

A wave of dizziness swept through him.

It cannot be!

His body broke into cold sweat.

It cannot be!

Yet the voice—he would never forget that voice, never in his whole life. That melodious voice that flowed over blood-red lips, that rippling laughter that made the tiny hairs on his arms stand on end.

He steadied himself with one hand against the wall and took an unsteady step forward, bringing him into the shadows next to the threshold, just out of the light. Breathing hard, he pressed himself against the wall. His heart thudded in his ears. The metallic taste of remembered fear filled his mouth. *Dear God. . . .*

He squeezed his eyes shut, balling his hands into fists. He tried to still the helpless trembling of his body, tried to calm his racing heart so he would hear something over the drum of his pulse. *You have to get a grip! Think! Concentrate!*

He opened his eyes again.

La Veuve Noire had brought one of her men, he now saw. Antoine, the best-loved of her pets. He stood behind her like a golden shadow, his eyes fixed on Lillian, his wife, who was wringing her hands behind her back.

Troy frowned.

There was something in her posture, something he remembered now but had not seen since France: that submissive half-bow of her head. Her eyes would be cast down, he knew, remembered.

He shook himself like a wet dog, willing the last roaring in his ears to subside.

He blinked.

". . . ran off like that. Do you not know, *chérie*, that nobody just slips away from Château du Marais? *Of course* I had to come and see how you are." The French sounded lyrical almost. "Quite the refined lady you have become, I see." The woman raised one of her perfectly trimmed eyebrows, waited.

His wife's answer was almost inaudible. "*Oui, maman.*"

La Veuve Noire smiled. She reminded Troy of a cat that had caught the mouse but enjoyed playing with it for a while before squashing it under her paw. "And married, I have heard. *Toutes mes félicitations, ma chérie.*"

"*Merci, maman.*"

When the Black Widow reached out and trailed one long, ruby-red nail over the younger woman's cheek, Troy saw his wife flinch.

"So shy, *chérie?*" The sound of the woman's laughter drifted up, making him feel sick. "Tell me, have you told your husband about the present I gave you? About that precious, precious gift? That magnificent toy?"

His mouth went dry as he realized the woman was talking about *him*. He swallowed.

"My present?" For the first time, his wife looked up. "I am sorry, *maman*. I no longer have it."

"*Non?*"

His wife gave the tiniest of shrugs. "He is dead, I suppose."

Troy's jaw dropped.

What?

She went on, her voice cool and uncaring. "I left him in

the garden somewhere, chained to a tree. He must have died after a few days. The chains were strong, *non?*"

Troy could hardly believe his ears. What kind of tale was his wife spinning now?

"Is that so?" *la Veuve Noire* asked slowly.

"Did you think I would have taken him with me? With his lame leg and everything?"

"You left him so the crows could pick his eyes out and chew the flesh from his body?" Disbelief tinged the Black Widow's voice.

His wife stood unmoved, her back ramrod straight. "If you search the gardens, you might still find the bones."

A slow smile started to spread over the woman's face. Gently, she patted his wife's cheek. "Very well, *chérie*, very well."

Warily, Troy rubbed his hand over his face. He did not know what kind of game his wife was playing right now, but he intended to put a stop to it here and now.

He rolled his shoulders, his head, and straightened to his full height. Placing a nonchalant expression on his face, he stepped out of the shadows onto the landing. "Ahhh, there you are, my dear," he said, giving his voice a hint of faint surprise. "We have already been missing you." Idly, he started to walk down the stairs.

At the sound of his voice, his wife's head whipped around. She stared at him as if she were seeing a ghost, her eyes round, her face suddenly deathly pale.

"And who might this be?" breathed the Black Widow in accented English.

He could see his wife swallow convulsively. He remembered how he had wanted to witness her fear all these past months. What he had not achieved then, happened now: Stark fear was written in her expression, flickered in her eyes.

In the past, he would have exulted in her terror.

Smiling, he turned to the Black Widow. "I am the lady's husband." He put his arm around his wife's waist and picked up one of her hands to place a kiss on its back. "Isn't that so, my dear?" He smiled down at her, tightening the grip on her waist, when he felt the slight shivers racing through her body.

"*Son époux? Enchanté!*" the woman simpered. Obviously she did not recognize him. And why should she? She believed him to be dead!

Out of the corner of his eye, Troy caught a fleeting expression of amused surprise on the face of her companion, and his own wife, standing transfixed. Very slowly, the Black Widow's golden shadow lifted an eyebrow.

Troy's wife jerked against his body, once, then stiffened.

The Frenchwoman tittered. "Don't you want to introduce us, *chérie*?" Despite her strong accent, she managed to infuse her words with malicious disdain.

"*Oui, maman.*" Her voice was faint. "*Maman*, Lord Ravenhurst. Lady Camille Abberley, my . . . stepmother." She looked up at him, and what Troy saw in her eyes made him think of a cornered fawn.

"Delighted, my lady." He bowed. "Much as I wish to talk to you further, I am afraid our hosts would send out a search party if we were not to return to them soon. May we call on you tomorrow, instead?"

The woman smiled, a smile Troy remembered quite well. This time, however, it was directed at his wife, not at him. "That will not be necessary, my lord. I will call on you, *n'est-ce pas, chérie?*"

Troy bowed again. "As you wish, my lady."

"Indeed." And with that, she swept around and walked into the entrance hall, her man following like a pet dog.

Only when Troy heard the entrance door close behind them, dared he to relax. "I did not fib," he said quietly. "We really should go upstairs." He felt strangely empty, as if the encounter with the Black Widow had frozen his mind and soul.

"Yes," his wife murmured.

She let him guide her up the stairs, back into Lady Holland's crimson drawing room. "Ah, there you are!" Luttrell greeted them. "Your husband feared you met with some mishap, my lady."

Something like a laugh bubbled from the lips of Troy's wife. "I should think not." When he looked down at her, surprised at her show of gaiety, Troy saw that her eyes glittered feverishly. "After all, what kind of mishap should befall me here in this house?"

"Who knows?" Luttrell shrugged, a droll expression on his face. "You might have been kidnapped by Lord Holland's Royalist forebear to be kept prisoner in the famous priest hole."

"To make her his ghostly bride," Drake added with a groan. "Dear God, Luttrell, don't tell me you're into these gothic novels where one horror stumbles over the other to come crashing down onto the poor, insipid heroine." His grimace transformed into a wide grin. "Don't you just *love* Mrs. Radcliffe's tales of horror?"

The rapping of Lady Holland's fan on the wooden arm of the settee cut into their conversation. "Lady Ravenhurst, you must come here and join us for one of Mr. Foscolo's delightful stories. Are they not delightful, Ibby?" she asked Miss Fox. "Mr. Foscolo, do tell us again what you did with that sausage." Impatiently she patted the empty seat beside her. "Do come, Lady Ravenhurst. Lord Ravenhurst, you can get your wife another cup of tea in case she wishes for some refreshment." Like a queen, the woman resided on her black and buttercup-yellow settee, overseeing that all her commands were followed in due course.

Troy accompanied his wife to the empty chair Lady Holland indicated. Her delicate dress rustled as Lillian sat down, hands demurely folded in her lap. Her cheeks were still pale, and Troy thought that a brandy would probably work more wonders than a mere cup of tea ever could.

Yet Lady Holland did not care for his malingering. She sent him off with shooing sounds. "The tea, my lord. The tea! Now, Mr. Foscolo, tell us again about the sausage."

The Italian's chest swelled. "It was garlic sausage. Very strong. *Fuerte*," Troy heard as he walked away toward the sideboard.

As he had been ordered, he poured a cup of tea for his wife, the earthy aroma of the brew strangely soothing. He added some milk and put a clean teaspoon on the saucer. When he turned, Mr. Foscolo had apparently reached an especially exciting point in his tale, for he waved his hands about, this way and that, nearly knocking Miss Fox's cup off its saucer.

With long strides Troy returned to the group on the settee. His wife looked wan, as though all of her color had been washed out. Still, her lips were lifted in an apparent attempt at a smile.

". . . hit bat *devant la fenêtre*." Mr. Foscolo slammed his fist into the open palm of his other hand. "*Bang!* Straight into *estómago*." He glanced around his rapt audience. "Bat. *Chauve-souris*." He made flapping motions with his arms, again endangering Miss Fox's cup.

"Yes, yes," Lady Holland swatted at his flaying arms. "A bat, we know. Ah, Lord Ravenhurst, there you are. My dear Lady Ravenhurst, you have the appearance of a wilting flower. Do drink some tea to refresh yourself, will you? Mr. Foscolo, go on."

"Sausage hit se bat. *Bang!*" His fist hit the arm of the settee and made Lady Eckersley jump. "Bat fall to ers, *sin sentido*."

Troy leaned down and handed his wife the saucer with the cup of tea. Her thank-you was no more than a whisper. Nodding, he straightened.

"And sen . . ." Mr. Foscolo paused and raised his finger, obviously to heighten the dramatic effect. "Signore Pratchett's cat et bat."

Lady Holland clapped. "Brava, Mr. Foscolo! Brava! What a clever cat that was! It must have taken the bat for a flying mouse." Her hearty laugh rolled around the room. "A very droll tale. Very droll indeed, don't you think, Lady Ravenhurst?"

The rattle of china made Troy look down. His wife's hands were trembling so much that tea had spilled from the cup onto the saucer.

"Lady Ravenhurst?" Lady Holland prompted.

"Will you excuse us, my lady?" Troy cut in smoothly. "It has been a long day and . . . surely you understand." He gave the mistress of the house a winning smile before he bent and retrieved cup and saucer from his wife to deposit them on a side table. When he took hold of her hand, it felt like ice. Trembling, brittle ice, ready to break any moment.

He said all the right things, made all the right excuses, declared himself enchanted by the evening and finally, finally, was able to whisk his wife out of the room, down the stairs. In the entrance hall they had to wait while the footmen brought his coat and her pelisse, and the butler sent for their carriage.

The night air was crisp and cool when they stepped outside, yet this did not seem to affect her. Only when they were seated in the coach, warm blankets over their legs, did her trembling increase until it gripped her whole body.

The coach rumbled down the drive of Holland House, and Troy's wife shook like a leaf in a storm. And for the first time Troy fully realized that she was, in fact, very much afraid of her stepmother. Terrified.

Unbidden, the knowledge roused his protective instincts. Before he had given himself time to think, he scooted over to her side of the carriage and put his arm around her shoulders. "Are you cold?" he inquired.

"Cold?" To his surprise she laughed, a short, shrill sound that made his own throat ache in sympathy. "I can never be cold enough again!" She choked. The laugh turned into a sob and she covered her face with her trembling hands. "Dear God . . . dear God . . ." She bent over as if in great pain, her breath coming in laborious pants. Troy's arm slid off her shoulder.

Self-consciously, he cleared his throat. "I take it that was not a polite family visit."

When his wife raised her face, he was shocked to see the glittering traces of tears on her cheeks. Never before had he seen her cry.

"A family visit?" she scorned him, her voice hoarse. "She brought *Antoine!*" She said it as if this would explain everything.

Troy frowned. He remembered the man's strange stare and his wife's ensuing nervousness. The betraying jerk against his body. "Antoine," he repeated. "And what is Antoine to you?"

"Antoine?" This time, her laughter bordered on hysteria. "*Mon dieu*, of course, the first thing you would think . . ." She halted, shook her head. In her lap, her hands slowly tightened into fists. When she turned to him again, anger had replaced the hysteria. "Antoine. You want to know about Antoine? Let me tell you about Antoine, my lord husband," she spat.

Troy felt his eyes widen in surprise.

"When you made your oh-so-gracious offer for my hand, I told you I was no longer a virgin, did I not? You made it quite clear that you think me no better than a common—how would you put it—a common trollop." She snorted, an unladylike sound. "My stepmother gave me this for my birthday. Another present of hers. An *initiation*."

Troy opened his mouth. "You—"

"It takes so little to make a girl into a woman, doesn't it?" she cut in, her voice as hard and cold as ice. "Just a few drops of blood on white linen. . . . She gave me Antoine, her beloved Antoine, for one night."

"My lady," Troy tried again.

Unheeding, his wife went on, her words cruelly precise. "At first she stood by to instruct him. Where to put his hands, his mouth. Where to lick, to bite. Where to apply pressure or not. You cannot say he took me by force, can you, when she insisted that he make me come and come and—"

"*Stop it.*" He took her by the shoulders and shook her. Beneath her clothes, her bones seemed fragile, like those of a small bird. "*Stop it!*" His voice sounded hoarse, even to his own ears, and his skin crawled with revulsion at the images she had conjured.

"You wanted to know!" she cried, her face deathly pale, her eyes black hollows in the near-darkness of the carriage. "You wanted to *know*. She stood by and let him have his way with me, the whole night, all those long, long hours, until my voice was no more than a croak, until my whole body ached and ached, just so that I would be a fitting heiress for her, that I would know what to do with the other present of hers, a toy all for myself, a—"

"STOP IT!" Troy roared.

For a moment she froze, while the blood pounded in his head, a wild, pagan rhythm that threatened to swallow him up. The wheezing breaths that filled the carriage might have been his or hers; Troy did not know.

"And now she is back," she whispered and went limp. Her shoulders slipped through his fingers as, in a rustle of muslin and silk, her body slid off the seat. Covering her face with her hands, she huddled on the floor of the carriage, rocking back and forth.

Troy swallowed.

At first her sobs were quiet, silent almost. But they increased in volume, a swelling sound that made his nerve endings quiver. Soon, loud, heart-wrenching sobs shook her whole body, filled the coach with her despair.

For Troy, it seemed as if suddenly the bottom of his world had dropped away.

Breathing became difficult.

Within a few short moments his whole world had been turned upside-down and, like in a kaleidoscope, the pieces had fallen to form a new picture. The woman whom he had thought to be incarnate evil, whom he had desperately wanted to prevent from marrying his cousin, that same woman had suddenly turned into a victim, had reverted back to a terrified girl, pushed beyond her endurance.

A memory flashed into his mind, the first sight of her in prison. Her reluctance, embarrassment. And her fear.

He had forgotten her fear, later. His own feeling of helplessness, his own abject terror and pain had left no room for considering others, had obliterated every other feeling but intense hatred.

But he remembered her fear now. Her fear in the prison, her fear on the stairs of Holland House. And yet . . . and yet. . . .

I left him in the garden somewhere, chained to a tree.
And yet she had tried . . . what?
If you search the gardens, you might still find the bones.
Troy's throat felt constricted. He swallowed, hard.
She had tried to protect him. To protect *him!*
"Dear God . . ." he murmured.

He looked down at his wife, to where she huddled in a weeping, miserable bundle. Her carefully arranged coiffure had come undone, the bundle of curls hanging askew where Lady Holland had picked the flowers. Troy's breath caught.

In another flash of insight he realized that she had protected Lady Holland, too, when she had chosen to fence with fat Prestwood Smith.

And all this time, he had thought her a copy of her stepmother, had felt his hatred justified and had finally ruined and nearly raped her. "Dear God . . ." He ran his hands through his hair. *What a mess. What a horrible, horrible mess.* The sounds of her weeping cut at his heart. Each sob was a stab at his conscience.

He bent and touched her back, felt her sobs reverberate in her bones. "Lillian." When she did not react, he scooped her up and sat her on his lap. God, how slender she was. Why had he not seen she was still more a girl than a woman? "Lillian."

She was a weeping, quivering bundle in his arms. Awkwardly, he patted her back. "It will be all right." His fingers were caught by a strand of her hair. The silky softness curled around his hand, while her flowery scent drifted up to tickle his nose. He tightened his arms. "Everything will be all right, Lillian."

Sudden as it had begun, her outburst stopped. From one moment to the next her body went stiff, her sobs halted. With fast, impatient movements, she wiped her hands across her eyes before she scrambled off his lap to sit on the opposite seat. When she spoke, her voice was once more controlled. "I beg your pardon, my lord."

Head held high, she sat on her seat, her back impossibly straight. Nothing betrayed the turmoil of moments before but the silvery traces of wetness on her cheek when she turned her head to look out the window.

Troy rubbed his neck. She reminded him of a mechanical toy, one of Weeks's marvels: Free the switch and she would spring to life, only to revert back to inanimation a few minutes later. Cool and impossibly controlled in all situations.

"We will be home soon," he said.

Her nod was almost imperceptible.

He shook his head, looked out the window, too. The rest of the drive they spent in silence.

Never had Troy been happier to spot his narrow house on Hill Street than this night. The welcoming yellow light that shone through the skylight above the entrance turned the old house into a comforting haven in the sea of darkness. Heaving a sigh of relief, Troy rushed his wife up the stairs and, as soon as Finney threw open the door, began issuing commands. "Tell the maids to prepare a bath for Lady Ravenhurst." He stripped off his gloves, gave them to a waiting footman and proceeded to shrug out of his coat. "I want a tray with tea and brandy brought to her room. Is Mistress Nanette already asleep? Send for her. I want her to take care of my wife, do you hear me?"

"Yes, my lord." Agitated color suffused Finney's face. "Immediately, my lord."

Troy turned to his wife. Red blotches still marred her face, and her eyes appeared unnaturally large. "It will be best if you retire for the night, my lady." He touched her arm. "Things will look much brighter tomorrow morning."

Even though she turned her head toward him, her glassy stare went right through. "If you say so, my lord," she said, her voice devoid of inflection.

Hurried footsteps on the stairs and the rustling of skirts announced the arrival of Nanette. The old woman was clearly agitated, worrying about the welfare of her ward. With a quick look to Troy, she hurried toward the younger woman and put a comforting arm around her shoulders. "Is everything all right, *chou-chou?*"

The quiet answer lacked any hint of emotion. *"Oui. Bien sûr."*

Troy cleared his throat. "Lady Ravenhurst's stepmother has arrived in London," he explained.

The head of the old woman whipped around, horror written on her face. "Is this true?" she whispered.

Clenching his teeth, he nodded. "Would you bring my wife upstairs? I . . ." He raised his hands. "Surely you understand."

Her old, clever eyes flickered over him, probed his glance before she nodded. He got the impression that she understood much more than he wanted.

She let Nanette pluck the remaining flowers out of her hair, let herself be peeled out of her elegant evening gown, the stays loosened and the straps of her thin chemise drawn down her shoulders until it slithered down her body and pooled at her feet, crushed silk, like the broken petals of a large flower. Shivering, Lillian closed her eyes.

Nanette clucked her tongue. "Here, here, *chou-chou,*" she murmured. "Sit down. Here."

Lillian sat stiffly on the stuffed chair, the material of the upholstery soft against her skin. She felt Nanette loosening the garters of her white stockings, her cheerful, rose-colored garters.

Roses . . .

Another tremor raced through Lillian's body. She had not wanted the roses; no, she had not.

"Hush, *chou-chou*. Hush now. You will feel much better after a nice warm bath." Nanette fluttered around her, removing Lillian's shoes and stockings. Finally, she ushered the girl to the waiting bathtub, from which scented steam rose up in lazy whirls. "Here now. The lavender will calm your nerves, *chou-chou*."

Shivering, Lillian sank down into the water. Yet even though it was warm enough to turn her skin all rosy, it could not melt the ice inside her.

She remembered Camille's blood-red lips curving into a smile, that malicious little smile so familiar to her. The way she had smiled when they had returned from the prison after Camille had chosen the man. The way she had smiled when Lillian had told her he was dead, having died of starvation while chained to a tree, to one of Camille's trees. . . .

Lillian shuddered.

Why had he chosen to walk down the stairs? What if her stepmother had recognized him? What if *Antoine* had recognized him? Antoine had acted as executor for Camille's punishments often enough, had wielded the whip or the cane, a helper to break another man's spirit.

Only, this man's had not been broken.

And if her stepmother ever found out, she would want to finish what she had started at Château du Marais all those months ago.

Vividly, Lillian recalled her first sight of him chained to Camille's construction, his body spread-eagled, arms and legs stretched tight so that movement was impossible. Her stepmother knew how to render a man helpless, how to reduce him to something less than an animal.

Lillian remembered the quivering of his flesh whenever the whips seared his skin, remembered the look in his eyes before she pressed the brand against his chest, the way his body had jerked at the touch of the hot iron, the smell of burnt flesh in her nose . . .

"Oh, dear God," she moaned.

"Hush, *chou-chou*, hush," Nanette was quick to soothe. "We are no longer in France, remember? That horrid woman cannot harm you now. Never again. Surely he would not let any harm come to you."

But what about him? Lillian wanted to scream. *She will want to harm* him! *Want to tear his flesh apart, want to destroy the man.* As she had destroyed all the other men. Her hand rose to cover her mouth, to choke back the sobs that rose in her throat.

She could only imagine what those weeks at Château du Marais had cost him. Ultimately, they had estranged him from his family, had made him a recluse on his own estate, had made him haunt London like one of the tormented. She had seen him in the grip of his demons on her wedding night, had caught a glimpse of his inner suffering then. She was sure, should he ever fall into Camille's hands again, he would not survive it a second time.

Her fists tightened until her nails bit into the soft skin of her palms. *I will not let this happen*, she thought fiercely. *I will not let her have him. Never!* She recalled how she used to dream about the plants of the overgrown garden reaching out and enveloping Château du Marais, smothering her stepmother under a green carpet; how she'd dreamed about dripping poison into Camille's drink, watching her die. *If only* . . .

But no, she would not have been able to do that, kill her own stepmother, when Nanette had taught her to heal, never to wound. With one exception: she had burnt that lily into her husband's smooth skin.

Her responsibility.
And I will not let Camille take him a second time!

Lillian let Nanette wash her with the sponge and, afterward, when the water had cooled and she stepped out of the tub, huddle her in a big soft towel. Sighing, Lillian closed her eyes and gave herself over to the luxury of having someone pamper her, rubbing her skin dry in soothing, wide circles. For a moment, she could almost imagine to be five again, could imagine her mother waiting in the room next door, welcoming her baby girl with open arms. Cheerfully, Lillian would hurl herself into the scented embrace, to be cuddled close on her mother's lap. She would snuggle her nose into her mother's curls, so much like her own, and breathe in the perfume of orange blossoms that would linger there.

A strand of her hair caught around Nanette's fingers. The short, sharp pain tugging at her scalp snapped Lillian back to reality. She opened her eyes, blinked once, twice. The warm, fuzzy feeling of the daydream evaporated faster than the steam rising from the bathtub.

Her mother was dead.

There was nobody to keep her safe.

Never again.

Only herself.

Somewhere in the distance, a church clock struck three. Wearily, Troy leaned forward in his chair and rubbed his hands over his face. His palms rasped over the stubble that covered his cheeks and chin. He should have got properly foxed hours ago. At least the alcohol would have stopped his thoughts from turning around and around in his brain until his head ached. Or perhaps it just ached from the numerous cheroots he had consumed, the smoke drifting crazily up to the ceiling. After four hours of steady smoking, the bluish clouds that wafted through the room blurred the soft light of the candles and made the air in the study oppressive.

Troy sighed.

"I have never heard that ghosts might be banished by cigar smoke," a soft voice said.

Troy's head jerked around.

Clad in a white nightgown, a tattered shawl around her shoulders, his wife stood in the doorway. Her hair was unbound; in flowing, curling strands it fell to her waist. "The Catholics use incense, I believe," she said.

Troy blinked. For a moment or two he could have sworn she was an apparition herself.

She regarded him solemnly. "You were not in your room. I thought you might be here." She lifted her shoulders as if in a shrug.

"Yes." His voice scratched in his throat, the price of hours of tobacco overindulgence.

Her eyes seemed huge. "We have to talk."

Talk. They had never talked before, had they? Only that one time, when he had made the offer of marriage in her grandfather's drawing room. He shook his head, tried to clear the haziness that fogged his brain.

His wife obviously took it as a gesture of refusal. "We *have* to talk," she insisted, her voice stronger this time. She raised her chin a notch, held it at a defiant angle.

Surprised, Troy lifted his brows. What had happened to the meek, submissive girl? "Then, by all means, come in," he drawled.

She slipped into the room and quietly closed the door behind her. Yet she remained standing with her back against the wood and watched him warily, as if he were a particularly dangerous animal who might pounce on her at any moment. The thought sparked his anger. Though, whether at her or at himself, he did not know.

"Damn," he muttered and, not for the first time, wished for a tumbler of port. Old, deep red port. He could almost taste the rich bouquet on his tongue.

His wife frowned. Had her features always been this delicate? He had never noticed. Troy scratched his stubbled cheek.

"Surely you see that we have to talk. Camille's . . ." She swallowed, the long, clear lines of her throat moving convulsively. "Camille's arrival has changed things."

With a show of nonchalance, Troy settled back in his chair, cheroot clenched between his fingers. "I don't see how. After all, she thinks I am dead, doesn't she?" He puffed on his cigar, inhaled the smoke, yet never let his wife out of sight.

Another frown marred her forehead. "But if she ever finds out otherwise—"

"Well," he interrupted, lacing his voice with arrogance as if his body were not drenched in cold sweat. "There is nothing she can do. I am an earl. She would not dare to lay a hand on me now." He raised his brows.

For a few moments his wife just stared at him. And then, the strangest thing happened: She laughed. It resembled in no way the short, shrill sound in the carriage. It was low and angry, full of scorn. Hands clenched into fists, she advanced on him, her gray eyes sparking with rarely shown emotion. "You cannot tell me you have forgotten what she is like. Do you really think any of that would matter to her? You being an earl and all that?"

Unexpected fury pounded through his veins. "But it matters to me, to *me*, do you hear?" he shouted, on his feet. "I will not have my pride taken from me again! I will not be demeaned again!" He towered over her, using his height to intimidate her, his fury like a red veil before his eyes. "Do you think I'm still a dog on a leash? *Do you*? A dog that can be whipped and branded and—"

His wife's sharply indrawn breath made him stop. All color leached from her skin, leaving her face ghostly pale.

And there it was again, the memory that bound them together and that stood between them like a solid wall made of mortar and stone: the white-hot pain of the brand on his body, her mark burnt into his skin.

A lily for Lillian.

With a bitter expletive, he turned away from her. He ran his hands through his hair and felt the remembered humiliation gnaw in his gut.

"There has never been anything that I regret as much as this," the voice of his wife came from behind him, haltingly, with the lightest of trembles.

Briefly, Troy closed his eyes. Intellectually he now understood she had been a victim just like him, but still, she had held the brand, she had watched and—

Tiredly, he shook his head. "I will not run away from that woman," he said hoarsely. "Damn it to hell, *I could have her hanged*."

Another woman might have been intimidated by his anger. His wife, however, was not. She walked around until she stood in front of him, and fearlessly she looked up at him, searched his face. "Do you think she cares?" she asked softly, her voice steady once more despite the tears shimmering in her eyes. "Do you not know? Do you *still* not know? My stepmother is mad. How else can you explain all of it? She thinks herself the mistress over life and death, a big black spider sitting in the web of her own making, waiting for another victim to tumble into her trap."

"Your stepmother is a woman, not a spider," Troy snapped impatiently. "And I will not run from her."

His wife continued, her voice imploring. "Nobody ever escapes her clutches. She has always hunted them down. *Always.* Even now, I still sometimes hear the song of her dogs in the night. If she ever finds out that I have lied to her, she will want to hunt you down, too."

"Do you think I'm so helpless that I—," he began, only to be interrupted by her.

"Do you not understand? You have seen how she is. Do you really not understand yet?" His wife put a hand on his arm, her fingers digging into his flesh as if to lend her words more emphasis. "Ravenhurst, I beg you, you have to leave London. It is *not safe*." He had never seen her so intense.

He looked down on her hand. Such a small, white hand, with elegant, slender fingers. Did she play the pianoforte? He did not have an instrument at Hill Street, but he could imagine her fingers dancing over the keys, stringing together note after note, creating melodies sweeter than the sound of birdsong.

Tentatively, he reached out and ran his forefinger over the back of her hand. Her skin felt as soft as down.

"I beg you," she whispered. All at once she sounded choked. He glanced up, and he spotted more tears glinting between her lashes.

The sight made his heart constrict, and his fingers closed over her hand. "She will not harm you," he said, his tone fierce. He would make sure that *la Veuve Noire* would never again come near his wife.

She closed her eyes. The tears spilled over and rolled down her cheeks. "She will not want to harm me. Don't you understand? She will want to harm *you*." She opened her eyes once more. Such beautiful eyes, shimmering with moisture. "I *beg* you. You are not safe in London."

She worried about *him*? About *him*.

One dark brown curl tumbled into her face, and Troy reached out to brush it behind her ear, carefully, gently. He remembered how she had cried in the carriage, a damp bundle of misery and desperation. All at once, he felt the urge to wrap her in his arms, to reassure her she was safe; that nothing would ever harm her again. But how could he do it, when it was *her* mark marring his skin, when it had been she who had held the brand and begun his degradation? Still, he wanted her to be safe from *la Veuve Noire*. "Then what do you suggest?" His voice was hoarse. If making her feel safe meant leaving London, so be it.

"Could you not ask Lord Allenbright and Mr. de la Mere to accompany us back to Bair Hall? We could tell everybody we are going to Cornwall with them. At least that would buy us some time."

"If you think so." Obviously, she had given this serious thought. "I am sure Drake and Justin would come with us. We could leave tomorrow."

"*No.*" Her grip on his arm tightened, her panic obvious. "Let us be gone this morning, before she has time to call on us."

"Is this wise?" Her locks twined silkily around his fingers as he brushed his hand through her hair. "After all, it will only serve to make her think we are afraid of her."

At that, his wife smiled. It was a sad, little smile that tugged at his heart. "Never fear," she said softly. "She already knows I am afraid of her. She has always known. It is what she wants."

Chapter 15

Bair Hall rose in the distance, with its familiar jumble of oriels and turrets and chimneys, its bricks blurring into a single rusty-brown. The shades of red, orange and apricot were lost, just like the delicate blue pattern among them, that diamond-shaped tattoo on the thick hide of the Hall. But like one of the fearsome, blue-painted warriors of old, Bair Hall was steadfastly standing guard over the earls of Ravenhurst.

Thoughtfully, Lillian put her chin on her updrawn knees. She sat on one of the tumbling walls of the fourth earl's fashionable ruins, the gardens laid out before her like a colorful carpet for a pagan queen. The wind picked up and tugged at her hair, until the long strands tumbled loose from their bonds.

They had told her that here in the north the weather might turn wild in autumn. Yet Lillian did not fear wild weather, just as she did not fear a wolf that might haunt the forest nearby.

Her husband and his friends were out, hunting that

wolf, which one of the villagers thought to have seen while collecting wood. A big, bad wolf, just like in a fairy tale.

Lillian smiled as she remembered Lord Allenbright's excitement over the hunt. His cheeks as rosy as a chubby boy's, he had fidgeted on his chair during breakfast, nearly knocking a tray out of the footman's hands. De la Mere, his nose stuck in the air, had kept teasing him, but for all his cool demeanor and arrogant drawl, Lillian had seen the loving indulgence shining in de la Mere's eyes.

She still found it strange to take her meals with the men and to live in the countess's apartments, which were so vast she sometimes felt lost among all their spacious splendor. Strangest of all she found the change in Ravenhurst's behavior toward herself. While still reserved, he had dropped his outright hostility. Sometimes, Lillian would catch him watching her, his face inscrutable. Since that night after Lady Holland's dinner party, they had not talked again. Now he seemed to be waiting—but for what?

Surely not for Camille.

Lillian frowned.

There was no sign of her stepmother. Camille had not followed them, and Lillian could almost believe that she had returned to France, defeated.

Almost.

With a shake of her head, Lillian banished her dark thoughts. She stood and stretched her arms wide. For a moment more she enjoyed the feeling of the wind caressing her hair, letting it dance like a living thing. In moments like these she could almost imagine herself to be a true pagan queen with the power of the earth coursing through her veins.

Lillian smiled at her own fancy.

But she did not live in a fairy tale, and much as she

239

would have liked to pick some flowers for her room, she knew that Nanette might need her help. For in the village several people had come down with a fever. Each day Nanette visited those who were ill, bringing them teas and salves for the chest and sometimes soup, too, from the kitchen of the Hall.

Lillian wrapped her arms around herself as the wind freshened even more. She should probably have taken a warmer coat than this thin spencer jacket.

And an umbrella, too.

A look to the sky showed dark clouds building ominously on the horizon and closing in quite fast. "Rain, rain, go away, don't come back till Christmas day," Lillian chanted softly, then laughed as she remembered the morning Lord Allenbright had come into the breakfast room, his arms full of small, wrapped parcels. "They were supposed to be for Christmas," he had said somewhat bashfully. "But just imagine you don't like them. That would ruin the whole festivities. Better to get it over with now." De la Mere had groaned and scolded, yet his friend had cheerfully proceeded to distribute the presents, while the dogs, picking up on his excitement, had jumped all around him.

Smiling and chuckling, Lillian skipped down the path. "Rain, rain, go to Spain, never show your face again. . . ."

"Bloody hell!" Drake cursed as yet another roll of thunder spooked his horse. He had trouble reining the nervous animal in and calming it down.

Troy's lips twitched as he regarded his friend. Under the steady downpour of rain, the rim of Drake's fashionable hat had finally caved in and now hung limply over his ears and into his eyes. At the moment Drake Bainbridge, Viscount Allenbright, looked more like some sort of oversized, angry dwarf than a fashionable gentleman.

"And not a bloody wolf to be found the whole day," Drake muttered. "Devil take that wood-picking fellow with the big imagination!"

At that, Troy laughed. "Did you really think we'd find a wolf in these woods? All the wolves of Britain were hunted down long ago, my friend. But I couldn't let my villagers sit trembling in their beds for fear of being devoured in their sleep."

"Then, by all means, let's call it a day," came Justin's drawl from the near darkness in the shadows between the trees. A flash of lightning illuminated his wet face. Rain dripped from his chin and nose. "For even if there were wolves lurking around here, they would be wiser than to stay out in this dreadful weather."

Troy had to admit that his friend was right. Not only were they all soaked to their skins, but it was also growing darker by the minute. It would not do if one of them fell off his horse and broke his bones. So they all turned their horses, wet and weary, toward home.

The ride back to Bair Hall slowly took on nightmarish qualities. Their wet clothes soon became uncomfortable, rubbing the skin underneath raw. Troy felt as though the cold was seeping into his flesh to settle in the very marrow of his bones. Their horses stomped onward, slick with rain, heads hung low. They felt clearly as miserable as their masters, who had to duck their own heads against the madly swinging tree branches, while above them the wind howled like a wild beast on the loose.

It seemed to take ages to reach the grounds of Bair Hall. By that time, Troy felt weak with relief when he saw the lights of the house merrily twinkling in the near distance. The horses, too, seemed to feel that the warm, dry stables were near, for they picked up speed once again.

The stables, however, when they reached them, were

strangely deserted. Nobody hurried out to take the horses, and when Troy poked his head into the hay-dusted warmth to holler for a man, nobody answered.

"Now, this is what I call interesting," Justin said to no one in particular, his normal nasal twang amplified so that it sounded like an oncoming cold. "What comes to mind is that saying about the absent cat and the dancing mice."

Troy frowned. "Let's walk the horses to the front of the house and see if we find somebody there."

The wary beasts protested when they were dragged away from the tantalizing warmth of the stables. "Come on," Troy murmured and tugged on the reins of his stallion. A niggling worry gently squeezed his heart, spread lower and settled in his stomach, a sliver of ice.

They reached the front of the house, the hooves of their horses crunching on the gravel, while the rain, merciless, pelted down on men and beasts alike. Even though the windows of the house flared with light, no door opened, no footman came hurrying outside.

Drake sneezed. "A day full of unexpected adventures," he said.

"I could well do without a few of them," Troy answered dryly, managing to keep his voice even. He handed the reins of his horse to Justin, then marched up the front stairs and opened the door. The creaking of the hinges sounded unnaturally loud in the empty entrance hall.

"Now, if this isn't strange . . ." Troy murmured. Tapping his foot, he looked around, but still there was no footman in sight. Troy frowned. Arms akimbo, he bellowed, "Oy! Anybody there?" His voice reverberated off the walls from where his ancestors threw him reproachful looks. "What the—"

"My lord."

Troy spun around.

Hill, his eyes round and large in his pale face, came to a halt on the threshold of one of the doors leading to the entrance hall. "Oh, thank God, my lord, that you are home!" he exclaimed. He was in such a jittery state that he even failed to show proper deference to his master. And when he came nearer, he was visibly shaking.

Unnerved by Hill's peculiar behavior, Troy felt his patience slip. "What the deuce is the matter in this house?" he asked harshly.

"Oh, my lord . . ." The old butler turned even paler. "There has been an accident. A dreadful accident. Everybody went down to the village to help."

"An accident?" The worry weighed like lead in Troy's stomach. "Whatever happened?"

For a moment, agitation seemed to rob Hill of speech. His eyes darted past Troy to his friends and the horses, and back again. A nervous tick made his left lid twitch. "The church," he finally managed. "A stroke of lightning hit the church. The roof caught fire, and the bell tower partly . . . it partly crumbled."

His words acted like a punch to Troy's stomach. "How is this possible?" he choked. "That church has withstood storms for several hundred years."

"I do not know, my lord." Warily, the old man shook his head. "But it did crumble, my lord, and the church roof came down. There are people hurt and dead, perhaps. I do not know. Most of the staff went down to see if they could help. To douse the fire at least. I stayed for your return, my lord."

"Damn it all!" The events of the day caught up with Troy, and he felt tiredness dragging his body down. "I trust that at least one maidservant stayed to look after my wife?"

Hill swayed on his feet. "Lady Ravenhurst?" His face lost all remaining color. "I have not seen her since the morning, my lord."

Troy swore—vile words he had learned in the army, in that French prison. Turning, he jumped down the stairs and strode toward Drake and Justin. "There's been an accident in the village. And my wife is not here."

Drake's eyes turned round, Justin's face grim. "Dear God," he said softly.

And for the first time it occurred to Troy that his wife might well have been involved in the accident. *She might be hurt. Or dead.* His heart missed a beat, only to start hammering in his chest the next moment underneath the skin that bore her mark. She might be dead. "I must go to the village," he murmured, and swung himself onto his stallion. His hands, when they picked up the reins, trembled.

Both Drake and Justin got back in the saddle. "We'll come with you," Drake said. "God knows what you'll find."

They rode fast and in strained silence. Troy felt neither the rain nor the cold any longer. His mind whirled with images of his wife's body, broken and bloodied, and he had to fight the bile that rose in his throat. The dark landscape, which he had loved for so long, suddenly seemed to have turned into a beast with a thousand eyes, ready to devour the unwary wanderer should his foot slip. The familiar landmarks became nightmarish visions of the netherworld, his father's ruins a bony finger raised toward the skies, a *mene tekel* in mortar and stone.

Thou art weighed in the balances, and art found wanting, it seemed to say.

And his wife was paying the price.

"No," he groaned. "*No.*" He spurred his horse on, faster, always faster. He could not rest, could never rest, until he had seen his wife. His hand crept up and splayed wide over his chest. *A lily for Lillian.*

"Troy!" Justin's horse drew even with his. "Troy, take heed! The ground's slippery."

Drake came up on his other side. "She will be all right, Troy. I am sure she will be all right. She might not even have been *near* the church when the accident happened. Heck, I'm sure she's spent the day wandering around your gardens!"

Yet Troy just shook his head and rode on at breakneck speed.

You art found wanting . . .

He had behaved abominably, and if his wife was now taken away from him, was paying for his sins, he would carry this guilt for the rest of his life.

There were lanterns lit all around the village, candles in the windows making the rain sparkle like diamonds scattered in the streets. Without conscious thought, Troy let his gaze stray to the familiar bump of the village church against the night-darkened sky, only to find it empty and void of all but clouds and rain.

The normally peaceful and silent night was filled with the sounds of men swearing, of the squelch of people's footsteps as they hurried through the rain, dashing to and fro, from house to house. Above, thunder rolled, and for a moment Troy was thrown back in time, to a bloodied piece of land somewhere in Europe, heavens knew where; he had lost track of times and places. In the end, all fields of death were the same; the stink of the gunpowder smoke, of burnt flesh, the cries of wounded men and animals, the roll of the drums and booming of the cannons all blending together into a symphony of death and destruction, of terror and madness, a man-created never-ending hell—

A flash of lightning made him start.

He blinked several times, and the vision of war vanished,

reverted to a small village struck by disaster. *His* village. *His* people.

He had no time to engage in private musings on his personal horrors.

With a dull thump and a splash of water, his feet landed on the muddy lane. "We'd best go and see who is in charge around here. The vicar most likely," he said over his shoulder, his voice loud and clear. He did not wait for his friends' answer, but strode down the lane, his tired horse stumbling in his wake.

Most of the people did not seem to recognize him in the flickering light. Some started, stared at him, wide-eyed, and mumbled a quick, "Good evening, my lord." Then they hurried on, their steps full of purpose as if they were bent on untold tasks.

Troy shook his head and pushed on. Never had the way through the winding lanes seemed longer; never had the time so dragged on until they finally reached the vicarage, a snug little building with potted flowers in front. Yet this night the rain had pelted down the flowers, had torn the blossoms off the stalks.

The sight made Troy shiver.

Impatiently he pounded on the front door. When it opened, it was not the kind old face of the vicar that greeted him, but the vicar's wife. "Your husband? Is he here?" Troy barked in lieu of a greeting.

With her frilled white cap and her large, round spectacles, Mrs. Norris looked like a startled owl. She blinked, once, twice, before she found her composure. "I'm afraid he is out, my lord. He's taking the rounds, looking after the sick and the wounded."

"Isn't that the doctor's task?" Exasperation made his voice sharp. "Why hasn't anybody sent for him? I doubt that your husband is very skilled in tending wounds."

Confusion registered on Mrs. Norris's face. "My husband? Of course not."

"Troy? What is the matter?" asked Justin as he and Drake stepped up beside him, the reins of the horses dangling from their hands. Seriousness had sharpened their features, creating sterner lines and angles.

"The doctor is still in Keighlin. The vicar is tending the wounded instead."

"That's the most caper-witted scheme I've ever heard," Drake remarked. "Why hasn't anybody fetched the doctor from Keighlin?"

Her eyes almost as large and round as her spectacles, Mrs. Norris looked from one to the other. "But they did, my lord," she said. "One of Lord Ravenhurst's stablehands tried to ride to Keighlin, but the river's swelled and the bridge's been washed away."

"Dear God." Troy rubbed his forehead, fighting the despair that threatened to swallow him up. His wife was missing, his village was in desperate circumstances, and he was as helpless as a kitten.

"Now look, we have to establish some sort of order," Justin said firmly. "Establish what exactly happened, how many are wounded, and then we have to organize the looking after them. Naturally, we must relieve your vicar. I doubt that the poor man is at all able to deal with such a crisis."

Troy nodded. "You are right, of course." He glanced at his friend. "But there is also that other matter." All at once, his chest felt constricted, and he had to take a deep breath before he could go on. "My wife. We have to find her."

"Your wife, my lord?" Mrs. Norris cut in, in a tone of total amazement. "Lady Ravenhurst? But . . . she is the one who is tending the wounded. My husband is only assisting her."

Slowly, ever so slowly, Troy turned back to look at the woman. It was still the vicar's squat wife with the frilly cap and the oversized spectacles, and yet it was as if she had suddenly turned into Pythia, talking in dark riddles that made no sense to the listener.

"I thought you knew, my lord," Mrs. Norris went on. "My Lady Ravenhurst has been helping Mistress Nanette look after the ill for some time now. She was the one who gathered all the herbs, they say. Tonight she was desperate to stay with Mistress Nanette, of course, but in the circumstances. . . ." Her voice trailed away. Her lips lifted in a quick, tremulous smile, while she pulled a white lacy handkerchief out of her sleeve and dabbed at her eyes. "I felt honored when she asked me to stay with her."

Troy swallowed hard. "Stay . . . with Mistress Nanette?" Apprehension sliced through his first relief that his wife was unharmed.

"She was in the church when it happened, you know." Mrs. Norris took off her spectacles as more tears spilled over and slowly ran down her withered cheeks. "She has such a good heart, Mistress Nanette—always thinks of others. She came to light a candle for those who were ill with fever."

"How badly was she hurt?" Troy managed to force the question past his constricted throat.

"Oh, my lord." Mrs. Norris pressed a hand to her mouth. Nevertheless, a muffled sob escaped. "She will not survive the night."

"*Sacre dieu!*" Justin's mutter was almost lost against Drake's sharp inhalation.

Troy closed his eyes. His beautiful, brave wife was somewhere out there, looking after other people, while the person she must love most in the world lay dying.

Drake's voice sounded flat when he asked, "Are there any more people who have sustained such grave injuries?"

With visible effort Mrs. Norris gathered her composure. "No, my lord, we believe not. Some of them were hurt by flying stones and such, and some were burnt when they extinguished the fire, but none so bad ... so bad that—"

"Yes. I quite understand," Drake said softly. "Troy ..."

Troy opened his eyes. "Would you make sure that there is enough dressing material and such? Bring linen down from the Hall, if need be." He turned to his friends. "I should like to see Mistress Nanette." To see if there was anything he could do. "Would you be so kind as to bring me to her, Mrs. Norris?"

She regarded him curiously, yet after she had dabbed at her eyes one last time, she stepped aside to let him in. "Of course, my lord."

He left his sodden coat and jacket in the hallway and, in silence, followed Mrs. Norris up the stairs to a room at the end of the corridor. The first thing he saw when she opened the door was the fire in the hearth. The flames flickered merrily as if the world outside had never turned into chaos. It was a snug little room, the blanket on the bed lovingly crafted to resemble a sea of woolen flowers. However, there was nothing cozy about the petite, old woman who rested on the pile of pillows. Her eyes were closed, her skin so white and transparent that Troy could see the net of blue veins underneath.

"I have given her some laudanum," Mrs. Norris whispered. "We hoped it would ease her pain and make ... her last hours easier." She padded to the bed and touched the old woman's bony hand. "Mistress Nanette? Lord Ravenhurst is here to see you."

The woman's lids fluttered, then her eyes opened, small and dark as a sparrow's. Slowly, she turned her head, and for the first time Troy saw the traces of blood that had dripped from her mouth to her chin. When she caught sight of him, a ghost of a smile flickered over her face.

"You are back, my lord." Her voice was the merest whisper.

"Yes." He stepped into the room, gave a nod to Mrs. Norris as she left.

"Have you . . . found . . . the wolves?"

"There were never any wolves in my forest." He reached for a nearby chair and sat down.

"And yet you . . . went out . . . to hunt them." This time, the smile stayed longer. "You have . . . a good heart . . . my lord." On the woolen blanket her fingers twitched.

He took hold of her hand, held it between his palms to warm her cold flesh. Gently, he stroked his thumb over her aged skin. Her bones felt fragile and tiny like a small bird's. "Hush." A cold, hard lump had become lodged in his throat. "You should not tire yourself thus."

"Ahh." Her eyes closed. "But then . . . there is only one . . . one more journey for me to take." She coughed, a painful, gurgling sound in her chest, and dark blood spilled over her lips. Her fingers spasmed in Troy's hands.

"Here, let me help you." On the small table beside the bed, he spotted a cloth floating in a bowl of water and a decanter of red wine. With one hand he reached for the cloth and wrung out the excess water. Gently, he wiped the blood from the old woman's face. "There. Would you like a bit of wine?"

She nodded, so he poured her a glass. Stabilizing her shoulders with one hand, he held the glass to her lips. She took just the tiniest of sips before she turned her head away. He put the glass down and, with great care, let her sink back against the pillows.

For a few moments, she breathed heavily, exhausted even by this small motion.

Troy's heart clenched painfully as he watched her. Compassion for the old woman mingled with memories of friends he had seen dying on the battlefields of the continent, young hopeful faces squashed and wiped out by a hellish war. He blinked and forced the memories back into the farthest recesses of his mind. Leaning forward, he took the old woman's hand once more.

At his touch, her lids flickered and opened. Her eyes glinted with something like humor. "See?" she whispered. "One last journey. And there is not much time left." Her gaze slid away. "Not much time." Her eyes flickered, widened, and suddenly her hand gripped him tight. Her eyes darted back to meet his. "Lillian. Will you take care of my little girl?" With a surprising boost of strength she straightened, while agitated color suffused her face.

"Mistress Nanette . . ." Troy tried to calm her and keep her down on the bed.

"Will you take care of Lillian?" Her nails dug into his hand. "*Ma petite fille* . . . Will you protect her? Keep her from harm?" The blanket slipped, revealing the bright red stain that blossomed on her white nightgown.

"Yes, yes," Troy soothed, hardly knowing what he was saying. "Of course, I will." If only she would lie down again, so she would not hurt herself even more.

"A rowan tree grows before your house," she muttered. "Guarding the gate from evil. . . . She will not be able to come and get my girl, *mon petite chou-chou*. No, she will not—"

"Nobody will get Lillian," Troy agreed.

The old woman's eyes, dark and ominous, burnt into his. "She is evil . . . *mauvaise, très mauvaise* . . . She took everything . . . everything . . . poisoned our lives."

"Who did?" He tried to steady her with one hand around her shoulders. "Not Lillian?"

Her voice sank down to a near inaudible mutter. "Camille did . . . Camille. He married her . . . *oh, mon pauvre chou-chou,*" she moaned.

"It is all right," Troy soothed. "Your girl is safe. Lillian is safe now."

"She took everything . . . destroyed everything . . . every last memory . . ." Abruptly, her grip on his hand relaxed. Her strength spent, she reverted to a tiny, frail old woman.

He helped her lie down, all the time crooning softly. "It is all right . . . everything is fine . . ."

". . . everything . . ." she murmured, as her eyes drifted closed. ". . . even the locket . . ."

Troy's hands stilled, and he thought his heart did, too. "The locket?"

"My girl's golden locket . . . her mother's locket . . . most precious. She would have taken it. *Mon pauvre chou-chou* . . ."

A sudden, clear image sprung up in Troy's mind: the light glinting on gold flying through the rain. His stomach clenched.

". . . the only keepsakes from her parents . . ."

He remembered the miniatures inside, small, delicate portraits, exquisitely done.

"The most precious thing in all the world . . ." The old woman took a shuddering breath before she drifted off into unconsciousness.

Troy slumped down on the chair, bent forward to rest his elbows on his knees. Groaning, he buried his face in his hands. If he had wanted proof of his wife's innocence, he now had it: the girl's golden locket. A locket he had bartered for safety and the fare to England.

She had given him the thing she held dearest in the world so that he might purchase his freedom. Even when he had hated her most, she had tried to help him as best as she could. Yet, as caught in her stepmother's web as himself, she had had only limited resources. He remembered her as she had been in the prison cell: a sad, gray shadow of the Black Widow, a girl more than a woman. How could he have ever expected a girl to fight a lifelong experience of malice and evil?

His lungs felt constricted. He drew a gasping breath.

And how could I have ever been so caught up in my own pain that I didn't see her suffering? How could he have seen only the bad: *his* humiliation, *his* fear, the degradation of the metal collar around his neck and, even worse, the abasement and the searing pain of the brand.

His hand splayed over his chest.

The searing pain—the sting of which she had later tried to take away with the oil and the salve. And even though she had indeed led him around the garden like a dog on a leash, in the end it had been *she* who had removed the collar. But he had been unable to see beyond his humiliation and the destruction of his pride.

Instead he had projected his own bitterness onto her, had used her as a scapegoat, as if by punishing her he could erase all the bitter memories and regain the feeling of his worth as a man. She had seen him at his lowest, no longer a man, but reduced to an animal, and for this he had wanted to revenge himself upon her. To show her his strength. His *manliness*.

Leaning forward, he tunnelled his hands through his hair, dug his fingers into his scalp. He could have laughed at the grotesqueness of it all.

For all he had achieved was to prove how weak he was. Not in physical strength, but in spirit. Only a weak-spirited man would have so clung to revenge that he had been blinded to another's suffering.

He shook his head and jumped to his feet. He had to do something. He could not just sit here and. . . . He rubbed his neck. Without his volition, his fingers slid around to his throat and then eased under the material of his shirt until he could feel the unevenness of the scar against his fingertips. *A lily for Lillian.*

He drew a deep breath.

His hand fell to his side.

He would get that doctor. Whatever the cost, he would ride to Keighlin and get the doctor.

Later, Troy would always remember this night with a shudder. Assured his friends would organize all the necessary things in the village, he rode back to the Hall and got himself a lantern and a fresh horse, a sturdy carriage horse that might manage the passing through a wild river. And on he rode, through the darkness and the rain, while the wind howled around him and dragged at his clothes. In the distance, the trees of the forest huddled together like a giant beast, ready to pounce. But he was not deterred, nor did he feel the cold biting his bones. Brighter than any flame, determination burned in him, urged him on, and on, and on.

This was the land of his birth, the land he had roamed since he was a little boy, the land that was in his blood. He knew this place inside out. He would not be delayed by whatever the elements threw at him.

He knew a ford further upstream, where the old road had been before his grandfather had the bridge and a new better road built. The rain had transformed the river into a raging, foaming monster that greedily lapped at the land beyond the riverbed. To attempt a crossing now was madness.

Troy shook the rain out of his eyes and calmed his nervous horse. He watched the river, observed the flood as he would an opponent on the battlefield. The water ran high, but not so high to hold him back. The current would be the greater threat. But his horse was strong, used to carrying heavy loads. Surely, it would be strong enough to withstand the river.

He urged the horse forward, into the foaming flood. Soon, the river reached greedily up, slurping and gurgling, slapped water against his boots—and still, he pressed the horse on. Inch by inch they defied the river; inch by inch they came nearer to the bank on the other side. And finally, with a sucking sound, the river released them, and the horse stepped free of the water.

"Good boy." Troy bent forward to sling his arms around the animal's neck. "Such a brave boy you are." The horse might lack the blood, but it certainly had bottom and bone.

Without faltering, it carried him on to Keighlin, where Troy proceeded to ring the doctor out of bed. Still a young man, with a shiny, pink face that was creased with worry, the physician might have been game for an adventure in the first place. More likely, though, he was loath to argue with a man who looked as if he'd just been dragged through hell. So the man packed his bag, saddled his horse and rode back with Troy.

By the time they reached Ravenhurst lands, the rain had stopped and the wind had chased away the clouds to reveal the pale twinkle of the last stars against the gray sky. Fatigue and exhaustion made Troy lightheaded. Yet unerringly, he led the doctor through the winding lanes to the vicar's house.

The vicar himself opened the door, his eyes growing wide as he saw who was standing on the threshold. Troy swayed on his feet and clutched the door frame to steady himself. "Mr. Norris. I've brought the doctor for Mistress Nanette."

The vicar took their coats and sodden jackets and brought them towels, so they could dry their hands and faces before he led them upstairs. In the little room, Mrs. Norris sat with the old woman—as did Troy's wife. *His wife.* Troy leaned against the wall to let the doctor pass. *Alive and well.* His vision seemed to blur as he feasted his eyes on the girl whom he had married, the girl who had saved him from the Black Widow's malice and cruelty. His hand reached up and clutched at his shirt, where underneath the material the lily bloomed on his chest.

A lily for Lillian.

She started when the doctor touched her shoulder, and when she half turned, her mouth formed a perfect circle of astonishment. She stumbled to her feet, awkward in her haste to make room. And Troy saw what toll the night had taken on her: mud and bloodstains soiled her erstwhile white dress. Her hair had come undone and hung in loose, matted strands around her face; her skin was gray with exhaustion. Still, to him she had never been more beautiful.

Then she spotted him and froze.

It took Lillian a moment to recognize him, damp and bedraggled as he was, so far removed from the immaculate gentleman. No, he looked more like a particularly large rat, drowned twice over. Strain and tiredness had etched deep lines into his face, lending him a haggard appearance and reminding her of how he had looked chained to Camille's construction. His cornflower-blue eyes burned with the same intensity as then, yet with an entirely different emotion. He stared at her as if he had never seen her before, his gaze curiously hungry.

Behind her, Nanette made a sound, and Lillian's head whipped around. The doctor had started to unbutton the old woman's nightgown, baring the blood-soaked bandage underneath. The doctor . . . they had not been able to get the doctor because the bridge had been washed away.

Very slowly, Lillian looked back at Ravenhurst. Like the young doctor, he was wearing only a sodden shirt and trousers. She took a step toward him.

With a barely suppressed exclamation, he strode across the room to her side. He searched her face, and then his arms were around her, enveloping her in warmth. She did not mind the dampness of his shirt, if only she could hold on to the warmth a little longer, a shield to protect her while her world came apart at the seams.

Just one little moment of brief protection.

With a sigh she rested her face against his chest. Strong and steady, his heart thumped against her ear as if to welcome her. As if this were the place God had created for her of this man's flesh and bone.

The flesh she had marked with her brand.

Lillian shuddered violently.

Immediately, his arms tightened around her. "Hush," he murmured against her temple. "Hush. Everything will be all right, my dear. Just hush." With a sob she let herself be pressed back against the strong wall of his chest, a haven in the midst of chaos.

She should have known, though, that in the end the coldness would return for her, that for her there would be no happily ever after.

When the doctor finally cleaned his instruments and put them back into his bag, Nanette had slipped deeper into unconsciousness. Ashen color tinged the doctor's round, young face, while he explained that the old woman was beyond human help. "Her life rests in the hands of the Lord."

Lillian stepped out of her husband's arms, while she felt the coldness gather in the corners of the room like a wild beast, ready to pounce and devour her whole. "Can I hold her hand?" she whispered.

"Of course. I am sure it would bring her comfort, even where she is now."

She took the chair that Mrs. Norris had abandoned earlier, and sat down beside the bed. With the ease of lifelong familiarity, Lillian slipped her hand into Nanette's and held on tight. The old woman's fingers felt so fragile within her own, the skin wrinkled and thin like parchment. Lillian's heart constricted as she stared at her old nanny's beloved face.

She hardly heard the door open and close as the doctor left the room. Yet when her husband put a gentle hand on her shoulder, she flinched.

Immediately, he removed his fingers. Deep grooves bracketed his mouth. "Can I bring you something?"

She shook her head.

She started when he brought himself a chair from the other end of the room and set it down beside her. "You do not need to stay," she said. She almost did not recognize her own voice, flat and dead.

"I think I do." He sank down on his chair. "Will you allow me this?"

She stared at him a moment longer. Why would he tempt her with illusions of warmth and security? They were just that: illusions. For her, there was only the cold. So she lifted her shoulders in a small shrug and turned her attention back to Nanette. "If you want to." It was all the same to her, for the coldness would return one way or the other.

Troy had to swallow several times to dislodge the lump that formed in his throat as he watched his wife holding on to her old nanny's hand, a small child holding on to her mother in the midst of a storm.

But the storm would swallow her up nonetheless.

He had failed her—bitterly, bitterly failed her. He had misjudged her, ruined her, forced her into a travesty of a marriage, and now he had even failed to protect her from this loss.

Tears burned in Troy's eyes as he picked up his wife's free hand, the hand of the girl who had saved him from the Black Widow's malice and cruelty. He cradled her fingers between his own and warmed them with his flesh. She did not protest, but neither did she look at him. And thus, they sat in silence through the rest of the night, until the candles had burned down and Troy's fingers had grown numb. Outside the birds broke into jubilant song. The blush of a new dawn colored the horizon, and together with the night, Mistress Nanette's life ebbed away.

Chapter 16

Troy saw to it that the old woman's body was brought back to the Hall. Then he ordered his coach so he could bring his wife home. She was very pale, exhaustion bleaching her skin of all color except for the shadows below her eyes, which resembled painful bruises. When she stood, she swayed on her feet, so Troy slipped his arm around her and pulled her against him to lend her the support of his body. Her eyes dim and flat, she let him guide her out of the house into the bright light of the new morning.

After the rain everything glinted and glistened, freshly washed, and it seemed to Troy that all things had taken on a new brilliance as if created anew. Beside him, his wife trembled like a leaf in the wind, a child lost in a world that no longer made any sense. He drew her tighter against him. "Everything will be all right," he whispered.

She did not react any more than would a statue carved out of ice.

And so, while waiting for his coach on the vicar's doorstep, Troy pressed his lips against his wife's dark curls and wished they had the kind of relationship where he could bundle her off to bed, hold her in his arms and offer her the comfort of his body. But in this, he had failed her as well.

He closed his eyes. "How I wish things would have been different," he murmured. But now all he could do was bring her home and make sure that a maid saw after her, that Nanette's body was washed and laid out, that candles were lit. Like an old gray mouse, Hill padded through the Hall, from room to room, to close the shutters, veil the mirrors and stop all clocks. Silence settled on the house. Even the Weimaraners remained hushed, as if they too knew of the young mistress's horrible loss.

Troy only washed, shaved and changed clothes before he went back to the village with Justin to oversee and help with the clearing work. Drake, meanwhile, remained at the Hall in case Troy's countess needed the comfort of a friend. It pained Troy that her friend could not be him.

In the afternoon, when their clothes were smudged with dirt and mud, Troy caught up with the doctor, who had gone from house to house, looking after the wounded and the ill. Yet all he had done was change a dressing here or there, and clean a wound that had ripped open again.

"Whoever looked after these people did a very fine job of it," the doctor said.

Bittersweet pain sliced Troy's heart. "My wife did," he said.

At that, the young doctor raised his brows. "Well, well, this is most unusual. Yet as I said, she did a very fine job. All broken bones are set correctly, all wounds are properly dressed and stitched. . . ."

Troy gave the rosy-faced young man a tight smile. "My wife is very knowledgeable in the art of healing." Another memory sprung up. How she had tended *his* wounds that first evening, had spread salve over his torn and burnt flesh. Only now, the pain was worse than when the brand had seared his skin.

261

Shuddering, Troy closed his eyes.

The young doctor left with the promise to come back in a few days. Troy was grateful for this; he did not know whether his wife would be ready to care for her patients herself.

Upon Troy's return, he found that his wife had several of her dresses dyed black. He refrained from pointing out that it was not seeming to wear full mourning for a mere servant. Mistress Nanette had clearly been more. Out of respect for the old woman, he found himself a piece of crepe to wear around his arm.

Until the funeral, his wife sat with her old nanny, the flower fairy having reverted back to the sad, gray ghost he had met in France. Whenever he thought of France, a vise constricted around Troy's heart. Because of his own fear and pain he had been unable to sense hers, had been unable to see past anything other than the violence he'd suffered. And yet, all that time, Lillian had tried to help him, to protect him. She had set him free—in more ways than one. Apart from Jus and Drake, she was the only person who had ever stood up for him—and that was not an easy feat in her circumstances.

He tried to envision her childhood and youth, spent in that hellish château in France, cut off from all human company, indeed, cut off from all humanity. How she had survived was beyond him. He marveled at her endurance in the face of the worst adversity, at the will of steel that even her stepmother had not been able to twist. And he admired the courage with which she had taken her life in her own hands when she had fled from Château du Marais, and once again when she fashioned a new life for herself here at Bair Hall. For she had clearly done that: the villagers asked after her, and his friends adored her. While his own anger and hatred had poisoned the atmosphere at the Hall, she had gone out and been happy, had made herself a flower queen of his fields and gardens. This was the girl who had freed him from Camille's shackles and had later lied to her stepmother to protect him from her—when it should have been him protecting his wife.

It humbled him.

And it filled him with deep gratitude toward the woman he had married. With gratitude and more—so much more.

But after all that had happened, how could he expect she would ever forgive him? For ruining her, for forcing her into this marriage, for nearly raping her on their wedding night. He shuddered when he thought of that. He despised himself for it, the self-contempt churning in his stomach. How could he ever have sunk so low? Driven by a base need for revenge, all unjustified. It was indeed he who needed forgiveness. It had never been her, never been Lillian, whose only sin consisted of being a girl, as much a victim of her stepmother as himself.

How could she ever forgive him?

He watched her during the funeral as she stood at Nanette's grave, still, as if she were one of the statues that adorned so many churchyards. A sad angel, clad in the bleakest of colors. Yet even wearing deepest black, she did in no way resemble *la Veuve Noire*. Her delicate features did not mirror her stepmother's malice, but revealed only loneliness. Deep loneliness. He wondered how he could have ever thought otherwise.

It seemed to Troy that he had woken from a long, dark dream. And now it was time to set his life to rights to prove to his wife that he was worthy of her after all.

How strange it was that life outside had not died, that the birds should still sing, that horse chestnuts, round and shining, would litter the park, and that the rowan tree at the gate would be aglow with a thousand red berries. Should they not all be withered and dead?

When Lillian wandered around the grounds she now knew so well, she, at least, felt withered and wilted, as if a part of her had died with Nanette. Whenever she stepped into the countess's sun parlor, she almost expected to hear the merry clicking of Nanette's needles; and when she stepped into the kitchen in the afternoon, she would wonder why it did not smell of melting wax, of mint and dried herbs. Never again would she feel cherished in lavender-scented embraces, would she see the petite figure of her old nanny slip through the woods with the light step of a young girl.

With Nanette, Lillian had lost the last bridge to her childhood and to happier years. Now there was nobody on this whole wide earth who had been present when Lillian had taken her first step or smiled for the very first time. Forgotten was the first word she had spoken, the first drawing she had made and the name of her first doll. Everything was lost in the past, the memories gone like sand in the wind.

And so, the coldness returned to reach for Lillian, to envelop her in its icy embrace until it had dimmed the pain.

What did it matter then that her husband wanted to leave for France? She did not know why he wanted to return there. She did not care. It did not touch her. Nothing ever would. Never again.

On the day he left, she stood on the front steps of Bair Hall together with his friends and their dogs, while the servants hovered in the entrance hall behind them. She noticed how the sun glinted on her husband's hair, little, dark flames dancing around his head. Her gaze wandered on, to the bright blue sky, which was dotted with a few white clouds, sheep of the air.

"My lady," her husband said.

She blinked.

He stood in front of her, on the step below so that their eyes were almost level. She had not heard him come so near.

"Lillian," he said. His warm, large hand cupped her cold cheek, and for a moment she was tempted to snuggle closer to that warmth. But then, the coldness from the stone beneath her seeped through her shoes, into her flesh, traveled upward until the cold erased his tempting warmth.

His thumb slowly rubbed over her skin, and she saw that his eyes were as blue as the sky. "Before I leave I wanted to tell you . . ." Even his voice was soft and warm. "I know it is too late this year, but I wanted you to know that you can fill this house with flowers if you wish. And that, should you prefer to change the decoration, you can do that, too." He regarded her solemnly, and his thumb rubbed over her cheek. Again she was tempted to cuddle closer to the warmth he offered.

Yet warmth, she knew, was an illusion. It was better to reach for the cold, to cloak oneself in ice. Feelings made one vulnerable, and Lillian could not afford vulnerability. Therefore she stood unmoving, proud and erect, until his hand dropped away and something like sorrow shadowed his eyes.

She watched how he hugged his friends, a display of camaraderie and affection, how he patted the dogs' heads and set their tails wagging. She watched how he climbed into his carriage, how the footman closed the door. She heard the cracking of the reins, the crunching of the gravel when the coach drove off. Her husband lifted his hand, waved, and then he was gone, too.

Lillian closed her eyes.

It seemed to her that the wind picked up and caressed her cheek until it had chilled her flesh and, like a jealous lover, had wiped out all memory of another's caress.

She went into the gardens then, roamed the grounds without aim, the wind her only companion. In time, the days and weeks blurred and melted into one. She watched the leaves of the trees turn yellow and fall, the Michaelmas daisy wilt. She saw the birds gathering and watched them leave for the warmer regions of the south. And when her gaze followed their path, she would sometimes pause and stand on the hill where the fourth earl's artificial ruins stretched to touch the sky. She would stand and look toward the south and remember the expression in her husband's eyes when he had taken his leave. She would pray for his safe return then, and told the birds to take her greetings with them.

To track down the single golden locket he had sold months before, proved remarkably easy. All it took was time and patience to find the ship that had brought him back to England. Troy bought himself a mean-tempered brute of a horse and rode along the coast, traveling mile after mile in search of his treasure. The wind blew into his face, the land rushed by, and frequently his stallion would attempt to take a bite out of its master. Troy thumped its nose and boxed its ears, and with time, they came to an understanding. He would catch himself talking affectionately to the mean old horse, his only companion on this quest.

As he slipped easily back into French, and because the months at prison had roughened his tone and accent, the fishermen in the small villages and the sailors in the bigger ports never suspected that he was one of the hated English. They threw him a curious glance or two, but a man who wanted to repay another a favor done in the past was not such an oddity that they would not help him. He found his captain in Roscoff, where the white chapel of Saint Barbe stood guard over the Roscovian sailors, pirates all, if legend was to be believed. This was the land where Saint Pol had overcome a horrible dragon, where Perceval had searched out the Holy Grail. A golden locket might not be as precious as the chalice that had held the blood of the Lord, yet it was precious enough to Troy, a magic talisman to heal and start anew.

Therefore he sat patiently in the shabby tavern, stood jug after jug of the cheap sour wine, listened to the captain's tales of woe, and finally added some placating gold to the wine. The captain, he found, had sold the locket to a pawnbroker in Le Havre, but the man would have had to send the locket inland, to Paris, perhaps. Sailors did not buy their *bien-aimées* such a golden trinket.

So Troy rode on to Le Havre, while his clothes took on the grubby look of one who lived on the roads. He ignored the dull throbbing in his leg as he pressed his horse on day after day in an easy rhythm that carried them from dawn till dusk. Dust and dirt darkened his hair to a dull brown. Yet while the knights of old could expect a hot bath after a day on the road and a servant who scratched the rust and dirt off their skin, the small pitchers of water Troy found in the rooms of the dingy inns on the way were barely sufficient to clean his hands and his face. When he finally reached Le Havre, he felt like one of the Roscovian pirates himself, grubby, limping, his face covered with several days' worth of stubble.

In one of the town's narrow winding roads, he eventually found Monsieur Fatras's neat little pawnshop, stuffed up to under the roof with small boxes, meticulously labeled. Monsieur Fatras himself was a small, spindly man, peering at Troy through a pair of round spectacles. With his tufts of white hair, he looked rather like an Irish leprechaun and turned out to be as cunning and wily. Yet he still had the *médaillon d'or*, for apparently he had been charmed by the portraits inside, carried out with loving attention to detail. In the end, though, Monsieur Fatras was much more charmed by the small heap of gold that Troy left on his counter; thirty or fifty times as much as he had paid the captain for it. And so the locket Troy had been given on a muddy road in the waning light of a rainy day almost a year ago, came back into his possession.

No, not into his possession.

Into his keeping.

He took his treasure and his horse and looked for an English ship that might carry them across the channel. He arrived in Portsmouth, reeking of old fish and the sea. After the time on a rocking ship, his horse was meaner than ever—and who else would ever want to buy such a brute of a horse? If Troy sold it, the stupid beast would likely end as an ingredient of fake French sausage: not the fate a man wished for a horse that had carried him to the treasure of his heart. Thus, selling was out of the question. A tough, tenacious animal, the stallion would carry him back home just as it had carried him through Brittany and back again. Besides, he had grown fond of the beast; it seemed to him a Brueberry reborn. And never had there been a more faithful companion than Brueberry the Horrible.

So Troy pressed his horse on, northward this time, English roads adding to the layers of French dirt and dust. It was exhilarating, this ride. With the wind in his face and the weight of the golden locket in his breast pocket, Troy felt freer than he had in months, years even. As the past slipped from his shoulders like an old, discarded cloak, his thoughts flew ahead of him, to the woman at Bair Hall, his wife.

His brave, beautiful wife.

And then he urged his horse on, to go just a little bit faster, until finally, finally the towers of Bair Hall rose in the distance like loyal guards.

Troy reined his stallion in to enjoy the view, to treasure the moment. *I'm home*, he thought, and deep gratitude filled him. *I'm finally coming home.*

When he rode through the gates, thrown open as if in an embrace, he saw that the rowan tree had shed almost all its leaves and was now adorned with bright red berries. The sight made him smile. *Rowan tree, witchen-tree, guardian of the house. . . .*

His smile deepened when he heard Nolan's voice behind him. "Afternoon, Master Troy. Happy return home."

Troy turned in the saddle to greet the old gatekeeper. "Good afternoon, Nolan. And thank you."

As he rode on under the mighty oak trees up the drive, he remembered the old woman, small and frail, who had reminded him of a fairy godmother from a children's tale. Her voice seemed to whisper on the wind that brushed through the trees above and rustled in the fallen leaves along the way. *For no evil shall come to a house that is guarded by a rowan tree. . . .*

Happiness let him forget his tiredness and the dust of the road. Never had there been a more beautiful sight than the entrance of Bair Hall when he came out of the tree-lined walk. He slid out of the saddle, careful of his bad leg. Yet even as his feet hit the ground, he realized the pain was almost gone. All that remained was a small, niggling ache as if of sore muscles.

A grin lifted Troy's lips. *Perhaps I have found my own, personal Grail after all.*

Sandra Schwab

While he hurried up the front stairs, Hill threw open the door. "Oh, my lord. I heard a commotion on the drive . . ." The face of the old man crinkled into an unbutler-like smile. "Welcome home, my lord."

"Thank you, Hill." Troy shrugged out of his coat and gave it to his butler. "Is my wife in? No? Lord Allenbright and Mr. de la Mere? Not in either. Hm, well, I need a nice hot bath anyway before I'm fit for civilized company." He grinned. He could have hugged the whole world—including Hill. Only, that would give the poor man the shock of his life. "Could you ask Mrs. Blake to send a tray with some food up to my room? I am ravenous, really. Oh, and will you send somebody to see after my horse?"

"Of course, my lord."

"And do tell them to take care, do you hear, Hill? It's a second Brueberry, that horse!" With that, he hurried up the stairs, taking two at a time. God, it was good to be home, to breathe in the familiar scent of wood polish with just the faintest hint of—he sniffed—old mortar and stone. And wet dog.

He wrinkled his nose, then laughed.

At least Drake's and Jus's mad dogs filled the house with life and bursting joy. Exactly what such a dignified, old building needed.

Flowers would be nice, too. Troy sighed. Of course, it was much too late in the year to fill the house with flowers. He would have liked it, though. Perhaps they could set up a hothouse somewhere in the park, so they would have flowers in the winters to come. He would have to talk with his wife about that.

His wife . . .

Whistling, he strode down the corridor to his rooms. After the days on the road, his large, clean bedroom seemed like heaven. A heaven of soothing dark green and

270

burgundy red, with the big four-poster decked in pristine white. No bedbug would worry him in *there*.

He gave a contented sigh. Yes, it was good to be home.

He looked back to the bed and tried to imagine the pale flesh of his wife between the sheets, her flowery scent soaking his pillows. But, no.

Troy shook his head to banish the erotic images that fogged his brain. It would take time before he won her trust, much time before he would be able to indulge in sensual games in his bed.

Sighing, he stowed the golden locket in his chest of drawers. What would she say when he gave it to her? Would she understand his gesture? Would she understand that he wanted to start anew? And, more importantly, would she forgive him all the truly ghastly mistakes he had made?

His reveries were interrupted by a maid who brought him a platter laden with sandwiches, cold meat and chicken legs, as well as a jug of wine. At the sight, his somber mood lightened. In the bathroom he could hear the footmen setting up the tub and filling it with buckets of hot water.

Happily, he munched on a cucumber sandwich while fumbling with the buttons of his jacket and waistcoat. They landed in a bundle on the floor, and he jumped around the room, trying to get his boots off his feet. "Phew. Guess I need a new pair of boots." He considered throwing the smelly shoes out of the window. But then they would land on the drive, and how would that look?

Shaking his head, Troy shed his shirt and left it on a chair before he got himself some fresh clothes and padded into the bathroom. The steam of the hot water and the scent of clean soap nearly made him dizzy with joy.

Quickly, he got rid of the rest of his clothes. Afterwards he could finally, finally sink down into the warm water. He let the warmth seep deep into his bones before he started to rub the grime of the road off his skin. Soon, the lather of the rosemary-and-lemon soap had dispelled all lingering unpleasant smells. And when he rose from the tub, he felt wonderfully clean from the top of his head to the tips of toes. He dried himself with the soft towel, rubbed his hair until it hung into his eyes in glorious disarray. After weeks his scalp no longer itched with dust and dirt. He truly felt like a man reborn.

With a grin he slipped into the fresh clothes, the white shirt billowing around his torso like a tufty, white cloud. *And now a nice glass of wine . . .* Whistling, he went back into his bedroom—and stopped dead.

"So I was right. It was you on the road," said *la Veuve Noire* and smiled. She lounged on his bed like a sleek, black cat with cruel, cold eyes. "Take him."

Only then did he become aware of the presence of the two men behind him who had stood like statues carved of stone on either side of the door. There were two of them and they had the benefit of surprise.

He never stood a chance.

But, oh, how he struggled. Even as rough hands twisted his arms behind his back, wrenched them until the pain made him gasp.

The woman's trilling laughter filled the room. "Did you really think I would not find out? *Och, mon petit niais,* it was so easy to find out. A question here, a question there—*voilà*. You will not slip away a second time, oh no. I will put you to such good use."

Lillian had been right all along.

Panic surged up in Troy as he sought to evade the rough hands, hands that had handled his body before. Remembered hurt and humiliation lent him strength.

Never again.

A shove of his shoulder. A loud clatter. He managed to get one arm free. His hand reached out. The ripping of material. Then a blow to his head, causing an explosion of new pain.

Dazed, Troy fell onto the bed. From a great distance, he heard the woman's voice, full of malice: "But of course we will leave a small souvenir for *ma chère fille*. . . ."

A searing pain at his ear, and then—darkness.

PART V

And on her lover's arm she leant,
And round her waist she felt it fold,
And far across the hills they went
In that new world which is the old:
Across the hills, and far away
Beyond their utmost purple rim,
And deep into the dying day
The happy princess follow'd him.

—Tennyson, The Day Dream

Chapter 17

Before Lillian had even reached the top step to the entrance of the Hall, the door swung open with a flourish. "Oh, my lady." Hill beamed at her, his old face creased with wrinkles of happiness. "The master has returned."

"Lord Ravenhurst has returned?" she echoed. Her heart missed a beat—only to start thumping uncomfortably loudly afterwards.

Hill stood back to let her pass. "Dusty from the road, but else fresh as a pin."

To freeze her hammering heartbeat, Lillian reached for the chill in the stone. "He rode?" The coldness trickled through her veins, but, oh, too slow, much too slow.

"Bought himself a mean old horse and named it Brueberry the Second." The old butler looked ready to burst with joy. "Oh, my lady, after all this time, the master is finally acting like himself again!"

His joy was so contagious that, despite herself, Lillian felt her lips curve into a smile and the precious coldness ebb away. "That is lovely," she said softly and crossed the threshold into the entrance hall. Yet the moment she stepped into the house she knew something was wrong. It might have been a change in the atmosphere, a whiff of perfume still lingering, but whatever it was, it made the skin of her neck prickle with unease.

Her smile faded as quickly as it had come. Concerned, she turned back to the butler. "Have there been any visitors today?"

"Visitors?" A puzzled frown appeared on Hill's face as if he found the concept of visitors to Bair Hall completely beyond his experience. "Like Lord Allenbright and Mr. de la Mere?" he asked carefully.

Lillian nodded.

His expression lit up. "There were no visitors, my lady."

"Nobody called?" she pressed.

"Nobody, my lady."

Uneasily, she glanced around the hall in an attempt to locate the source of her apprehension. Apart from the first earl's bear having a more munched-on look than ever before, she could not detect any differences.

"Are Lord Allenbright and Mr. de la Mere in?" she asked with mounting anxiousness.

"No, my lady," Hill answered in dignified tones, apparently quite relieved to be back on familiar turf. "They went for a drive in the gig, and Mrs. Blake packed them a basket for a picnic."

"I see." Lillian hurried toward the stairs. "And Lord Ravenhurst is in his room?"

"He sent for a bath, I believe."

"Thank you, Hill." Her stomach churning, Lillian gathered up her skirts and rushed up the stairs. She did not care whether her exit looked undignified or what the old butler might think about it. She just wanted to see her husband, wanted to reassure herself that he had come home safe and sound. Never before had the stairs seemed so numerous, the way into the wing with the private apartments so long.

An eerie silence reigned in the empty hallways of the upper floor. For a breathless moment Lillian felt as if caught in a nightmare of deserted corridors with closed doors. It made her hasten her steps until she was almost running.

Finally, *finally*, she reached the door to the master bedroom. Here, however, Lillian hesitated. Her fears suddenly seemed childish and fanciful.

She stared at the solid wood of the door.

She was a grown woman, not a child prone to tears because of a bad dream in the middle of the night.

And then, it came again. A feeling of unease washed over her, stronger than before, and left her so weak-kneed she nearly stumbled.

"Dear God," she murmured. "Dear God." When she raised her hand to knock on the door, she saw that her fingers were trembling. She only managed a weak rap against the wood, which Ravenhurst surely did not hear, for she received no answer.

A second knock, louder this time, also brought no reply.

Perhaps he was still in the bathroom, was still soaking in the bathtub; perhaps he could not hear her because of that. Perhaps. . . .

Yet her clammy fingers had already clenched the doorknob and turned it. The door swung open, revealed a view into the room in dark green and burgundy red, an empty room, a silent room. No splashing of water to be heard.

Her heart leapt into her mouth.

Where is he?

She strode into the room, looked around.

It was still empty, still silent. Yet the creases in the bedspread of the large four-poster, a carelessly discarded dirty shirt across the padded chair, a small dusty bundle of luggage, all revealed that he had been here. And sure enough, the room smelled of soap, the rosemary and lemon he preferred, underlaid by a hint of . . . a hint of . . .

Lillian went icy cold.

No. No, it cannot be!

She scanned the room once more.

A silver box on the floor in the corner, the cheroots spilled over the expensive carpet.

A tear in the dark, heavy bed curtain.

A splatter of blood against the white of the bedspread.

Lillian gasped.

No. Please, God, no!

An icy fist clenched around her chest, pressed the air from her lungs until her knees buckled and she sank down to the floor, panting. "No," she sobbed. "No. Not him." She thumped her fist onto the thick carpet, again and again. "*No*," she howled. "You cannot take him, too!"

Breathing hard, she let her chin sink on her chest. *Damn you, Camille, damn you. I wish I had poisoned you after all!* Bitter remorse cut through her. If only she had been stronger. *But you weren't. And now he has to pay the price for it.*

"No." Lillian fought against the panic that welled up inside her. *Think, Lillian! Think! If she has taken him, she would not leave like that. Surely she would leave a message. Something.* Lillian blinked. Yes, a message. Her stepmother relished power games. If Camille had found out about Ravenhurst, if she had abducted him, she would want Lillian to know what she would be doing to him. There *had* to be a message.

Stumbling, Lillian came to her feet. "Where?" she whispered. "*Where?*"

Frantically, she looked around the room, searched his

bathroom, his dressing room, raced through the adjoining door into the countess's dressing room, where the wardrobes were full of her clothes, through the door into the bedroom, and farther into the countess's sun parlor at the far end of the wing. And there, on the table, she spotted the letter. It leaned against a small bundle, something that resembled a handkerchief marred by rust-brown stains.

With trembling fingers, Lillian picked up the letter and opened it.

Chérie—
I believe I have something of yours. If you want it back you have to come to me. Meet me at the big boulder in the forest. I have left you something so you see that I am speaking the truth.

C.

Lillian swallowed hard before she dared reach for the small bundle on the table. It weighed next to nothing, yet the brown stains had stiffened the fabric, and it revealed its contents only reluctantly. Carefully, Lillian smoothed the material, rubbing her thumb over the corner where the fabric was still clean and white, over the neat, tiny stitches of the monogram. *MS*, intertwining, for Murgatroyd Sacheverell. Again and again, she rubbed her thumb over his initials and stared at the tiny thing that nestled in the stained folds of the handkerchief.

At first she did not recognize the thing, alien as it looked, all smeared with brown and red, at places so dark it was almost black. It might have shriveled a bit, so it took some time before the shapes began to make sense, before Lillian's mind was able to supply the missing bits.

Camille would never cut off a piece of flesh she still

might have some use for, such as a finger, a tongue or even a toe.

Lillian closed her eyes.

Instead, she had cut off the lower part of his ear.

Acid bile rose in Lillian's throat, choked her. "Damn you, Camille," she whispered. "Damn you for this."

Nanette had been wrong all along: Troy would not be able to protect her from harm, for he himself had fallen prey to malevolence, to evil. *Again.*

There was nobody to keep her safe.

Only herself.

Only me.

Taking a deep breath, Lillian straightened. All the fear and horror seemed to slide off her and was replaced by a crystal-clear coolness, so different from the paralyzing, numbing cold that had held her in its icy grip for so long.

She put the bloodied handkerchief back on the table.

She knew what she had to do.

She retraced her steps all the way to his bedroom and from there into his study. His gray greatcoat hung discarded over the backrest of the leather-upholstered chair as if he were about to return for it any moment. In one of the drawers of his desk Lillian found the small pistol that Allenbright and de la Mere had given to him as a present, the same model de la Mere had enthused over on the evening of Lady Holland's dinner party. Her husband's voice echoed in Lillian's head: *I do not think my wife is in need of a pocket pistol. Or any other weapon, come to that.*

He had looked so handsome that night, tall and strong, as if nothing could harm him.

"But you were wrong," she murmured as her fingers closed around the cool metal. A pistol small enough to fit in a woman's reticule, small enough to fit in the pocket of a man's coat, unseen.

She took his coat then. The thick material settled heavily on her shoulders, fell down to her feet. She had to roll up the sleeves. Yet the coat was warm and draped enough that the pistol would go unnoticed.

With long, determined strides she went out of the room, to the main staircase and down into the entrance hall. As the coat flapped against her legs, a feeling of power surged through her. This time, she would not stand by and watch.

"Hill." Loud and clear, her voice rang in the hall. "Have Lord Allenbright and Mr. de la Mere said where they would be heading? Good. Send a footman to fetch them. I want them to come to the clearing with the great boulder in the forest. They must come armed, do you hear me? My stepmother has abducted Lord Ravenhurst and she is. . . ." Lillian faltered.

"My lady?" Eyes wide, Hill stared at her.

Lillian straightened her shoulders. "Quick, Hill. Do as I say. Else she will kill him."

The old butler's face turned pasty white. "Kill him? M-my lady . . . one of the footmen could go . . . surely . . ."

She considered this idea for a moment. But the footmen were all either old men or young boys. "No." She shook her head. "Send somebody to fetch Lord Allenbright and Mr. de la Mere. Quick!" With that she hurried toward the door.

"My . . . my lady!" Hill spluttered. "Surely you do not want . . . you cannot . . ."

"Oh, I *must*, Hill," Lillian said grimly. "After all, I have known her for most of my life. There is nobody who knows her as well as I do."

She rushed out of the door, down the drive of Bair Hall. She knew where the clearing was Camille had spoken of, yet she also knew that it would take her the better part of an hour to walk there. She tried not to think of what would happen to him if she took too long, if Camille grew impatient and displeased. Lillian had to force herself not to run, for exhausting herself would help neither her nor her husband.

Doggedly she marched on, through fields and meadows, not caring that the hem of her dress, of her coat, became wet and muddy.

Her mind whirled with images of her husband—from the dirty, bedraggled prisoner to the proud earl, from the hateful stranger to the reclusive man under whose roof she lived. She remembered the moments of his intense anger, but also the moments when she had caught glimpses of the other man—the man with the quick humor, the strong sense of family, of honor. The man who believed in friendship and loyalty, who suffered the gradual destruction of his forebear's hunting trophies without ever batting an eye. The man who could cast his own inner torment aside and show compassion, who would brave the elements to fetch a doctor for a dying woman. The man who, despite all that had happened to him, was still capable of tenderness.

Lillian bit her lip and clenched her hands into fists so she would not start crying.

Everything needs balance, whispered Nanette's voice in her head. *One to do the healing in a place where another does all the wounding.*

And he had been wounded so very dreadfully in the past. She simply could not let it happen again. And so, she thrust the images of her husband aside and marched on, one foot in front of the other, into the shadows of trees. She did not care whether the dead leaves of the past years stuck to her clothes, whether she had to press through thorny hedges, or whether cobwebs caught in her hair.

She walked on and on, her back straight, her head held high. And finally, the trees thinned out, and with one last stride Lillian stepped out into the clearing.

They had bound him to the boulder, his back pressed against the stone, the rope around his hands fastened on a tree behind, stretching his body taut. His legs were spread wide and ropes around his ankles secured them to the pegs that were buried deep in the earth. He was conscious and still wearing his shirt and breeches, she saw, with no marks of a beating yet visible. On the side where they had cut off his earlobe his shirt was soiled with blood, and between his teeth glinted the metal of one of Camille's bridles.

Lillian hoped they had not heated it before they had shoved it into his mouth.

"Ah, look whom we have here." In perfect, melodious French. Across the clearing, her stepmother smiled while idly playing with a small knife. "It is a pleasure to have you here, *chérie*." Maurice and Antoine stood behind her, patiently waiting for orders.

Black silk rustled as Camille slowly came nearer.

"We have . . . ahh . . . *regained* your little present." The tip of her knife pointed toward the bound man. But Lillian's attention remained fixed on her stepmother.

"So I see."

"I have decided to take it back with me." The blood-red lips curved some more.

"To France?"

"*Naturellement*." Suddenly, Camille's eyes narrowed. "But now that you have spoilt it, I do not know whether it can be of use to me any longer." As if in thought, she touched the tip of the knife to her lips. "What do you suggest?"

Lillian forced her spine to remain straight and erect. "I do not know, *maman*."

Camille threw her a look full of disdain. Then her black silks swirled around her as she turned to saunter up and down the clearing. "I have thought—as it is such a nice specimen—that it would be a shame to send it to the mines straight away. For the moment, its tongue can be put to so much better use." A coy smile flashed over one black-clad shoulder. Antoine's and Maurice's faces remained expressionless.

To the third man present Lillian did not dare look.

"I have thought," Camille continued in a singsong voice, "as it will be even more stubborn now, to keep it on the floor." Abruptly, she turned to beam at Lillian. "For even with its arms and legs bound and restricted, its body can still be of so much good use, lying there, waiting for me to take my pleasure from it."

As the pictures her stepmother evoked blossomed in Lillian's mind, a wave of nausea threatened to engulf her. She saw Troy's body, bruised and battered, reduced to an instrument, a sex toy.

Camille's eyes brightened with pleasure.

Trust her to notice any weakness.

"It will give me great delight riding it, I think," the cruel litany went on. "Pressing my nails into its flesh and seeing the blood spring up. And when I tire of that, it still has its clever tongue to bring me enjoyment, *n'est-ce pas?* But perhaps we should get rid of its teeth first to ensure it will not get any ideas."

The back of Lillian's dress felt clammy as cold sweat drenched the material, trickled over her skin in endless streams. She wanted to scream and to cover her ears. She was alone and at Camille's mercy. Lord Allenbright and Mr. de la Mere would not be able to come in time.

"And then . . ." Her stepmother halted, flicking the knife through her fingers, and bestowed a loving glance on Maurice and Antoine. "I think we will chain it differently and I will let my pets enjoy it some." She whirled around to face Lillian. "What do you think? Is that not a splendid idea?"

Lillian clenched her jaw and forced the terrible pictures aside.

"Afterwards, when *everybody* has grown tired of it, I will send it to the mines, of course. It is in good shape. It should do for a few more months, even years." Camille's smile could have been a study of malice. Her eyes glittered like diamonds, and her half-opened lips looked as if she had already celebrated a barbaric ritual where she drank the blood of her victims.

Lillian slid her trembling hands into the pockets of the wide coat. With an effort, she straightened her shoulders, forced herself to breathe slowly. She must steady herself. She *must*.

A soft breeze tickled a stray lock across her cheek, and from the heavy material around her shoulders rose a whiff of sandalwood and oakmoss, her husband's very own scent, and for a moment it enveloped her like a warm embrace.

A moment was enough to steady her nerves, to reach for the core of steel inside herself.

Her face cool and smooth once more, she let her lips curve into a parody of a smile. "*Extraordinaire.*" Inside the pocket of the coat her fingers closed around metal. "But it sounds like very much work for very little pleasure. Why don't you just let him go?"

The trilling sounds of Camille's laughter filled the clearing. "Oh, *chérie*, you are priceless!" All at once, the laughter stopped and the woman's expression changed. "Why?" she almost snarled. "Because you need to take control over them, else they will crush you like a nasty little bug." Her eyes glittered feverishly. "Just as my father crushed my mother because she did not bear him any male heirs. As my first husband tried to crush me." Camille giggled, her voice suddenly high and thin like a little girl's. "But, oh, I didn't let him. How could I let him do such things? I couldn't let him go on hurting me, oh no, no, no. So I hurt him back, in the middle of the night, when it was dark outside and silent." Briefly, she put her index finger against her lips. "Sshhhh. Hush, hush," she continued on in a whisper, "so the servants wouldn't hear. They never heard screams at night, you know. And they didn't hear his, either. But I heard, oh yes, I heard them, his screams, and they were like music. Like music when I took the control away from him." She stared at the small knife in her hand as if only now she'd become aware of it.

Compassion welled up inside Lillian for this woman, who was still a frightened girl deep inside.

Everything needs balance . . .

Her fingers let go of the pistol, and she reached out both hands to her stepmother. "*Maman*—"

Camille's head whipped up, and a snarl twisted her face. "I thought I taught you all about control, *chérie*, but you have disappointed me. You *spoilt* it! You spoilt it, and now I am taking it back with me. And for the rest of its measly life it will never again slip my control!"

Lillian's breath caught. Her hands fell to her sides, while the blood seemed to freeze in her veins. *Not him! Not* him! Her moment of compassion passed. Whatever her stepmother had endured as a young girl, she had repaid it a hundred-, a thousandfold, had brought death and despair over innocent men. She would not have *him*, as well.

Lillian slipped her hands back into the pockets of her coat and firmly gripped the cold metal inside. Despite the icy fear that gripped her heart, her voice remained calm, without the hint of a quaver. "Then why have you summoned me?"

Obviously, this question amused Camille. "Oh, *chérie*, is that not obvious?" Sunlight glinted on her raised knife as she turned toward the rocks. "I invited you so you could watch when I take its balls." She threw her stepdaughter a little smile. "Surely you knew. They will be my good-bye present for you." She nodded to the men behind her. "Strip it."

"No! Don't you dare touch him!"

A little surprised, Camille turned back to her stepdaughter. Surprise was replaced by open amusement as she spotted the pistol in Lillian's hands. More laughter trickled up, filled the clearing. "Oh, *chérie*, you would not dare. So put it down before you hurt yourself."

Her laughter still hovered in the air when the shot echoed across the clearing.

The blood did not show on the black dress, but it had been too short a range for the bullet to miss its mark.

Surprise widened Camille's eyes. "You . . ." Blood bubbled over her lips, ran down her chin. The soft breeze that gently stirred the air played a little with black silk before she crumpled.

Lillian's gaze fastened on the fallen figure of her stepmother. The boom of the shot still rang in her ears, deafening her, threatening to swallow her up. She gulped and clutched the suddenly slippery pistol tighter.

One shot.

She had one more shot.

Lillian raised her head to look at Maurice and Antoine.

For a moment, they remained frozen, then they turned and feral snarls robbed their faces of all humanity.

One shot.

Coldness washed over Lillian.

She could not possibly take both of them down at the same time.

Time seemed to slow, their movements sluggish, almost leading her to believe she had an eternity before they would strike. And strike they would, for it was hate that blazed from their eyes.

They are going to kill me, Lillian thought numbly. *They are going to kill me and then they will kill Ravenhurst, and everything will have been for nothing.*

Yet at that moment two other shots rang out, one after another, so quick that they almost blended into one. Antoine and Maurice were struck in mid-stride, their momentum making them somersault and roll over on the grass.

"Bloody *hell!*" For once, shock robbed Justin de la Mere's polite voice of its nasal twang.

The pistol dropped from Lillian's nerveless fingers, landed on the ground with a dull thud. She turned, and with a sob she flew across the clearing toward the bound man at the boulder, the fabric of her long coat flapping behind her like the wings of an agitated bird.

"Oh, Ravenhurst . . . Troy . . ." She did not notice the tears that were streaming down her face as her hands fluttered over his body and reached up to free him of the bridle. "Troy . . ." When she could not reach the rope that tied his hands, she grew frantic. She sobbed and whispered and clung to him, desperate to set him free, deaf to the soothing noises he made.

"Lillian, it's all right. Everything is fine."

Gentle hands closed around her shoulders and drew her away. "Here, my lady, let me." Lillian looked up and through the blur of her tears she recognized Justin de la Mere, his stern features rendered soft by an emotion she could not fathom. He gave her a little squeeze and a smile, then went to work on the fetters, while Lord Allenbright cut the ropes that imprisoned Troy's arms and hands.

Lillian waited next to them, shivering so violently that

her teeth chattered, and fastened her eyes hungrily on her husband.

At last, he was free. He stood and rubbed his wrists where the ropes had chafed the skin. Then he raised his head and his gaze met hers. His eyes, Lillian saw, burned like two bright blue flames.

With two long strides he was before her and hauled her up into his arms. "Lillian," he whispered against her ear. "Oh, my Lilly." The voice was hoarse, yet unmistakably his.

She buried her face in the curve of his shoulder and muffled her sobs against his shirt. She did not care that his friends would watch her tears soaking him to the skin. He was here, in her arms, alive, and that was all that mattered. She clutched him as tightly as she could, horrified at how near she had come to losing him.

His strong, long fingers stroked her hair, while he pressed fervid kisses on her ear and cheek and every part of her face he could reach. Finally he lifted her head, so his mouth could close over hers, desperate. Her lips yielded gladly, opening for him, welcoming him, as his tongue thrust deep.

Troy felt his wife's body tremble in his arms, or perhaps the tremors wracked his own body; he did not care. Only her warm, living softness could erase the memories of the hell of the last few hours, could chase away the all-consuming fear that had enveloped him when she stepped into the clearing, small and vulnerable, her face as pale as chalk.

He tasted the tears on her lips, in her mouth, in his own. Gently, without breaking the kiss, he set her down, freeing his hands to frame her face so that his thumbs could trace the salty cascade that streamed down her cheeks. Tenderly, he brushed her closed eyelids with his fingers, the wet lashes feather-touches against his skin.

"Hush," he murmured against her lips, "hush. It's all over now, Lilly." He stroked the hair out of her face, loving the silky texture of the curls. They twined around his fingers, tickled the backs of his hands. "Hush," he crooned. "Hush, my love." Once more, he enveloped her in his arms, rocked her back and forth while he rained kisses on her face, her mouth. "Everything is fine now."

Finally he drew away so that he could look at her. He brushed at the wetness that clung to her lashes and drank in the sight of her face, red and swollen from crying. It was the most beautiful thing he had ever beheld.

She reached up to stroke his cheek. He leaned his head into the caress before he captured her small hand in his own and pressed a kiss to the center of her palm. Intertwining their fingers, he brought their joined hands down to rest over his heart, while his free hand tilted her chin so she was forced to meet his eyes. "Listen to me, Lilly," he said slowly and clearly. "*Listen.* You did it. You set us free."

She blinked, her gray eyes still glistening with tears.

"She cannot touch you now, never again. And you did it all by yourself, do you hear?" He pressed her hand tighter against his chest so that she could feel the rapid beating of his heart. "Through your courage you freed yourself. Your stepmother can no longer harm you or anybody else. In the end, you were stronger than she was."

Under his fingers her face crumpled again, and he drew her into his arms and against the solid comfort of his body. With hands and lips he soothed and cherished her, knowing she would feel guilty about the death of her stepmother, for his wife was made to heal, not to hurt.

Only when she had grown silent did he raise his head to throw a look over his shoulder at his friends. "And thank you, too."

Justin looked a bit sheepish. "It was nothing. You would have done the same for us."

"We are just glad that we came in time," Drake added and reached out to squeeze Troy's free shoulder tightly. "You look a mess. Why don't you take your wife and go home so she can clean you up. We will take care of this." He jerked his chin to where the three corpses lay. Then his lips wrinkled in an attempt at a weak smile. "And do lock your firearms up somewhere safe in the future."

"Perhaps." Troy grinned. "Or perhaps you should learn to be faster than my wife." He pressed a kiss onto the crown of her head, safely tucked into the shelter of his arms. Vividly he remembered the feeling when he had seen the glint of the pistol in her hands. His brand-new pocket pistol—four barrels, two shots—which could be hidden so nicely under a wide coat. He had been horrified, his fear for her increasing in leaps and bounds. Before, they probably would have let her go. Yet with the pistol, she had endangered her own life. Her precious, precious life. The fear for her then had been worse than the feel of the bridle in his mouth, worse than anything he had and would suffer at the hand of *la Veuve Noire*.

Yet at the same time, a fierce pride had filled his being. Pride in his wife, in her wits and courage, pride because she had fought like a lioness, because she had fought for *him*. Without reserve.

He pressed another kiss onto her lovely, riotous curls. "Or perhaps I should teach her how to shoot properly. You should have turned the breech, sweetheart."

"What?" She looked up, all red and blotchy, and indignation rose in her eyes.

He grinned and kissed her nose. "The breech of the pistol. You need to turn it before you can make the second shot."

"Oh."

He laughed and then bent his head to kiss her mouth, hard. "Let's go home, my dear. Could I borrow one of your horses?" he asked, turning to his friends. "I have no idea where they left theirs."

Justin rolled his eyes. "All right, all right, go then and take mine." He had recovered enough for his voice to regain its usual nasal quality. "Drake here can show you the way. Somebody has to get the magistrate anyway. So shoo, shoo, away with you. Your wife looks ready to drop from exhaustion at any moment."

Troy looked down at his wife, who was leaning against his side, her head resting on his shoulder. He smoothed a hand over her hair, then hoisted her up in his arms.

Lillian gasped. Her eyes flew open, and she found her husband staring at her. "Hush," he said, even though she had not opened her mouth. "You look a mess. Lean your head back and relax." He frowned. "There's a tear in your dress and the hem is all muddy up to your knees."

"I hurried so. I didn't heed where I stepped. I . . ." Her voice caught.

"I know." His lips brushed her forehead. "It's over, Lillian. Forever."

She nodded and huddled closer. Closing her eyes, she murmured: "Your wound . . ."

"Hush. It's just an earlobe." The echo of a laugh rumbled in his chest. "Considering everything else, I feel that I can gladly live without it." Another brush of his lips, soothing. "Hush now. I can still carry you." When she swayed gently from side to side, she knew that he had already begun walking.

It was nice, she thought, being thus held by him. It made her feel protected and cherished, surrounded by warmth, inside and out. And strength. Strength to lean on, to count on.

Burying her nose against his throat, she breathed deep and inhaled the smell of his sweat, sharp and musky, with an underlying memory of sandalwood and oakmoss. Content, she nuzzled his skin and let his scent calm her.

You set us free, he had said, and his eyes had conveyed so much more than that.

You set us free.

Not just from Camille, but from the past. It was as if that one shot had blown away all barriers between them, all remaining anger and hatred; as if that one shot had wiped the slate clean. As if a happily ever after would be possible even for her.

It did not take them long to reach the horses beside the soggy path, where the waning sun glittered in a thousand puddles. The light transformed the water into molten silver.

Lillian blinked. "Oh, look," she murmured sleepily, "it looks like pools of diamonds."

Smiling, Troy settled her on the saddle in front of him and drew her firmly against his body, with her bottom snuggled into the vee of his spread legs.

"Or," she added in the same dreamy voice, "as if bits of the sun have fallen from the sky and settled on the earth."

Clasping the reins with one hand and securing her around the waist with the other, Troy put his chin on her shoulder. "I seem to remember a fairy tale where things like that fell from the skies," he replied in a husky whisper.

She chuckled and turned her head to look at him. "But those were stars. I would prefer the sun to stars, wouldn't you?"

"Hmm, who needs suns and stars when there are flowers? Candytufts, and marigold, and roses, and honey-

295

suckle, and lilies . . ." He blew a soft kiss on her cheek. "*Especially* lilies." His eyes had warmed to the loveliest of blues with tenderness.

Lillian felt an answering smile tugging at the corners of her mouth. She threw a quick glance to Allenbright, who was riding in front of them and pretended sudden deafness.

Her husband's warm breath caressed her neck, tickled her ear. "One very special Lilly in particular," he murmured. And then Lillian felt the delicate, moist pressure of his tongue circling the shell of her ear, and a fiery shiver raced through her body.

As if in silent answer, the hand on her waist tightened.

Lillian looked back at him, saw his gaze, darker than before, fasten on her mouth. His eyes flicked up to meet hers, and a private, soft smile played around his lips. Slowly, ever so slowly, he bent his head and—

"The road," Allenbright said to no one in particular, "is very muddy. In such conditions a fellow might very easily slip from his horse if he does not take heed."

Immediately, Lillian felt a blush blossoming on her cheeks. Troy just chuckled and contented himself with nuzzling her temple. "I think that was for my benefit," he said, his voice muffled against her skin. "And I'm afraid he's quite right." He sighed and drew away. "No more cuddling until we are at home." But he winked at her, his eyes twinkling with happy mischief.

Utterly charmed, she leaned back against his chest and rubbed her hand over his arm around her waist. As she looked at Lord Allenbright's straight back in front of them, she remembered the day in the gardens, when she had come upon him and Mr. de la Mere. *A love so beautiful* . . . For the first time, the memory did not hurt.

You set us free.

She felt her husband's body moving behind her, and a rush of deep happiness flowed through her.

Lord Allenbright left them at the crossroads to Keighlin, headed off to get the magistrate. Troy and Lillian rode on to Bair Hall, while overhead the North Star twinkled in the darkening sky. "I have thought . . ." Lillian murmured sleepily.

"Yes?" Her husband tightened his arm around her.

She turned her head to look up at him and found that dusk had turned his features into planes of gray and deep shadows. "I have thought . . . Could we invite my aunt and my grandfather for Christmas?"

She saw his teeth flash in a quick smile. "Of course." He pressed a sweet kiss to her cheek. "Whatever you wish."

The rest of the way they rode in peaceful silence. And when they passed through the high arch that was the entrance to the grounds of Bair Hall, the boughs of the rowan, heavy with berries, bowed low in silent welcome. Troy cuddled Lillian closer. "Your Nanette once told me that it would guard us from evil." He smiled down at her. "And it did. It kept us both safe, and now there's no need for fear anymore."

"Yes." Lillian rubbed her head against his shoulder like a contented cat. "Bring us home, Troy."

The house, when they reached it, was blazing with lights and was a place of general mayhem. Even the usually immaculate Hill had forgotten to smooth down his hair, and now gray tufts stuck into the air, lending him the air of an agitated owl. Upon throwing open the door with unusual force, he ogled Lillian and Troy as if they were ghosts, risen to drag him down to hell. "M-master," he stuttered. "I mean . . . I mean . . . M-my . . . My lord."

"Hill." Troy nodded, his arm clamped around his wife.

"Will you please send someone to take care of de la Mere's horse and—"

A maid, rushing by, caught sight of her master, one side of his neck and shirt sullied with blood. She came to an abrupt halt, her eyes going round as saucers before she threw her apron over her face and started to wail.

"Oh dear," Lillian said.

Hill looked this way and that, obviously confused about what to do first. "Oh . . . oh . . . Well . . . I. . . ."

Lillian straightened her back and fixed the butler with a penetrating stare. "Hill. Lord Ravenhurst needs rest. And a bath. So please inform the household that he is alive and back, and do send somebody to prepare a bath for each of us. And ask Mrs. Blake to prepare a tray with some wine, bread and cold chicken."

The butler hurried to bow. "Yes, my lady, at once." They watched him walking briskly away and making shushing noises to the wailing maid as if she were a panicky hen.

Troy frowned. "Lady Ravenhurst," he began. As he looked down at her, Lillian nearly burst with the urge to reach out and soothe the troubled line between his brows. "I am afraid I brought you back to bedlam."

"Is that so?" Tentatively, she reached up to cup his cheek in her palm, her thumb caressing his skin. "I am sure you will feel better once you have had your bath."

The lines of his face gentled. A smile warmed his eyes as he put his hand, so large and strong, over hers. "And you, my Lady Ravenhurst? What—"

"I, my lord, will look for my herbs." She stepped back, but smiled up at him. How could she not smile when her hand remained caught between his warm, strong fingers. "Or do you wish me to send for the doctor to tend your wound?"

"I—"

Gently, she freed her hand from his. "So please excuse me, my lord." It would not do to let him distract her with tenderness so that she forgot the important things like his bloodied ear. A shiver of remembered fear raced through her.

"I will see you soon," she murmured, and fled up the stairs.

Chapter 18

How much time later was "soon"? Troy wondered as he sat in the big bathtub and the water swirled all around him. Even a glass of mulled wine had not been able to dull his yearning to hold his wife in his arms once more, to reassure her and himself that they had come out of this particular battle alive. He scowled at the soap in his hands in frustration, working up a lather to wash his chest and arms. All the while, he muttered curses, but that did not help much either. Should he march into her room and demand an explanation? He had thought that she would feel similarly.

Moodily, he eyed the decanter of wine on the table.

Perhaps he should just drink himself into a stupor. Get foxed, fuddled, top heavy. And then he might just forget the feeling of her softness in his arms.

He hung his head and groaned aloud—which probably accounted for the fact that he did not hear her enter. When she spoke, her soft voice, tinged with concern, almost made him jump.

"Ravenhurst? Are you all right?"

"Yes," he mumbled and busied his hands with the soap.

"Splendid." From the corner of his eye he saw that she had already bathed and changed. She was wearing one of the pale, plain dresses she so liked, with small printed flowers scattered over the cloth. Her flowery scent drifted up his nose as she came nearer, carrying a small tray, which she set down on the table beside his wine.

"I have come to see after your wound."

"Yes." If he bowed his head any lower, his nose would touch the water. Great.

He heard her come up behind him, heard her indrawn breath as she caught sight of his back. Well, he had forgotten that. The scars.

A hesitant finger brushed over his skin. "Oh, your poor back," she murmured. The fragrance of assorted flowers enveloped him just like that first time when her scent had banished the stench of the prison cell—a glimmer of hope, even though he had not known it at the time. But he knew it now. He knew her worth and her measure, his very own guarding angel.

His exasperation at her delay dissolved. Only the yearning remained, the burning desire to reaffirm life with her in the most basic way there was between man and woman.

The welts, Lillian saw, had healed to white ridges in the skin, crisscrossing his back, the lines broader and ragged where metal-adorned straps had taken skin and flesh. All at once, she felt so faint that she had to sit down rather quickly on the stool beside the tub. The warm scent of him rose up to tickle her nose, to settle on her hair and in her dress. She could grow drunk on his scent alone. "Have you . . ." She licked her dry lips and tried again. "Give me the soap, and I shall wash your back."

He handed her the slippery bar without a word, without even looking at her. She had to force her hands to cease trembling before she could guide the soap over his skin. The fresh scent of rosemary and a hint of lemon balm drifted up as she worked up a lather. Putting the soap aside, she laid her hands on his back, felt the muscles move under the warm, wet skin. Carefully, she kneaded the flesh, followed the line of his spine with a fingertip. When she had cleaned his back as thoroughly as humanly possible and felt she had no excuse to prolong the joy of touching him, she took the sponge to wash the lather away. Rivulets of water chased the bubbles downward, revealing once more the white lines on his golden skin.

Lillian's bottom lip trembled, and quite suddenly tears blurred her vision. She could no longer refuse herself—not after all that had happened today, not after coming so near to losing him, this man who had gripped her heart so tightly that she could no longer cloak it in icy numbness. She leaned forward and pressed her lips to his back, rubbed her cheek over the scars. "Oh, your poor back," she murmured.

"Lillian." Troy groaned. He shifted so he could clamp his hand around an arm and draw her around and against his wet chest. In the blink of an eye, his mouth was moving hungrily over hers, nibbling and sipping just as if he were a man lost in the desert and she the only well to quench his thirst. Her hands clutched at his shoulders, fisted in his hair, and a thousand butterflies exploded in her stomach. She was floating, and he the steady rock of her salvation.

Her fingers dug into the firm ridge of his shoulder. As if in answer, he ran the tip of his tongue along the seam of her mouth, scalding her lips, making her blood sing, and . . .

Her eyes fell closed. She moaned, and without her volition her body pressed against the hardness of his muscles. "Troy . . ."

"Mhm-hmm?"

She felt his other arm come around her, felt his hand stroke over the curve of her hip, the indentation of her waist, her ribcage . . . higher, always higher, the stroke of his hand pulling her body as tight as a bow and making her tremble in his arms. "Troy?"

"What?" he whispered against her lips, just as his hand closed around one breast, the tip already thrusting out and awaiting his touch.

Lillian opened her eyes wide, saw him smiling at her, that wonderful, wonderful smile. "Don't be afraid, my Lillian," he murmured tenderly, just before he closed his fingers over her nipple, rolled it between thumb and forefinger.

Lillian shrieked with pleasure. It was as if a firestorm raced through her body, bringing her alive, oh God, so *alive*.

His mouth swooped down and moved hungrily over hers. When she gasped, his tongue slipped inside like a small, nimble fish. Instantly, her mind whirled with the taste and smell and feel of him, with the deep, urgent sounds he made at the back of his throat when she touched her tongue to his, when her hands fisted in his hair, kneaded his scalp.

Abruptly he broke off the kiss and rose, making her world lurch as he swung her up in his arms. Her eyes widened in surprise. She looked down and saw the water streaming from his body, as if he were Neptune himself, risen from the foamy sea. "Oh my," she murmured.

He stepped over the rim of the tub, his movements full of purpose. "Yes?" He looked down at her, desire a bright blue flame in his eyes.

"Oh my," she repeated and pressed her face into the hollow of his throat. His skin was damp, and the smell of rosemary mingled with the scent of musk and sweat. His heat and his strength surrounded her, made her feel small and protected. Tightening her arms around his neck, she reveled in the warmth. She whimpered a little in protest when he laid her down among the cool linen of the bed.

"Shhh." His hand brushed over her hair. "Shh." He sat down beside her, and his mouth sought hers, sweetly, gently. She closed her eyes and lost herself in his gentleness.

Unhurried, his hands followed the curves of her body, making her sigh with contentment. But then he caught her lower lip between his teeth and tugged—and just like that, her body turned boneless, with liquid fire racing through her veins.

A firestorm, indeed, urged on by his large hands on her body; a firestorm that burned away all memories of red blood on white linen, memories of what had gone on *before*.

Her back arched as he moved his mouth lower, licking and kissing her throat as if it were a new and exotic kind of pastry. He fumbled with the fastenings of her dress and the shift beneath, the touch of his fingers on her naked skin a sweet torment that made her whimper.

When he finally drew the garments over her head, her sigh mingled with his satisfied groan. "God, you're beautiful." His voice had turned rasping. "So very, very beautiful. All milk and honey and . . ." She opened her eyes then, looked at him as he rose above her, broad-shouldered and magnificent.

And then she remembered another time when he had risen above her, his skin clammy with cold sweat, and half-hidden by the curly hair on his chest the lily, the burnt flesh—

With a stricken sound she reached out and covered the mark with her hand, feeling the heavy beats of his heart against her fingertips. The warm glow of the moment evaporated like water on a hot stone.

A lily for Lillian.
Her responsibility.

Tears welled up in her eyes.

"Lillian, no," his voice cut through her guilt. He feathered gentle kisses over her face. "It is all right," he said, his voice tender. "It is all right."

"I am sorry, I am so sorry." The tears overflowed and ran in bitter, salty streaks down her cheeks. Ice filled her heart, froze the blood in her veins.

He rolled to his side and wrapped her in his arms, bringing her face down onto the welcoming curve of his shoulder. But the tears came harder and harder.

She felt him press his mouth against her hair. "It is all right, Lillian."

"How can you say that?" she sobbed. "How can it be all right?"

His hands came up to cradle her face, and he held her away from him. "Because we can make it so." His eyes burned into her, willing her to believe. "We can make it right again. We have already started, don't you see? Can't you *feel?*" He moved his body against hers. "Can't you feel the rightness, Lillian?"

She stared at him, felt the fire rekindle where their bodies touched, skin to skin. She shivered.

A crooked smile lifted his lips. "We can make it all right, Lillian," he whispered, before his mouth came down and claimed hers. His tongue seared her lips, coaxing them to open for him, and when they did, the sensual, moist glide of his tongue against her own made her dizzy with yearning.

"Touch me," he coaxed. "Touch me, Lillian, and make it right again."

Yet still she hesitated, suddenly shy of touching him like that, intimately and with tenderness. After all this time, how could she still be capable of tenderness?

He kissed her jaw, her throat, nibbled at her earlobe, then slid lower and brushed his mouth over the upper swell of her breast. "Touch me," he murmured against her skin. "Like this, just like this . . ." And his tongue whirled over the rosy tip of one breast, making it tingle and burn and muscles deep in her stomach contract.

And how could she *not* touch him after that? How could she not smooth her hands over his arms, down the curve of his back, and over his sides? And how could she not smile in delight as she felt the muscles bunch under her questing fingertips and hear her husband groan with pleasure.

With *pleasure*.

It was then that Lillian finally understood. She could not hurt him, would not hurt him if she touched him like this, with tenderness and the intent to give pleasure. Only pleasure from now on.

She took a deep breath, and the last of Camille's fetters sprung free.

Dizzy with joy, she continued her exploration of her husband's body. She learned the taste of his skin, the salty tang of his sweat, and inhaled the scent of him mingled with the musk of his arousal. And under *his* hands and *his* mouth she felt the fire within her flare up again. Together, they fanned the flames, making them burn higher and higher, until he finally slipped into her so he was buried deep, deep inside.

A smile spread over his face then, of such intensity as she had never seen. It was as if he were lit from within. It was there in the glow of his eyes and the soft curve of his mouth.

Lillian felt an answering smile lift her own lips.

He sighed, a sound of utter contentment. Then he wriggled his forearms under her shoulders and cuddled her close, all the time looking at her, looking.

Watching.

It is said the eyes are the mirror of the soul, and in that moment it seemed to Lillian as if this were indeed true: For once, his eyes were clear and untroubled. Free of anguish and pain.

They had slipped from the past, both of them, and had finally arrived in the present. The man Lillian held in her arms was not the prisoner in the stinking cell, was not the man in chains whose blood had dripped onto Camille's floor, was not the earl whose eyes had burned with hate and wrath, was not even the husband she had wed on the wrong side of town.

The man Lillian held in her arms was Troy.

Just Troy.

Lillian reached up to stroke the damp hair at his temple. "I love you," she whispered. For a moment, he leaned into the caress like a kitten, and she almost expected him to purr. Then he turned his head and placed a lingering, open-mouthed kiss in her palm. Smiling, he looked back at her. "I love you, too," he said.

And then—he moved.

Their gazes remained locked. Even when the flames of their desire licked at their skin and their breathing became pants and moans, even then did they not look away. They made love with their bodies, their eyes and their souls. And the flames consumed them both.

Later, they lay among the rumpled sheets, Lillian's head on Troy's shoulder. With one arm, he held her close, while she gently stroked his chest and played with the springy dark hair there. More often than not, however, her fingers strayed to the brown mark on his skin. Now that most of the candles had burned down, it was almost invisible, flickering in and out of existence as the light danced over them.

She pressed a tender kiss upon it, as if the touch of her lips could undo the pain she had inflicted so long ago.

"It no longer hurts, you know." His lips brushed her temple and he took up her hand. "And it does not bother me now. In fact"—smiling, he kissed her palm—"I like it. Your mark upon me." He threaded his fingers through hers and brought their joined hands back to rest on his chest. His strong, brown hand engulfed her slender fingers, swallowing them up. His thumb gently stroked over the pulse at her wrist.

"I have got something for you," he finally said.

Surprised, Lillian raised her head. "For me?"

He nodded, intently watching the play of their fingers. "I went to France with a purpose." Only then did he look at her. There was an odd expression in his eyes that Lillian could not interpret. "I will be right back." His fingers slid from hers and he left the bed.

Lillian huddled in the blankets, suddenly feeling bereft. Her gaze was drawn to his firm naked buttocks as he went around the room. To the graceful curve of his back, toned with muscles. And then there was that spot on his neck, just below the hairline, that small, vulnerable-looking spot. Her fingers twitched with the urge to stroke the skin there, to lay her hand over that stretch of flesh, to take him into her care.

Mine, she thought. *Mine*.

He rummaged in the top drawer of his chest and came back with a small velvet bag. Upon his approach, Lillian settled higher among the pillows against the headrest. The mattress dipped as he sat down on the side of the bed, his face somber.

Worried by his expression, Lillian reached out to touch his hand. At that, he smiled a little, yet when he looked at her, he grew serious again.

"You once gave me something," he began. "A precious

gift it was. But it took me some time to understand its full significance. At first it was just gold to pay my way to freedom. And that, of course, was precious for me. But I did not understand . . . how much more it was." His gaze never left hers, and she saw how very blue his eyes were, that intense cornflower-blue that so easily touched her soul. She remembered that last smoldering look on a muddy lane in France and the sight of glinting gold flying through the rain. "Nanette . . . Nanette made me see its real worth." He swallowed. "A gift of your heart. So much more precious than mere gold."

Lillian blinked. A lump rose in her throat and rendered her powerless to speak.

"So I went to France to get it back. For you. To give you back that gift of the heart." He reached out and tenderly wiped away the single tear rolling over her cheek. "A heart for a heart." He opened the velvet bag and let its contents fall into his hand.

But Lillian did not look down. Her gaze remained locked with his, even as her eyes welled over, even as he slowly raised his hands and the cool metal settled on her skin. Carefully he fastened the chain and made sure that no hair would be caught in the tiny rings.

She did not need to look down to know what it was. She had worn the locket for so many years that the weight of it felt instantly familiar.

"It is a bit dented at one place," Troy said huskily, "but the miniatures are still there. I give it back to you, my Lilly, and I thank you for the gift." He leaned forward. "And I thank you for my life."

A sob caught in Lillian's throat.

"Twice, if I recall correctly." A smile tugged at his mouth. His hands came up to frame her face. "I love you, my Lilly," he murmured before he kissed her.

The tears now flowed freely over Lillian's cheeks. Wet, hot tears, as she threw her arms around him and hugged him tightly. "I love you, too," she whispered shakily against his lips. "So very much." His warmth surrounded her, and she let the heat of his body seep into her skin until it warmed her heart forever.

They had overcome the past, and now the future was theirs.

Windfall
CINDY HOLBY

1864: Jake awakens from months of unconsciousness with his body healed, but his mind full of unanswerable questions. Is there a woman waiting somewhere for him? A family? A place he belongs? Shannon walks away from her abusive father and the only home she's ever known. Can a soldier with no past be the future she's prayed for? Grace tries to be brave when the need to capture a traitor rips her lover from her arms. Will it take even more courage to face him again now that his seed has blossomed within her? Jenny's grandfather's beloved ranch becomes a haven for all those she holds dear, but now the greed of one underhanded land baron threatens everything they've worked for. How can she keep the vision of her murdered parents alive for the generations to come?
